About the Author

Karen Legasy lives in Ottawa, Ontario, Canada with her longtime life partner, Pam. They have one adult daughter, Lisa. Having grown up in northern Ontario in a loving family of six, Karen enjoys the outdoors and spending time in nature. After a successful career in government, Karen is pursuing fiction writing as her next vocation.

Acknowledgments

I would like to acknowledge Humber College for its gem of a Correspondence Program in Creative Writing. Many thanks to author Elizabeth J. Duncan, my teacher and mentor who provided insight and guidance while drafting *My Forever Hero*. Many thanks also to author Kim Moritsugu, a teacher and mentor from Humber College who taught me many things about the craft of writing that were fundamental to writing this novel.

I feel very fortunate to have worked with Lauren Humphries-Brooks as my editor. She provided lots of excellent insight and suggestions that helped me to bring out the best that I could with this story. Thank you Lauren.☺

Maureen Bellgard, thank you for hosting Pam and I in Canberra while I was researching this book, and thanks so much for giving the manuscript a read to ensure I got the Aussie slang right. You are the best.☺

Bella Books, with publishers like you, these lesbian stories can be told. I am so grateful to be part of your team of authors and appreciate all of the work you do to make books like *My Forever Hero* happen.

A big thank you goes to my life partner, Pam, for supporting me in this project, turning me into a cat person by bringing Sydney and Tazzie into my life for seventeen years, and being the first reader of a completed draft. To my parents Elmer and Patricia, sister Linda, and brothers Lawrence and Joel—you are the best and I was so lucky to be born into this family. I would also like to acknowledge Jeff and the fun times we had together. I hope you are resting in peace Jeff.

My
Forever
Hero

KAREN LEGASY

BELLA
BOOKS
2017

Bella Books, Inc.
P.O. Box 10543
Tallahassee, FL 32302

Printed in the United States of America on acid-free paper.

First Bella Books Edition 2017

Editor: Lauren Humphries-Brooks
Cover Designer: Judith Fellows
Cover Photo: Taken by Pamela Laidler of Ottawa, Ontario. Photo taken in Sydney, Australia.

ISBN: 978-1-59493-579-4

Dedication

To Pam, my forever hero

CHAPTER ONE

Marlee Nevins feared she was going to drown until a shark nudged her surfboard and bared its teeth.

"Holy shit! Holy fuck!" Marlee yanked her limbs out of the water as the great white circled then dove.

"You're not getting me, you bastard!" She ripped off a neoprene bootie in desperation for a weapon to strike back if charged and clung to her board.

Marlee screamed as a jolt from beneath pushed her into the ocean in one big splash and left her defenseless. Disoriented, gasping for air, and nose burning from inhaling salty water, she broke surface a short distance from her overturned board. The shark was mangling it, allowing her a chance to back away with thrashing arms and hyperventilating curses. She started to swim for her life.

Marlee had been trapped in the water off the coast of New South Wales for over six hours, initially caught in a riptide then drifting farther out to sea after many futile attempts to make it back to shore. The solitude of the secluded morning beach had followed her into the far horizon where nothing was in sight, not even a seagull, until the shark showed up.

Marlee swam like hell. Heart-pounding tremors roared in her head as she raced against the waves. Marlee had never been this scared before. Her lungs about to collapse, she finally stopped to get her bearings.

Head thrashing from side to side, she scanned the rolling waves for other triangle fins. There were none. If she could keep in control and stay at the ready to wallop against an attack, maybe her grisly death could be put off for a little longer.

The shark swam around shreds of fiberglass floating on the surface. Marlee whimpered as she envisioned her horrific end. She struggled to keep her head above the waves, arms weakening and legs all but dead weights. Her bootless foot felt numb and her anxiety level peaked with the realization she was likely to die a painful death.

The shark dove, its dorsal fin disappearing beneath the surface and leaving no trace. Marlee held her breath, expecting an ambush from below that would remove her legs and redden the water. Heart pounding and head throbbing, Marlee squeezed her eyes shut and prepared to meet her end.

Hope all but lost, the roar of an approaching motor renewed Marlee's determination to fight back. The blond ponytail of a female driver flapped in the wind as a speeding watercraft seemed to come out of nowhere and bounce across the waves. Was it for real or was she hallucinating?

"Help! Over here!" Marlee waved her arms, trying to flag down the driver just as the triangle fin resurfaced and started swimming toward her.

"Back off! Leave me alone or I'll kill you, you motherfucker!" Marlee tried to look as large as possible in the water. Appearing bigger was supposed to help with warding off enraged black bears in the bush, and she desperately hoped it would be the same for an attacking shark in the ocean. Large teeth threatened and Marlee stared into the darkness of its dilated pupils. She had nothing to defend herself with other than her neoprene boot-covered fist. She kept her wide eyes focused on the dark orbs until they dipped below again.

A sputtering water scooter stopped behind Marlee and a woman's voice called out. "Give me your hand."

Marlee reached behind, keeping her eyes glued to where the shark went under until she felt someone grasp her arm. She swung around and grabbed onto the seat as the watercraft began to pull her away. The engine gave one final roar then choked and died.

"Damn," the woman said. "We're out of bloody petrol. You'll have to climb on behind me. Hurry!"

Marlee mustered all her remaining strength, but it wasn't enough to pull up out of the water and onto the seat. "I can't."

"You're a woman?" The words came out in a screech of shock as she whipped around and stretched out both arms. "Grab onto me. I'll help pull you up."

Marlee seized the outstretched hands, and felt herself being raised as she struggled to kick her legs to get onto the watercraft. She managed to get her stomach slung over the seat then felt grasping arms scooping her legs out of the water.

"Oh shit, it's coming at us," the woman said. "You have to get all the way on and sit up. Hurry. Now."

"Holy fuck!" Marlee felt the woman clawing at the back of her wetsuit as she struggled to get upright on the seat. Luckily the shark stopped just short of ramming them and began to circle.

The woman tried starting the engine, but it was futile. The tank was dry. "Where the hell are you, Josh?" She looked around; hyperventilating whimpers escaping her throat.

Marlee collapsed against the woman's back, arms wrapped around a firm waist and clinging for life as her cheek rested on the blond ponytail. When she noticed an approaching sailboat, she perked up and began to wave.

"Stay still." The woman's voice was stern. "He'll be here in a minute, but we can't let ourselves tip over before then. Be ready in case the shark rams us."

Marlee lowered her arm and could have grabbed onto the triangle fin because the shark was so close. It brushed up against the side of the personal craft and the two women had to shuffle on the seat to keep from tipping.

"If it goes under, the bloody bastard could flip us," the woman said. "Josh is almost here."

"Who's Josh?"

"He's my fourteen-year-old son." She shook her head. "I thought for sure you were a boy not much older than him."

Marlee was used to being in control during dangerous situations and felt ashamed at having to rely on the help of strangers. "I'm sorry."

"It's no time to feel sorry," the woman said. "Pull yourself together and work with me."

"Tell me what you need me to do."

"Stay still and hold on to me. What's your name and where are you from?"

"Marlee Nevins from Canada."

"A stupid Canadian tourist." She spoke over her shoulder. "That explains it. Does anyone know you're here?"

"Yes, and no." Marlee sighed.

"Don't give me ambiguous answers." Her lips quivered as she watched the circling shark. "Is it yes or no?"

"Nobody knows I'm out here," Marlee said. "They just know I'm visiting Australia."

"Anyone with half a mind should realize you never go out on the water without a buddy." The woman groaned.

"Okay, it was my fucking mistake." Marlee didn't need this. "I got us into this so if it attacks anyone, it'll be me." Marlee held on and used her body to shield her rescuer against the shark.

"Just keep staring it down and don't break eye contact," the woman said. A wave rocked the scooter, almost knocking them over, and the shark went under. A sailboat edged up to them.

"Toss me a line, Josh. Now."

"Hurry up, Mum. The shark's still there." He threw the rope.

The woman caught it and tugged to pull the water scooter to the small step at the rear of the craft. The wide blue eyes of a teen boy stared down at them as Marlee struggled to get on the vessel, her legs rubbery and feet numb. She wobbled onboard before collapsing into one of the seats in the cockpit.

Marlee watched her rescuer climb aboard and pull Josh into a firm hug "Thank you, darling. You saved our lives. I love you."

"I love you, too," he said. "Holy shit, did you see the size of its teeth?"

Marlee sat stone-faced as she tried to get her bearings. It appeared no else was on the boat and land beckoned in the distance.

"I'll get us some towels." The woman wrung water out of her ponytail as she looked at Marlee. "Are you all right? Do you need any medical attention?"

"No." Marlee leaned back and flopped her head against the seat. "I'm okay."

"Good. We'll take you in." She disappeared into the cabin.

"Who are you?" Josh's baby blue eyes examined Marlee.

"Hi." She offered a jittery hand. "I'm Marlee from Canada."

"Hey." He shook her hand.

"I'm so glad to meet you and your mom." Marlee's teeth were chattering and her body felt numb. "How did you find me?"

"I spotted you on the water with my drone." He picked up the control and showed it to Marlee. "You were on your surfboard, then disappeared, and Mum noticed the shark. She freaked."

"I bet." Marlee shivered in the warm sun as her cold, wet body craved heat. "What's your mother's name?"

"Abigail. You should have seen her when she saw there was a shark about to attack you. She jumped on the water scooter even though it wasn't safe."

"She's my hero," Marlee said. "And so are you."

Abigail returned and handed Marlee a towel. "We'll head back in now." She stood at the controls. "I'll take us from here, Josh."

"Sure." He went into the cabin.

Marlee watched Abigail ensure the water scooter was properly tethered at the back of the boat then braced for an awkward ride back to shore. She struggled to lower the zipper on her wetsuit, hands shaking and teeth chattering as she stared at her feet.

"I lost one of my booties." Marlee raised her naked foot. "I lost my new board too. I guess it's a sign because I sure won't be doing that again."

"I hope not," Abigail said.

"Thank you, Abigail. Your son told me your name. You saved my life." Marlee studied the attractive blonde at the controls. The bikini hugged Abigail in all the right places, highlighting firm round breasts and a tight bottom.

"You need to drink something." Abigail leaned toward the cabin opening. "Josh, could you please toss me up a couple bottles of water and some fruit?"

Marlee accepted water and a banana for sustenance as her body trembled during the silent ride back. A relaxing respite from her stressful position as a sergeant with the Ottawa Police Service had turned into a nightmare. She had chosen Australia for her three-month personal leave because their summer was her winter and she'd always dreamed of visiting the land down under.

Marlee had planned to master surfing while in Australia. Learn how to ride the waves and find balance to become a stronger person. After a few lessons, she bought a surfboard and had been practicing on her own away from others so she could feel comfortable making mistakes.

Her number one rule on the job was to never let her guard down because an error in judgment could mean death. Dying was something Marlee had prepared herself for, as she took many calculated risks in her work. For her, dying young meant being a hero, risking her life to save someone else's. Dying over some stupid stunt hadn't been in the plans and she was ashamed. Especially since she'd also put this beautiful stranger in danger.

Marlee gulped three bottles of water, devoured two bananas, some cheese, and a slice of pizza on the cruise back into shore. She was parched and starving after over six hours adrift in the ocean. And she was impressed with Abigail, still looking out for her after the rescue.

Marlee looked for that type of behavior in a partner—someone who would risk dying for her and make sure she was okay. Her dangerous work required it. This had been dangerous play, however, and the parameters were totally different. Marlee owed this woman her life.

CHAPTER TWO

"We should probably take you to the hospital to get checked," Abigail said as they lingered at the edge of the parking lot back at the marina.

Marlee stood on wobbly legs in bare feet, having removed her only bootie, and just wanted to get back to her place. "I'm okay so there's no need to bother." She looked around. "Is there a taxi stand nearby? I have to get back to my car."

"We'll give you a ride." Abigail approached her vehicle, a dark brown Toyota Prado with blackened windows. Josh was already in the backseat.

Marlee was too exhausted to refuse. "Thank you. My car is in the parking lot on the other side of the bay."

"I don't think you should drive." Abigail fastened her seatbelt. "I'll take you to your place so you can rest for awhile. Will anyone be there because you shouldn't be alone just yet?"

"I'll be okay. Really." Marlee gave Abigail directions to her apartment then leaned her head against the side window and closed her eyes. Her heart was pounding, head throbbing, and body twitching with every reminder of her near death at sea.

She wanted to roll up into a ball and cry, but she also wanted to lash out and hit something. She was furious with herself for being so careless and burned with shame.

When they pulled up in front of Marlee's low-rise apartment building, Abigail put down the windows then turned off the engine. "I'll go in with you to make sure you're going to be okay."

"I'll be fine." Marlee unzipped the key pocket on her wetsuit and dug out the only two keys she had in this country—one for her rental car and the other for her apartment.

"I imagine you'll be fine," Abigail said, "but I want to make sure. Josh, can you wait here? I'll only be a few minutes."

"Okay." He got into the front passenger seat, focused on a game on his phone as Marlee stood at the open door.

She squeezed his arm. "I owe you and your mother big time. I won't forget this and want to find some way to thank the two of you."

"Sure, whatever." Josh smiled without looking up.

"Let's get you inside," Abigail said.

Marlee's apartment was on the ground level of a neatly kept complex with large balconies, gardens of flowers and shrubs on the landscaped grounds, but no common space for residents. Most of the tenants were foreigners spending time along the warm coast while the winds of winter blew on the northern side of the equator. It was a pleasant place, not too expensive, practical, and quiet. So quiet, in fact, that Marlee had yet to get to know any of her neighbours beyond a few words or a wave.

"Come in," Marlee said as she opened her door and stepped into the small entryway she feared she'd never set foot in again. The apartment was dark, as she'd left for the beach before dawn and she hadn't bothered to open the curtains. She hadn't put on the air conditioner or opened any windows either.

"Let's get some light and fresh air in here." Abigail pushed by her and started opening curtains and windows. "Don't you have air conditioning?"

"I never put it on when I'm going to be out for the day." Marlee dropped down onto her sofa.

"You need to get out of that wetsuit," Abigail said. "A hot shower will do you good. I'll wait here while you have one then take Josh home and come back to make sure you're fine."

"I'm okay." Marlee struggled to stand up, touched by Abigail's caring. "You've already done so much and I don't want to hold you up anymore. I really want to thank you and Josh properly. Do you have an email or phone number where I can reach you?"

"Let's not worry about that for now. Is there anyone you can call to come over right now?"

"No." Marlee had been in Australia for almost seven weeks, but had kept mostly to herself.

"I'll wait until you're done in the shower." Abigail crossed her arms.

"I'm sorry for ruining your day," Marlee said. "I'll be quick."

"Just be careful," Abigail said. "If you feel like you're going to pass out, please sit down and call for me. I'll be right here." She sat on the couch.

Marlee refused to cry as warm water rinsed away the taste of salt and soothed her body. She put on her favorite T-shirt and a pair of clean cargo shorts then hurried back to the living room.

Abigail jumped off the couch and put her hands on her hips. "You're a police officer?"

Fuck. Marlee had given no thought to putting on the T-shirt she'd gotten at an Ottawa Police charity event. She just wanted to wear something comfortable and familiar. Her plan had been to hide the fact she was a police officer in Canada, but she couldn't lie to Abigail.

"Yes, but I'm on personal leave while visiting Australia."

"A police officer should know better than to go out on the water alone without telling anyone." Abigail shook her head.

"I screwed up, okay?" Marlee dropped to the couch and ran a hand through her short brown hair. "I feel like shit and I'm sorry."

Abigail sat down and touched Marlee's shoulder. "I'm sorry too. I shouldn't have reacted like that. Are you going to be okay while I drop Josh off at home?"

"I'm fine." Marlee peered into deep blue eyes and held them for a minute. Who was this tall, attractive woman with piercing eyes that felt so safe and warm? She had a sudden urge to hug her. Was there a husband waiting for her at home?

"Can I have your keys then?" Abigail got to her feet. "I think you should go for a nap and try to get some rest. I'll come back within the hour and let myself in while you're sleeping."

"Really, I'm okay." Marlee stayed sitting. Her knees were weak. "I've already troubled you enough and I'm sure you have other more important things to do."

"You're my priority right now." Abigail grabbed Marlee's keys from the table and folded them in her hand. "I'm responsible for you now that I've saved your life."

"I think it should be the other way around," Marlee said. "I owe you my life. How can I ever repay you?"

"That won't be necessary." Abigail was at the door, her hand on the knob. "Do you need help with anything before I leave?"

"Thanks, but no. Go ahead. I'm sure Josh is anxious to get home. You must be so proud of him."

Abigail smiled. "He is special. I'll see you later."

As much as Marlee wanted to stay on the couch and wait for Abigail's return, overwhelming fatigue set in. She mustered up her last bit of strength to get to the bedroom and climb between the covers before falling into a deep sleep.

Darkness was all around when Marlee awoke, crying and writhing against the sheets as though fighting for her life. She felt like she was suffocating and her arms met resistance as they flailed about.

"Marlee!"

That voice. Where was it coming from? Marlee drifted from the nightmare to a sluggish awakening with someone straddling her. "Where am I? What's happening?"

"You're in your bed," Abigail said. "You're safe now. Try to calm down."

"Let me go." Marlee pulled her arms out of the grip and struggled to sit up. Her eyes were starting to adjust to the grey of the room and Abigail's silhouette in the light of her cell phone. "You came back."

"I said I would." Abigail climbed off the bed. "You were in a deep sleep when I returned and I eventually fell asleep on your couch until I heard your lamp crashing to the floor."

"I dreamt I was back in the water, sinking to the bottom of the ocean." Marlee rubbed her eyes. "You saved me again."

"I just woke you up this time." Abigail placed the lamp back on the table and turned it on, giving the room a soft glow.

"I can't believe you're here," Marlee said. "You don't even know me and you're helping me again. I'm such a bother."

Abigail sat on the edge of the bed. "Sometimes people have to rely on the help of strangers. And you're no bother. I'm sure you would do the same."

"What about your family? Josh. This would have been traumatic for him too. Where is he?"

"He's with his father," Abigail said. "He's in good hands."

"And you?" Marlee asked. "You could've died. You should be at home with your son and husband instead of looking after me."

Abigail stood up. "Josh's father and I are divorced. It's the middle of the night. I think we should try to get some more sleep. Do you need anything before I go back to your sofa?"

"Please stay here," Marlee said. "The couch isn't comfortable and I could use the moral support. You make me feel safe." Marlee shifted to the far side of the bed and laid down, closing her eyes with the touch of the pillow. "Please?"

Abigail hesitated.

Marlee lifted her eyelids halfway. "I owe you my life. The least I can do is share my bed." She had been able to coax many women into her bed over the years, but this time it was different as the beautiful blond woman eased between the sheets.

"Thank you." Abigail kept to her side of the mattress. "This is much more comfortable than your couch."

"I'm glad," Marlee said.

A faint fragrance of coconut shampoo and Abigail's soft breathing brought Marlee a sense of comfort as she drifted back to sleep.

Daylight was squeezing through the closed blind when Marlee opened her eyes again. She raised her arms in a stretch and remembered how close she'd come to dying the day before. Her back was to the center of the bed and as she rolled over, Marlee was disappointed to realize Abigail was gone.

It wasn't until she was out in the kitchen, gulping a full glass of water, when Marlee heard a key in her lock.

Abigail pushed open the door, juggling a cardboard tray. "Hi. I got us some coffee and breakfast."

"How nice. Thank you." Marlee cleared a space on the table, her heart palpitating. "It's Monday morning. Shouldn't you be at work?"

Abigail sat down. "I have some flexibility. How are you feeling this morning?"

"Like shit. And like a loser."

"Stop feeling sorry for yourself." Abigail's stare was chastising. "You should be thankful you're alive."

"I am grateful, but I'm furious with myself for being such a stupid tourist."

"I shouldn't have called you that. I'm sorry."

"Don't worry about it." Marlee's cheeks burned as she studied this attractive woman, her matching pink-painted fingernails and toenails very ladylike.

"I thought for sure you were some young guy out there, not much older than my son," Abigail said.

"It wouldn't be the first time I've been confused for being a guy." Marlee ran a hand through her hair.

"Do you have any kids?" Abigail sipped her coffee.

"No, it's just me. I don't even have a pet. But I do have lots of pet peeves." Marlee's tone turned macho, a defense against her waning confidence around this sophisticated woman.

"And what are some of your pet peeves?" Abigail stood up.

"The behavior of tourists, having one bare foot, and getting attacked by sharks." Marlee grinned.

"I can see you're feeling better." Abigail smiled. "It's time for me to get to work."

"Yes, please do." Marlee followed Abigail to the door and gave her a heartfelt hug. "How can I ever thank you for everything?"

"By surfing with a buddy next time." Abigail reciprocated the embrace.

"I owe you and Josh big time and won't forget. I know I'll never be able to repay you, but I want to…"

"Stop right there." Abigail stepped back. "We only did what every decent human being would do in the same situation. There's no need to feel indebted to us."

Marlee held her gaze. "You're not going to get away with this without some kind of thanks from me. I'm a cop after all and don't like to let people get away with things."

"It's really not necessary." Abigail had the hint of a smile as she left.

CHAPTER THREE

Marlee was desperate to talk to someone, Kerry or Gabe, but her late morning was the middle of the night in Ottawa, and she didn't want to wake them. Kerry would be fast asleep with Diane, her long-time female partner. Her big brother Gabriel would be in bed with his wife. Other than Kerry or Gabe, Marlee had no one else she could call. There wasn't even an ex she could reach out to. There was no way she'd call Stacy after she'd left Marlee broke and broken.

A fluorescent blue sky and glistening sun did nothing to improve her mood that was better suited to dark clouds and rain. She made herself a grilled cheese sandwich and turned on the TV to watch the local news. There was no mention of a shark attack or near drowning of a *stupid* Canadian tourist. At least that was positive.

Marlee had reclined on the couch and was drifting off to asleep, but was revived by the sound of a light tapping then a key in her door.

"Hello." Abigail's head peeked around the entry.

"You're back." Marlee wobbled to the door and pulled it open.

Abigail, freshly dressed in a navy skirt and blazer outfit, stayed outside and paced. "I realized I forgot to return your keys." She handed them to Marlee.

"You must think I'm such a nuisance." Marlee felt Abigail's warmth as she clutched the keys and grinned.

"I was the one who forgot to leave them. I'll pop by again later this evening and we can fetch your car if you're up to it."

"I'm supposed to be the one who owes you," Marlee said. "It's very nice of you to offer, but I won't let myself trouble you anymore."

"Then be ready to go when I come by at seven." Abigail swung around and left.

Marlee spent the remainder of the day lounging on the couch and puttering in her apartment, even folding some clothes to avoid thinking about her near disaster. She was at a loss for what she was going to do with the next part of her stay in Australia now that surfing, and anything to do with the ocean, was over. While tidying in the kitchen and periodically glancing at the TV in the living room, a breaking news item caught her attention.

"Abigail Taylor, founder and CEO of AbTay Biosystems, is accused of terrorist links. The world-renowned geneticist is suspected of tampering with company research to engineer bioweapons."

Marlee dropped her tea towel and rushed over to the couch to watch a scrum of reporters swarm an approaching woman. She had a blond ponytail and was wearing a navy suit. It couldn't be…

"Dr. Taylor, are these allegations true? Did you authorize work for the genetic engineering of bioweapons?" Abigail held her head high and didn't flinch as she pushed her way through the cluster of journalists. She disappeared inside her office tower.

When the news moved on to the next item, Marlee rushed to her computer. It didn't take long to get to the homepage of AbTay Biosystems with its technical divisions and ten-year-anniversary proclamation. There was a picture of Abigail, smiling and looking like a corporate spokesperson, along with a short biography. She had her PhD in Genetics and Genomics and was a renowned expert on DNA profiling. Her family situation only mentioned a son, Josh.

Marlee browsed the website, but it was so scientific and outside her sphere of knowledge that she left it to search what else the Internet might have on Abigail. She was considered a pioneer in her field, one of the richest women in New South Wales, and cherished her privacy.

An ex-husband, a dentist named Dr. Keith Hampton, was mentioned in a few hits. They had divorced over eleven years ago and there were no recent posts linking them except to say that they shared custody of Josh.

AbTay Biosystems had been founded six months after the divorce, experiencing exponential growth since inception. Abigail had built a multimillion-dollar corporation focused on developing products and technologies that were foreign to Marlee, with the exception of some work involving DNA profiling for forensics. Marlee wasn't an expert in that area, but she recognized some of the terminology.

There were thousands of hits for Abigail Taylor and the top ones were the day's accounts of the breaking scandal at her company. All major news organizations in Australia were covering it and sensationalizing the potential links to terrorism by bringing in experts to discuss threats of bioweapons. Crimes involving weapons like genetically modified viruses to target a specific population were so much more sophisticated than what Marlee was used to in her life as a local police officer. It scared her.

Marlee contemplated Abigail's shocked reaction at discovering she was a cop. The way she'd jumped up off the couch and put her hands on her hips had seemed a little over the top. Maybe there was more to it than just letting on a police officer should have known better than to go surfing alone. After all, if there were any truth to the charges, a police officer would be the last person Abigail would want to be around, even one from Canada.

But why had she offered to bring Marlee to her car tonight? It didn't make sense. Marlee wondered if Abigail thought she was an undercover officer on assignment with the Australian police and the rescue was staged.

Marlee felt jittery, wondering if she could be in for another life-or-death situation, and a sense of uneasiness grew. What had she gotten herself into? She owed this woman her life, but there was no way she was going to get involved with anything that could put her in a difficult situation. She hoped Abigail would agree and understand that while Marlee was indebted to her, she would have no part of any criminal activity. In the meantime, Marlee decided not to tell Abigail about seeing the news and act as if she was still a *stupid* tourist.

Years of police training reminded Marlee she needed to let someone know Abigail would be picking her up. She was getting ready to contact Kerry when her neighbour in the next unit walked by the kitchen window. Although they'd only exchanged names and the occasional greeting, Marlee was desperate to trust him. A flight attendant for one of the major airlines, Tyler Bennet had a rolling suitcase in tow as he stopped to unlock his door.

Marlee stepped into the hot sun. "Welcome back."

"Hey." Tyler pushed his door open and put his hands in his pockets.

She assumed each realized the other was gay and because of it, shared a collegial view of life. At least that's what Marlee hoped as she struck up a conversation.

"You've been gone for a while. Where'd you go this time?"

"I took the long haul," Tyler said. "Sydney to LA. It was good to spend a few days there. I even took in a hockey game." The way he said game rhymed with dime. "I saw some of your family because the Kings were playing the Canadiens."

"I doubt it," Marlee said, "but if it had been a women's team, I may have had a few sisters on it."

Tyler laughed. "I'm starving. I just ordered a pizza for dinner and it should be here soon. Why don't you join me, especially if you have some cold beers you could share? My fridge is empty and I forgot to pick some up."

"Sure, why not?" Marlee said. "I do have a few cold ones, as it happens."

"Good on you, mate." Tyler hit his hands together. "I'll get settled in and you can pop to my unit as soon as the pizza arrives."

It was almost five when Marlee grabbed four chilled beers and headed next door. She would have less than two hours to chat up Tyler and gauge if he could be trusted as a confidante.

"How long are you here for?" Tyler asked. They were sitting out back, sipping beer for dessert.

"About another five weeks." Marlee hadn't yet told Tyler much about herself as she tried to keep the focus of the conversation on him and details of his latest travels.

"Where are you headed after this?" Tyler asked.

"Back to Canada. And you?" It was Marlee's understanding that all the apartments were short-term rentals. "What's your story?"

"You don't want to hear my sorry story," Tyler said. "The short of it is I needed a place in a hurry to get away from a controlling ex. I haven't told many people that I'm here because I don't want him to find out where I'm staying."

"Was it that bad?" Marlee asked.

"Worse. I sure hope you don't tell any of your surfing buddies I'm here because they might know my ex." Tyler tilted his head back and drained his bottle of beer.

"I don't have any surfing buddies." Marlee's beer was still more than half full. "Besides, I've given up surfing."

"No kidding. I thought you loved it, especially with the fancy board I saw you hauling around."

"Well I won't be lugging it around anymore. I got myself into a fancy mess with it and the board is history."

"That's too bad. I noticed your car wasn't in the lot. Did you get into a bingle?"

"More of a pickle," Marlee said, unsure of what he meant, but thinking it sounded similar. "Let's just say I lost it at sea."

"Did it get swiped?"

"Sort of." Marlee was conscious of the time and starting to feel comfortable with Tyler, so decided to wade in with the hope he could be trusted. "Did you see the news about Abigail Taylor?"

"Who hasn't?" Tyler said. "I thought we were talking about your board. Did she steal it or what?"

"She spent the night at my place." Marlee hadn't meant for it to come out like that.

"No shit?" Tyler's green eyes widened and his mouth dropped open. "You scored with the test tube lady?"

"No, of course not." Marlee had seen various references to Abigail being brilliant and reclusive, and acting as though she lived in whatever test tube she was studying. "I kind of ran into some problems on the water yesterday and she was out on her sailboat with her son. They rescued me. I had no idea who she was. Now she's coming to pick me up in less than an hour so I can get my car because I wasn't able to drive it home yesterday."

"You're jiving me, aren't you?"

"No, and please don't tell anyone about this. I wanted to let someone know. Just in case."

Tyler's jaw had fallen even further. "Do you know how private she is? People have been trying for years to find out more about Abigail Taylor, but she's very guarded on her personal life. I can't believe she's coming to pick you up. Are you sure it was her?"

"Yes, positive," Marlee said. "She dropped off my keys this morning and then I saw her on the news wearing the same business suit."

"Wow, you've already given her your keys. I didn't think she was a lesbian. She is gorgeous though."

"Nothing happened, really," Marlee said. "I never touch straight women. We hardly even talked to each other. She just wanted to make sure I was okay, but she was a bit taken aback when she found out that I'm a cop."

"A cop. Wow. Do you think she's guilty of having terrorist links?"

"I don't know and I don't want to know. Abigail Taylor saved my life and I owe her everything."

"That's sounds pretty dramatic. What really happened to your board?"

"Let's just say I went out on the water without backup and I should have known better." Marlee wanted to forget about it.

"What's this with words like backup and wanting to let someone know, just in case? You're making me nervous." Tyler ran a hand through his short, neatly coiffed light brown hair.

"There's nothing to be nervous about," Marlee said. "Being prepared is in my blood, or at least I thought it was, and I just wanted to tell someone where I'm going. I should have known better yesterday."

"Are you here on assignment to bring down AbTay Biosystems?" Tyler leaned forward, elbows on his knees.

Marlee straightened up. "No, not at all. I would never do anything to hurt her. I owe her."

"I suggest you don't say that to her. According to the tabloids, she has a reputation for having high expectations and being hard on staff who don't meet them."

"I can believe that," Marlee said. "She scolded me for not having a buddy out on the water yesterday."

"She was right on that one. Surfers should always go with someone."

"I can't imagine why she insisted on bringing me to get my car tonight of all nights, when she has so much else going on in her life right now."

"Do you want me to go with you?" Tyler asked. "If I hadn't just had three of your beers, I'd offer to take you myself."

"Thanks, but I'm okay." Marlee stood up. "I should get going because she'll be here soon. Please don't tell anyone about this. I want to watch out for myself, but I owe this woman and if there's anything I can do to help her..."

"My lips are sealed." Tyler slid fingers over his mouth, as though closing a zipper.

Marlee's stomach churned as she stood out front and waited for Abigail. She was nervous, but there was also some excitement and a bit of adrenaline mixed in. She could have just taken a cab to get her car, but she was curious. The trauma of her near death the day before had been overridden by the shock of realizing she'd been rescued by Abigail Taylor.

A late-model white hatchback Volkswagen Golf pulled into the lot. Marlee was watching for the dark luxury SUV they'd driven in the day before, and was surprised when the vehicle came to a stop in front of her. The driver's darkened window eased down and an emotionless Abigail waved her over.

"You seem to be doing much better," Abigail said as Marlee buckled herself in.

Abigail wore a snug white T-shirt and beige mid-length shorts, her ponytail fed through the back of a white ball cap. Her feet sported delicate slip-on sandals and balanced on the pedals of what would have been the passenger side of a car in Canada. Even dressed in casual clothes, Abigail had an air of sophistication that awed Marlee.

"I am, thank you." Marlee felt sloppy in her baggy T-shirt, comfortable cargo shorts, and well-worn sports sandals. "How was your day?" She could hardly imagine.

"Hectic." Abigail eased her foot off the clutch as they merged into traffic. "It's good that I had an excuse to leave or I'd still be at the office."

"What kind of office do you work in?" Marlee let on she hadn't seen the news.

"A busy one." Abigail stared at the road as she geared down for a roundabout. "What did you get up to today?"

"Nothing much."

They drove the rest of the way in silence. When they got to Marlee's subcompact rental car, Abigail pulled up beside it and parked then also got out.

"Thank you so much for everything," Marlee said. "I owe you my life and will never forget it." She wrapped her arms around Abigail and squeezed. There wasn't much of a hug returned so Marlee pulled away. "I'd like to take you and Josh out for dinner."

"That isn't necessary," Abigail said. "I'm sure you would have done the same for us." She got back into her car and put down the window. "Take care of yourself and enjoy the rest of your visit in Australia."

Marlee watched the white car disappear in traffic and wondered if she'd ever talk to this bizarre woman again.

CHAPTER FOUR

"How did it go?" Tyler stepped out of his unit in a waft of aftershave as Marlee put the key in her lock.

"Okay, I guess." Marlee pushed her door open then leaned against the frame, fighting off a sneeze from Tyler's cologne that reminded her of cinnamon. "She brought me to my car and now here I am. I'll probably never see her again."

"You'll see lots of her if you keep up with the news," Tyler said. "Did you tell her you saw her on TV?"

"No. I decided to play dumb to see if she'd bring it up, but she didn't."

"No kidding. What did you talk about?" Tyler used the top of his right foot to scratch the back calf of his left leg.

"Nothing much. She's a strange woman."

"Sounds like it," Tyler said. "What are you up to tomorrow? Want to go to Manly Beach with me?"

"I'm done with surfing," Marlee said.

"Good, because I hate surfing, but I love hanging at the beach. I have a few days off and am hoping to feast my eyes on some half-naked hunky male specimens. I'm sure there'll be lots of bikini watching for you too. It'll be fun. Will you come?"

"Sure, why not." Marlee liked Tyler and needed a friend. Besides, it had been a while since she'd let herself relax.

He rubbed his hands together. "Perfect. We'll go early to get a good spot. I'll pop by around ten in the morning."

Marlee fought off exhaustion to search the web a bit longer before bed. She plopped on the couch with her laptop and began browsing. This appeared to be the first time Abigail was associated with any criminal activity, and the only connection was through her company. There were many other hits linked with various universities all over the world where Abigail had been an invited guest speaker or asked to sit on a panel. Everything was focused on her professional life and there was little to be found on the personal side.

Eyes weary and beginning to droop closed, Marlee finally shut down her computer and climbed into bed, welcoming a deep sleep that lasted all night.

The next morning, Marlee hoped to touch base with her best friend Kerry for a chat before going to the beach. It would have been just after supper in Ottawa so the timing was good. Marlee set her laptop on her small coffee table and was about to try connecting with Kerry when a knock on her door interrupted her. She rushed to answer, hoping it was Abigail and wondering what she wanted.

"Ready?" Tyler had a beach towel draped around his neck and a small backpack slung over his shoulder.

"It's only nine thirty." Marlee's heart rate calmed. "I thought you said ten?"

"Maybe I did, but I'm ready now. It's supposed to be a scorcher and there'll be lots of people fighting for a good spot near the water."

"Okay, let me get my things."

The beach was starting to fill up by the time they got there, but Tyler managed to stake out space near a huddle of sculpted, bare-chested men.

"Ah, just look at those budgie smugglers," Tyler said. "What a view."

"Excuse me?" Marlee was coating her legs in sunscreen and paused to look at Tyler, raising her eyebrows above large plastic sunglasses. She wore a light cotton shirt over her two-piece bathing suit. "Budgie smugglers?"

Tyler laughed as he spread his towel on the sand. "The guys over there." He motioned with his head to the group of men in skimpy swimming briefs. "Their suits are called budgie smugglers because it looks like they have a budgie stuffed down the front. I love this kind of bird watching on the beach."

Marlee shook her head. "I'm not into birding." She wondered what had she gotten herself into now. "I hope you're not wearing one of those skimpy suits too, because I'm a cop and might have to arrest you if it looks like there's any kind of smuggling going on."

Tyler laughed. "I'd never wear one out in public. I'd be too afraid my budgie would get away on me." He looked Marlee up and down. "I can see you're not afraid of anything getting away from that skimpy bikini. You look fabulous in it, by the way."

"Thank you." Marlee removed her shirt. "It's not like I have to worry about my little bird breasts popping out."

"You dykes have it so easy," Tyler said. "You could let yourself get totally turned on by some cute chick on the beach and nobody would notice."

Marlee sprawled out on her towel. "Well it's not what I'm here for. I have to make sure I have a nice tan when I get back to Canada. Would you mind putting some sunscreen on my back? I just want enough to make sure I don't burn."

"So why are you visiting Australia by yourself?" Tyler spread the lotion on her back.

"Why not?" Marlee wasn't used to awkward male hands putting lotion on her back and was happy for it to end.

"Are you trying to get away from an ex?"

"It's more like I was trying to get away from myself," Marlee said. "I just needed a change of scenery."

"Do you have someone back in Canada?" Tyler took off his shirt and reclined on his stomach. "Would you mind slathering some on me?"

"There's an ex I was happy to leave behind." Marlee spread sunscreen over his well tanned back.

"Oh, that feels good. Could you give it a little scratch too?"

"Forget it." Marlee tossed the tube of sunscreen by her pack, relieved to have her hands off Tyler. "Besides, my nails are too short for that."

"Was it messy with your ex?" Tyler stayed on his stomach and rested his head on his hands.

"She took everything so there wasn't anything to leave a mess." Marlee flattened her towel then lay on her stomach beside Tyler.

"What about you? Is that why you're here? Because you were a mess?"

"Not really," Marlee said. "It was quite the opposite. I felt like I suddenly had space to reinvent myself. Why not go halfway around the world to do that?"

"It sounds a bit like running away to me. I know I sure felt like escaping when I dumped my ex. On one of my flights to LA, I almost didn't return. I thought about heading over to San Francisco and hanging out there for a while until I got my head together."

"It's different with me," Marlee said. "I knew I needed a change, but somehow didn't have the strength to walk out on Stacy myself. By the time she did it to me, there was nothing left—literally. I had to pay off her debts and she got to keep all the crap. In the end, I didn't care. I just wanted out."

"Who needs the crap anyway?" Tyler shifted on his towel and picked up a brand-new copy of a Jonathan Kellerman paperback. "I think I'll read for a bit, or at least pretend to as those guys play volleyball over there."

"Why don't you see if you can join them?" Marlee said. "I'll watch your stuff."

"You sure you don't mind?"

"Not at all." Marlee was looking forward to some time to herself to think about her life. "I'm still reeling from finding out who Abigail was and everything."

"You must have thought she was hot." Tyler stood up. "Test tube lady or not, she has a great body that I imagine any single lesbian would love to get their hands on."

"Have fun," Marlee said. She had certainly noticed Abigail's beauty, but refused to let herself focus on it. She wanted to keep any feelings for her hero pure and simple, with no complications of lust.

Marlee stretched out on her towel and buried her face in her arms to relax. She needed to think about the rest of her stay in the country and what she wanted to do with her time. The thought of going back out onto the water made her shudder. As much as she would have liked to properly thank Abigail and Josh, she was relieved that she could put this behind her. No one needed to know about her surfing disaster and no one would believe she'd fought off a shark. In the end, it was best she hadn't spoken with Kerry this morning.

"Hey, your back is getting red." Tyler poked a finger on Marlee's back and she twitched.

"I must have fallen asleep." Marlee bounced up. "What time is it?"

"It's time to get out of the sun," Tyler said. "Let's wander over to a restaurant and get something to eat. I'm hungry after playing with those hunks. Did you see how good I was?"

"Sorry, but I slept most of the time you were gone. Did you have fun?" Marlee slipped on her shorts and reached for her shirt.

"It was okay, but I didn't really fit in with them." Tyler pulled on his T-shirt and gathered up his towel. "It was a bit awkward because they all seemed so straight."

"That's too bad."

"No big deal." Tyler slung his pack over his shoulder. "Shall we go?"

They chose a burger place and were comfortably seated in a booth, glancing at a large muted TV screen, when Marlee saw Abigail being scrummed by reporters again.

"Look at her," Marlee said. "The poor woman. It's like she's being attacked. I wish I could somehow help her."

"How do you know she's innocent?" Tyler sipped his diet cola. "Maybe she deserves what she's getting."

"I don't think so," Marlee said. "I owe her my life and the least I can do is sympathize since she won't let me do anything else."

"You're starting to sound dramatic," Tyler said. "What exactly did she do to save you?"

"I got caught in a riptide and drifted for hours until she rescued me." Marlee refused to mention the shark.

"It doesn't sound like she risked her life to save you. I heard she has a nice boat. What was it like?"

"I hardly remember the boat," Marlee said. "It was scary in the water and I'm sure I would've drowned if it wasn't for her. Now it looks like she's drowning in all of this controversy."

"I'm sure it was no big deal to give you a lift back into shore," Tyler said. "It doesn't sound like she wants anything from you so I'd just move on. Did you at least get a selfie with her?"

"No." Marlee would keep the memory to herself.

They lounged on the beach for the afternoon, Tyler reading his book and Marlee thinking about Abigail. It had been like a dream, being pulled from the water and then finding out who her rescuer was. It wasn't a dream, however, when Marlee realized how aroused she was just thinking about Abigail's aura of elegance. Tyler was right and moving on was for the best. The last thing Marlee needed was to fall for this straight woman so far from her world.

Marlee and Tyler settled on sharing leftover pizza and beer for dinner back at their building. It had been a good day, and Marlee was glad they'd met. At least she'd have someone to hang out with for the rest of her stay. She had enjoyed his company; it was like they had known each other forever. That's exactly what she needed—a good friend with no strings attached.

Marlee had just settled down on her couch when she heard a light tapping on her door. She rushed to the door and flung it open.

"What do you want?" Marlee expected Tyler and cringed when Abigail recoiled. "Oh my God, I'm so sorry, Abigail. I didn't think I'd ever see you again and was expecting it to be someone else."

"Don't apologize." Abigail turned to leave. "I thought you were all alone and didn't mean to interrupt anything."

Marlee grasped her arm. "Please come in. I'm by myself and you're not interrupting."

Abigail stopped, her body tense, and pulled her arm away. "You told me you didn't know anyone here, that you were all alone. That doesn't seem to be the case."

Marlee's face reddened and she began to babble like an excited teenager. "I realized how pathetic it was so after you left I made a point of getting to know my neighbour, Tyler. He's a flight attendant and had been away, but just came back last night. It turns out we really hit it off and spent the day together at Manly Beach. Please come in."

Abigail hesitated. "It's probably best if I leave."

Marlee rushed out and around Abigail. "Please don't go. I want to help you. I saw you on the news."

Abigail stopped and stared into Marlee's eyes. "You can't help me. I thought just maybe you could, but now I don't think so. I can't trust anyone."

"You can trust me." Marlee peered back. The warmth of Abigail's eyes was mesmerizing. "I owe you my life and want to somehow repay you. I'd die before betraying your trust."

"You're a police officer," Abigail said. "How do you know you can trust me?"

"I can see it in your eyes." Marlee grabbed onto Abigail's hands. "I know you're a good person."

"You don't know anything about me. What kind of police officer are you?"

"An experienced one," Marlee said. "I base a lot of my decisions on instinct. I've had to over the years."

"Where was your instinct the other day?"

"I don't know, but it came back to me when I stared that shark in the eyes. I knew it was going to kill me. You risked your life to save mine. I don't need any more proof than that. I want to help."

"It feels like no one can help."

"I can if you let me." Marlee squeezed Abigail's hands. "When you were on the news this afternoon, I wanted to jump into the TV and rescue you. Sharks of a different kind were ganging up, wanting a piece of you, and I felt powerless. Please let me help."

Abigail eased away. "I need to think. Can we go inside before someone sees me?"

CHAPTER FIVE

Abigail accepted a cup of chamomile tea and wrapped her hands around the hot mug as though she was frozen. "Since I imagine you've heard all kinds of things about me, why don't you tell me a bit about yourself?"

Marlee sipped her tea. "There isn't much to tell. I was born and raised in Canada and have been a police officer for fifteen years."

"Why are you in Australia?"

"I've always wanted to visit the land down under. I needed a break from things and managed to get a three-month leave from my job. It just seemed like the right time to come to Australia."

"How much longer are you here?"

"Another five weeks." Marlee wondered why all the questions.

"Have you ever been married?" Abigail wouldn't let up.

"No. I've never been all that good at picking the right relationships."

"What about Tyler?" Abigail put her tea down and crossed her arms. "How would you define your relationship with him?"

"I needed a friend and he was there." Anyone else and Marlee would have stopped the interrogation, but she was willing to put up with the questioning to keep Abigail around. She was curious about where this was leading. "I like him and we have fun together."

"As in a casual fling?" Abigail's lips were puckered.

"Not that it's any of your business, but no." Marlee was annoyed by the insinuation. "We're both gay."

Abigail leaned back into the couch, face softening and hands resting on her lap. "My apologies for all the questions, but I want to be sure."

"About what?" Marlee leaned forward with interest.

Abigail straightened up again. "I'm not a lesbian, in case that's what you're wondering."

Marlee felt like she'd been slapped. "That's not what I was thinking. Please don't make any assumptions about me."

"No, I guess I shouldn't. I don't want to assume I can trust you either."

Marlee stared into Abigail's tired blue eyes. "I will not betray your trust."

Abigail scoffed. "I wish I could see trustworthiness in you like you say you can see it in me."

Marlee put her hand over her heart. "You have my word."

"I really want to believe you, Marlee. There's no one else I can trust right now except for Josh and I want him kept out of this. What type of work have you done as a police officer?"

"Everything from issuing traffic tickets to uncovering drug grow-ops." Marlee sensed she was being interviewed for a job and straightened her shoulders. "I also spent a few years working in our forensics unit."

Abigail leaned forward. "That's good to know. What type of work did you do?"

"I've been involved with a number of crime scene investigations that included liaising with colleagues from forensics for the collection and management of DNA samples. I've also had some experience with our fraud unit, especially for credit and debit card scams."

"Have you ever been investigated for anything?"

"Like what? Do you mean something criminal?"

"Yes, but really anything inappropriate." Abigail leaned back.

Marlee looked Abigail in the eye. "I do my job by the book and have a clean record, if that's what you're wondering."

"What about being accused of wrongdoing?" Abigail's gaze flitted away. "Something you didn't do, but were blamed for?"

"Sure, lots of times when I was a kid." Marlee tried to lighten the mood. "My brother was a little rascal and always trying to get me into trouble with our parents."

"Are your parents still alive?"

"Yes, but they divorced years ago and we're not close."

"How many siblings do you have?"

"Just one brother. Gabriel. He's two years older." Marlee's eyes lit up. "He's happily married and I have two beautiful nieces."

"Are you close to them?"

"Yes. And what about you? Other than Josh, who is your family?"

"It's just the two of us," Abigail said. "Except for Josh, my work is my life and I can't believe this is happening to me."

"What's going on? How can I help?" Marlee wanted to reach out and offer a comforting touch, but kept her hands to herself.

Abigail's eyes were red and moist, but there were no tears. "I can't trust anyone right now. Someone in my company is betraying all of us by tampering with our research and trying to engineer bioweapons."

"Have you gone to the police?"

"They've come to me," Abigail said. "Many times. They've been anonymously tipped that my company is engineering bioweapons and think I'm involved. But I'm not. The informant must be someone who works with me, but I can't be sure."

"What makes you say that?" Marlee's jaw clenched at the thought of someone betraying Abigail.

"Somebody hacked my email account to make it look like I'm involved in this despicable activity." Abigail sat forward, hands gripping her knees.

"Can I see the emails?"

"There was only one and it had me approving proposed research into genomic alteration for the development of personalized bioweapons."

"So you're being framed." Marlee focused on practical investigative techniques. "Have you noticed anything out of the ordinary, even the smallest things, from any of your staff? Maybe someone near your office when they shouldn't be, or offering to help with work that's not really in their domain?"

"No, nothing. I'm at a loss. All my research, everything I've worked on is at risk of becoming a weapon that could have horrifying results."

"In what ways?" Marlee was starting to feel nervous, especially since she didn't know much about Abigail's work.

"Cancer growing at exponential rates, genetic manipulations that cause birth defects, new diseases with no cures—the horrors could be endless." Abigail's shoulders were hunched and her voice started to shake. "Editing genes to encourage widespread growth of diseases and disorders instead of eliminating them. All my work…" She buried her face in her hands and started to sob.

Marlee moved to Abigail's side, wanting to offer some consolation. "I may not be an expert in genetics and all that science stuff, but I do have experience in uncovering crime." She put a hand on Abigail's shoulder. "I know exactly what to do."

"You do?" Abigail flung her head up, eyes wide as she looked at Marlee.

"Yes." The only thing Marlee knew for sure was that she needed to sound in control, like she had a plan. She'd used that strategy many times on the job. "I'm going to help you catch the scum responsible for this."

"Do you think you can?" Abigail asked.

"Yes." Marlee knew she could help. Whether or not they would catch the culprit was a little less certain, especially working in another police jurisdiction and on her own.

"I sure hope so." Abigail sighed.

"That's why you came back, isn't it? Because I have experience tracking down criminals?"

"That's part of it," Abigail said. "You did say you owed me your life. You're my last chance for trusting somebody in this. Please don't let me down."

"That will never happen." Marlee locked eyes with Abigail. "I'd die before betraying you."

"I don't expect you to do anything like that, but I appreciate the sentiment." Abigail's eyes moved away from Marlee's. "I want to pay you for your time."

"That won't be necessary." Marlee didn't want to be Abigail's employee. She needed to be her associate and in a position to call the shots.

"Money's not a problem," Abigail said.

"I'm not in this for any money and my role has to be much bigger than hired help if this is to work."

"And what do you expect your role to be?"

"To do whatever it takes to catch whoever is responsible and clear your name."

"I won't have you taking on my battle and implicating yourself in a scheme that could ruin your career." Abigail shook her head as though it was out of the question.

"We need to work together and our partnership must be based on trust." Marlee wanted to be taken seriously.

"Yes, but I want to keep you away from being associated with me. I didn't save your life to screw it up."

"My life's already screwed up," Marlee said. "I need a drink. Can I get you a glass of red wine?"

"Yes, thank you, that would be nice." Abigail followed Marlee to the kitchen. "What I really mean is for you to work with me, but secretly because no one in my company knows about you right now and that could be helpful."

"I suppose." Marlee poured the wine, starting to relax. "I'm nobody here until I open my mouth and people hear my accent. Then I become the tourist."

"At least you can go wherever you want and when people find out you're a tourist, I don't imagine they start to follow and take pictures." Abigail smiled and nodded thanks as she accepted her wine.

"Cheers." Marlee tapped their glasses together.

Abigail sipped as she returned to the couch. "I can't go anywhere without being hounded and harassed. Even coming here I had to make sure I wasn't being followed by a reporter."

Marlee joined Abigail on the sofa, determined to somehow help this woman. "We'll figure this out together."

"Let's hope so."

They drank their wine in silence, Marlee deep in thought about what to do next. As Abigail emptied her glass, Marlee began to ask questions.

"Do you have any suspicions who could be doing this?"

"No, none." Abigail shook her head. "Everyone seems so passionate about their work and the thought of having their research hijacked for unscrupulous means sends tremors through the ranks."

"How well do you know your employees?"

"Some of them I know very well, but I'm ashamed to say I don't even know the names of others I see often. There's too many. At last count, we had over twenty-five hundred."

"Are they all located in the head office in Sydney?"

"Everyone with access to our most important research," Abigail said. "We do have a satellite location in Canberra for proximity to federal government offices. Staff in Canberra lack security clearance to access our protected database of research in genome editing."

"Do you know everyone who has access to that database?" Marlee wondered how much control she had over her employees.

"Yes. At least, I thought I did because I cannot believe that any one of us who has access would be so deplorable." Abigail stifled a yawn.

"Can I get you a coffee or another tea?" Marlee didn't offer more alcohol because Abigail would be driving.

"How about another glass of wine?" Abigail stretched her shoulders.

"I could do that, but then I couldn't let you drive home." Marlee headed to the kitchen. "You'd have to either take a taxi or spend the night."

"I can't take a taxi. The driver would recognize me."

Marlee got the bottle of wine. "Then you'll have to spend the night here."

"I don't think so." Abigail leaned forward, as if to stand.

"Why not?" Marlee filled Abigail's glass. "This can be a test to see how much you trust me."

Abigail's eyebrows furrowed. "How so?"

Marlee had gotten ahead of herself, drowning in relief and adrenaline as she thought of helping Abigail, and felt her cheeks reddening. "Sorry, I didn't mean to sound so cocky. I think you're very attractive and I have a bit of a reputation. You'll be safe. I'll sleep on the couch."

"And I'm to believe this, as you're trying to get me drunk?"

"Of course." Marlee smirked as she handed over the full glass.

"Cheers." Abigail raised her glass, the corners of her mouth slightly lifted. "What have I got to lose?"

Marlee and Abigail spent the next two hours discussing strategies for an internal investigation into five high-ranking AbTay Biosystems staff, each of who had their own close cadre of workers. They reviewed some files of detailed information on key staff members, including performance appraisals, employment history, and personal bios. Executive employees at AbTay Biosystems were all impeccable with nothing out of the ordinary, except being extremely talented and brilliant people.

Between finishing their wine and then drinking lots of coffee, both had managed to remain clearheaded and focused on the task at hand. They decided Marlee's involvement would be kept quiet, a secret weapon against the mole. Nobody in the company knew she existed and her apartment would be Abigail's hiding place from the world. Their contact would be by cryptic messages through their phones and in the darkness of night, which meant Abigail had to be gone before daybreak.

"You need to get a few hours of sleep before you go," Marlee said. "Why don't you head into bed while I tidy up and get the coffee ready so you can have another cup when you leave."

"I'll never be able to sleep now." Abigail set her empty mug in the sink. "I'll get some rest at my place after I've showered and unwound a bit."

"I guess I had more wine than you," Marlee said. Abigail had taken small sips of her second glass of wine then poured most of it down the sink when the coffee was ready. "You should be okay to drive if you want to head out now."

"Thank you so much for your help." Abigail smiled.

"We'll do this together. I know we can. I want you to have a key to my place so you can come in whenever."

"Are you sure?" Abigail accepted the key and held it in the palm of her hand. "I wouldn't want to walk in and interrupt something personal."

Marlee smiled. "If I thought you'd be interrupting anything, I wouldn't give you a key. Besides, the only personal thing going on in my apartment these days is when I'm in the bathroom, and I always close the door."

Abigail laughed, folded her fingers over the key, and left. Marlee went to bed, the sweet sound of Abigail's laughter playing in her ears as she fell asleep.

CHAPTER SIX

"Hey." Tyler's head popped out of his unit as Marlee returned from a late-morning jog. "Isn't it a bit too hot for a run today?"

"I want to be hot stuff so have to keep my body in shape." Marlee unlocked her door and pushed it open. She reached inside for the hand towel she'd left on a hook.

"Did you see the news this morning?" Tyler stepped outside and edged up to Marlee.

Marlee froze. "No, not yet. Why, what's going on?"

"Your 'friend' has been brought in by the police for more questioning." Tyler used his fingers to put imaginary quotations around the word friend.

"Oh no, I didn't see it." Marlee put the towel on her face and held it over her eyes, soaking up sweat and hiding her emotions. She had to let on Abigail was in her past, a brief acquaintance.

"You okay?" Tyler tugged on the towel.

"Sorry, I just had to catch my breath." Marlee draped the towel around her neck, anxious to get back inside and look at the news.

"I'm heading down to the beach again this afternoon. Want to come?" Tyler's messy hair and wrinkled T-shirt made it obvious he'd just gotten up.

"I think I'll give it a pass today," Marlee said. "I have a few things I want to do around here."

"Like what? Surely you're not talking about housework or anything like that on a fabulous day like today?"

"The days are always gorgeous around here. I have to go now. Nature calls."

"Sorry, don't let me hold you up." Tyler went to his door. "Will I see you later?"

"Enjoy your day at the beach." Marlee wouldn't commit to anything now that Abigail needed her.

Once inside, she rushed to her computer and brought up some news sites. It didn't take long to see pictures of Abigail, head down and being ushered into the police station as though a criminal. Marlee wanted to reach into the screen and hug her broken hero, but instead hit her fist against the table in frustration.

She quickly showered and then started going through what they had reviewed the night before. One senior staff member, Hannah Williams, had done her master's and PhD under Abigail's supervision and quickly risen up the ranks to become the Vice President of Genomic Sequencing. The thirty-five-year-old whiz was single and didn't have any children. She had been born and raised in Melbourne then moved to Sydney to attend university and made the city her home ever since. The two had worked closely on a number of research projects over the past ten years and jointly published many research-related documents. Marlee made a note to find out more about Hannah, especially since Abigail scoffed at the idea of her being involved with any type of conspiracy. She spent the rest of the day trolling the Internet for information on bioweapons.

By suppertime, images of Abigail leaving the police station were splashing across news sites. Head held high and softer lines around her mouth, she rushed to a waiting car. Marlee caught a glimpse of a woman at the wheel, and based on the photo in the file, it was most likely Hannah. Her hair was blond too and kept in a ponytail like Abigail's. The two women could have been sisters they looked so much alike.

After a dinner of garden salad and chicken, Marlee began developing an action plan for her investigative approach. At this point, Abigail was the only person she could question to try to uncover any motives, methods, or identities of potential suspects. It would be a challenge because while she had access to Abigail's internal files and the Internet, it wasn't the same as being able to scout out an informant or rely on any kind of electronic surveillance. Her biggest problem, however, was that uncovering corporate wrongdoings was out of her league and she didn't really know what to do other than scope out a framework for next steps.

Abigail sent a text indicating she'd be dropping by around midnight. Marlee's stomach churned in excited anticipation of seeing Abigail, especially after what must have been a nightmarish day of police interrogation. She tried to get some sleep before Abigail's arrival so she'd have the energy to work all night, if necessary. She got out of bed just before midnight and was startled to find Abigail seated on her couch, computer open and beautiful blue eyes scanning the screen.

"Sorry, I didn't mean to scare you." Abigail's face glowed in the light of her laptop. "I hope you don't mind that I let myself in."

"Of course not." Marlee was rather pleased Abigail felt comfortable enough to use the key, but slightly unnerved she hadn't heard her come in. "How long have you been here?"

"Not long. I figured you were sleeping and didn't want to disturb you. At least for a few more minutes." Abigail sipped a coffee and motioned to another on the table. "I got us each an espresso."

"Thank you." Marlee was flattered that Abigail thought to bring one for her. "I'm so sorry you had another terrible day. How did it go with the police?"

"They don't believe me." Abigail bounced one leg up and down. "Why should they? It's my company and somebody under my watch is a traitor. I should know who it is and who they're working with."

"Why did they bring you in for questioning today?" Marlee resisted the urge to put her hand on Abigail's leg.

"They said it was to go over things again." Abigail leaned back into the couch. "I spent the afternoon in a small room with a police interrogator. The interview started with him implying that I was guilty. He wanted me to admit spearheading experiments in genetic manipulation for the purposes of engineering bioweapons. They think I'm in it for the money because the potential for financial gain is endless with all of the terrorist activity across the globe. Every time I tried to deny it, he'd cut me off. It was as though I couldn't speak unless I was going to admit guilt."

Marlee recognized the technique. Although she hadn't worked in interrogation, she'd heard all about the work of her colleagues and the procedures they used to elicit a confession. "Would you like me to see if I can get a police contact here and pay a visit to the station to try and find out about the inside word on you?"

"No, please don't." Abigail shook her head. "I won't risk having them know about you because I don't trust anyone."

"You think the police could somehow be involved?" Marlee's computer began to chime and she realized Kerry was trying to connect with her. "It's my friend in Ottawa. I'll call her back later."

Abigail continued with the conversation as though the call hadn't happened. "I don't know what to think anymore, but I do know that I don't trust anyone. It's a wonder I'm even here."

"Please don't say that." Marlee made eye contact and leaned forward. "You have to believe me if we're going to solve this. I don't know what else I can say or do to prove to you that I won't betray your trust."

"I'm sorry." Abigail touched Marlee's arm then closed her eyes. "I'm tired and shouldn't have said that. I think I need a nap. Why don't you call your friend back while I lay down for a bit?"

"Take my bed. I changed the sheets this afternoon so it's nice and fresh for a little nap."

"Thank you." Abigail smiled as she raised her heavy lids.

"Are you okay?" Marlee spoke in a low voice, keeping their eyes locked.

"Yes." Abigail released her gaze and got up. "I'm overtired, I think. I'll see you in a bit." She went into the bedroom and closed the door.

Marlee was overdue to speak with Kerry, her best friend in Ottawa, so launched a video call on her laptop.

"G'day mate." Kerry flashed a smile with her attempt at an Australian accent.

"Hey there, it's good to see you and hear your voice." Marlee felt a twinge of homesickness as she returned Kerry's smile and fought the urge to tell her about Abigail.

"I hope I didn't wake you. I forget what time it is in the land down under."

"It's late, but no worries. I couldn't sleep and was listening to music with my headphones. I just noticed you called."

"I hope you're behaving and enjoying the weather south of the equator because we're freezing our butts off up here."

"That's why I'm here." Marlee winked. "What's new in Ottawa?"

"I'm sure you'll be glad to hear we have tons of snow. Let me show you." Kerry brought her computer up to her kitchen window to give Marlee a view of her white backyard.

"I'd show you our nice lawn and summer weather here," Marlee said, "but it's dark out right now so you wouldn't see much."

"How's the surfing coming along?" Kerry sat back down at her dining room table and grabbed a mug of tea.

"I've decided it's not for me and got rid of my board." Marlee wanted to tell Kerry about her near-death encounter with the shark and meeting Abigail, but couldn't bring herself to talk about any of it just yet.

"That's too bad," Kerry said. "What are you going to do with the rest of your time there?"

"Lots of things. I finally met one of my neighbours and we hung out at Manly Beach yesterday."

"Nice. Is she hot?" Kerry bit into a cookie.

"I wish. Tyler's a gay flight attendant. He dragged me to the beach so he could watch the male species."

"That sounds like fun." Kerry snickered. "What about the women? I can't imagine you watched the guys too."

"I'm not interested in getting involved with anyone because I don't want to break any hearts when I leave."

"I didn't ask you about getting involved with anyone." Kerry's tongue snapped against the roof of her mouth. "I thought you wanted to 'pick up as many women as possible while down under the sheets,' to quote you. How's that going?"

"As a matter of fact," Marlee lowered her voice, "there's a hot babe in my bed right now."

"And you're sitting there talking with me?" Kerry smirked. "You're full of shit."

"It's true. It's not the first time she's been in my bed either."

"I thought you were listening to music when I called. What's that all about?" Kerry persisted.

"I couldn't sleep. What time is it in Ottawa?"

"It's just after one in the afternoon," Kerry said. "So what's her name?"

"She's Australian. How's Diane?"

"Diane's fine." Kerry leaned into her screen. "So she's going to be known as the woman from Australia? That's all you're going to tell me? How long have we been friends?"

"Okay, her name is Abby and she's great in the sack. There, are you satisfied?" Marlee looked up to see Abigail by the door, her mouth open and eyes wide, ready to bolt.

CHAPTER SEVEN

Marlee slammed her laptop shut and rushed to prevent Abigail from leaving. "Please, just let me explain."

"So I'm great in bed, eh?" Abigail dropped her head against the unopened door. "Fuck."

"It's not what you think." Marlee's cheeks throbbed to the tune of her pounding heart. "I was speaking to my best friend, Kerry. I don't know what came over me. I can be such a jerk."

"How can this be happening? What's wrong with you?" Abigail's words were harsh.

"I'm sorry. Please. I want to help you." Marlee was losing it, the terror at sea catching up to her. "I haven't been able to think about that day and how close I came to dying." She gripped Abigail's arms and began to sob. "It was a miracle when you came. Please don't leave."

"I'll stay for now," Abigail's voice softened. She put her arms around Marlee. "Let's talk and try to figure this out."

"Thank you." Marlee clung to Abigail as if the core of their beings were melding. It was an intimacy she'd never experienced with another woman. Abigail's soft skin, the aroma of her coconut shampoo, and her heated embrace made Marlee long to crawl deep inside this cocoon and never leave.

The blare of Marlee's computer alerting of a connection attempt tore them apart and back to reality.

"I have to answer," Marlee said as she grabbed some tissues. "It's Kerry and she'll worry if I don't." She lowered the light and wiped her tears before accepting the call.

"Hey, sorry about that." Marlee sniffled. "We're having some technical difficulties."

"Have you been crying?" Kerry squinted.

"Of course not." Marlee strengthened her voice.

"What's going on?"

"Nothing."

"Is everything okay?" Kerry's head tilted, her eyes widening.

Marlee didn't know what to say, whether to tell the truth or to keep making things up. She looked at Abigail for guidance.

"You can blame me," Abigail said. "I walked in on your conversation about my behavior in bed and she slammed her laptop closed. I think your friend was embarrassed."

"Abby? I can't see you." Kerry's nose almost touched the screen.

"And you won't because I'm naked."

Marlee grinned, pleasantly surprised by Abigail's ease at playing her lover, and carried it further. "The Australian scenery is amazing right now and things are starting to heat up down under, if you catch my drift."

"Too much information." Kerry pulled back, squishing her face. "I'll leave you two alone now. Just don't let things heat up so much that you get burnt."

"Say hi to Diane for me." Marlee waved, exited the program, then approached Abigail and took her hands. "Thanks. Kerry knows me and I didn't want her to worry. Your response was perfect because it made me look like the stud I was claiming to be."

Abigail pulled her hands away. "I saw the way you looked at me. I can play along with being your lesbian lover if that's what you're telling your friends in Canada, but don't get your hopes up. It's not me and it'll never happen."

"I know." Marlee replayed the way Abigail looked at her when pretending to be naked. She didn't dare hope the attraction was mutual, but still. She'd gotten goose bumps.

"Can I at least call you Abby?" Marlee's strategy for getting out of awkward situations was to grin and spit out words in hopes of lightening the mood.

"Please don't." Abigail plopped on the couch and folded her arms. She seemed out of breath. "If you must, I prefer Tay."

"Tay." Marlee smiled. "I like that. Does anyone ever call you Dr. Tay?"

"No. My childhood friends from school used to call me Tay."

"Tay has a nice sound to it and is more personal than Abigail." Marlee felt her cheeks heating up. "Not that I'm reading anything into it."

"Good." Abigail's facial expression softened and her eyes risked meeting Marlee's. "Let's talk about how you're doing. You had a very traumatic experience on the water. Have you discussed it with anyone?"

"No." Marlee pulled her eyes away. She grabbed a chair and sat facing Abigail, hands on knees and fingers digging into her legs.

"Why haven't you told Kerry?" Abigail leaned forward and tapped Marlee's knee.

"I don't know." Marlee felt the first few teardrops splatter on her legs before the gush began, and all words were lost. She didn't want to think about how close she'd come to dying, let alone talk about it. It was too soon and she wasn't ready.

"I'm sorry." Marlee shook her head. She wasn't used to crying like that. It was embarrassing.

"There's no need to apologize." Abigail's voice was soft. She pulled Marlee up and folded her into another embrace. "We're here for each other."

"I haven't been here for you." Marlee's heart felt like it was going to beat out of her chest as she clung to Abigail. "I wanted to hear all about your day and show you the plan I've put together. Tonight's been a disaster."

"I don't agree." Abigail caressed the back of Marlee's head. "We've made good progress tonight."

"Progress?" Marlee leaned back to look at Abigail. "How do you define that?"

"I'm ready to trust you now." Abigail smiled, her eyes sparkling. "I'd say that's a lot of progress."

"What made you change your mind?"

"I believe we can help each other." Abigail backed away and sat on the sofa.

"Let me show you my plan." Marlee got her computer and began to illuminate files.

Abigail reached over and lowered the screen. "I'm really looking forward to seeing it, but first I want to talk about how we can help you."

"I'll be okay as long as I stay off the water." She reopened her laptop.

Abigail stood up and slapped a hand over the computer to close it. "We need to get you back on the water as soon as possible. It's time to call it a night. We'll head to the boat first thing tomorrow morning and spend the day on it to go over your plan then."

"I don't know." Marlee started to quiver. "I think it'll be better if we stay here."

"No, it won't." Abigail took the computer from Marlee. "You're shaking at just the thought of going back out onto the water. Trust me on this, okay? I won't let you fall overboard or face another shark attack."

"Why don't we sleep on it?" Marlee wasn't ready to commit.

"Okay. You take the bed and I'll sleep here."

"No, I'll sleep on the couch," Marlee said. "It's the least I can do after my silly remarks to Kerry."

"How can I be sure you'll stay on the couch?"

"You won't trust me on my word, but want me to trust you on your boat?" Marlee raised her eyebrows.

"Okay, I trust you." Abigail covered a yawn. "Now let's get some sleep."

Marlee's favorite volunteer T-shirt was clean so she offered it up. "I thought you might want to put on something more comfortable and wear it to police me."

Abigail frowned as she took the shirt. "If you need policing then maybe I should leave."

"I'm sorry. It was an attempt at a bad joke. Go change and I'll set up my bed on the couch."

Marlee got herself a pillow and blanket then waited on a chair until Abigail came out of the bathroom. She wore Marlee's long T-shirt as a nightgown and carried her folded clothes in front of her chest.

Marlee tried not to stare. "I'm relieved you're going to let me help you. I'd do anything for you. I want you to know that."

"I know." Abigail's eyes met Marlee's. "I do appreciate that you're trying to help me. Have a good night."

"You too." Marlee couldn't help but notice that even though her black T-shirt was baggy on Abigail, it wasn't loose enough to cover the hardened nipples beneath.

CHAPTER EIGHT

Marlee stood beside Abigail's boat, its exquisite wooden deck and navy hull glistening against the reflection of the harbor lights in the early morning dawn. The salty mist, scavenging seagulls, and smell of fish reminded Marlee that she was at the sea. Her trepidation at stepping aboard wouldn't let up, and she hesitated on the wharf while Abigail busied herself in the cockpit.

"Permission granted to come aboard." Abigail started the engine and readied to ferry. She looked at Marlee. "Do you need help?"

"Maybe." Marlee's legs trembled and her breathing quickened. She was terrified, consumed by images of drowning or being eaten alive by a shark.

"Give me your hand." Abigail reached out.

"This is embarrassing." Marlee grabbed hold and stepped on. "What kind of police officer am I anyway?"

"You're human and there's nothing to be ashamed of." Abigail guided Marlee to a seat in the cockpit, giving an extra squeeze of support before turning back to the controls. "I'll get us out on the water then we can move around *The Cavity*."

Marlee gripped the edge of her bench, preferring to remain seated. "I'd rather stay here instead of moving into the cavity of the boat."

Abigail laughed. "*The Cavity* is its name. I guess you haven't spent much time on boats?"

"Nothing as big as this, but I've spent many hours in a canoe. I even made love in one once." Marlee was nervous and cursed herself for blurting out the inappropriate statement. "Sorry, I didn't need to say that."

"If we're going to trust each other, we have to be ourselves and not worry about what we say." Abigail focused on the horizon, the hood of her red waterproof jacket flapping in the wind. "Just because I'm not interested in having sex with you doesn't mean I'm a prude and will be offended by any of your comments."

"That's a relief." Marlee studied the shrinking shoreline and tried to keep herself calm by focusing on the woman before her. "As you witnessed last night, sometimes I can't control my tongue." Marlee's cheeks inflamed again. Why did she have to mention her tongue? "I know you're not a lesbian and I never hit on straight women because they stopped giving out toasters years ago."

"Toasters?" Abigail shut down the engine and readied to lower the anchor.

"It's another poor attempt at a joke," Marlee said. "The saying is that if a lesbian converts a straight woman, she gets a toaster. Now I'd better shut up before I really embarrass myself."

"We can't let that happen. Now might be a good time for a tour of the boat."

"Okay, I guess." Marlee's comfort level dropped when Abigail prevented her from entering the cabin and redirected her to walk the narrow gunwale along the side of the watercraft to reach the open deck at the bow.

"Let's sit in the forward and relax a bit." Abigail led the way across the teak wooden-planked deck to two facing benches aligned with the tip of the bow.

"This is nice, but it's a bit breezy out here, don't you find?" Marlee lowered onto a seat then gripped the metal side rail with one hand and the teak bench with the other.

"I love the wind." Abigail sat opposite Marlee, rolling her head back and eyes closing, her ponytail swaying in the breeze. "I love listening to the swish of water lapping against the hull, the tickling of the wind on my skin, the taste of salt on my lips and the smell of the fresh air. They're all so empowering. Being out on the water in this boat always helps me relax. It's one of my favorite places to be."

Marlee couldn't relax and her teeth were chattering. "How did you come up with the name of *The Cavity* for the boat?"

"I didn't." Abigail smiled, her eyes still shut. "Josh and his father named it. Keith is a dentist and Josh had just gotten his first cavity."

"My brother's a dentist too."

"Really?" Abigail opened her eyes.

"Yes. What about you? Any brothers or sisters?" Marlee knew the answer, but asked anyway.

"No." Abigail straightened up. "You look cold. Why don't we head into the cabin? There're lots of windows and a nice space to work. I'm anxious to hear about your plan."

"Good." Marlee followed Abigail below deck, overwhelmed at the attention to detail on this entirely automated sailboat yacht. There was a raised saloon with big windows letting in light that flickered around the room and danced upon the maple dining table. White leather benches with enough seating for twelve bordered the table.

"This is really nice." Marlee's mouth was dry.

"Let me show you the rest of the boat before we start to work."

Marlee noted that the bathroom, its shower and vanity sparkling clean, was fully equipped and would be a luxury anywhere, let alone this far from shore. "How long have you been sailing?" They stood at the entrance of the master bedroom.

"I feel as though I grew up on the water." Abigail pushed through and sat on the edge of the bed, folding her arms over a healthy cleavage covered with a low-neckline T-shirt. "My parents loved to sail and almost every Sunday we'd head out onto the water. Of course, we had a much smaller boat, but we were happy and comfortable. I wish they were still here to enjoy this one."

"What happened to them?" Marlee leaned against the doorframe, fighting to keep her eyes away from Abigail's chest. The fluffy bed had a white duvet and purple pillows that beckoned. There was a small porthole window at the head of the bed and Marlee focused on the bright circle, longing for a light at the end of this tunnel of lust.

"They both died much too young," Abigail said after a short pause. "It's been almost twenty years, but I still miss them a lot." Abigail took a few deep breaths.

"I'm so sorry about your loss." Marlee moved into the room and sat on the bed. "What happened?"

"Cancer is such a monster. It eats people up and spits out their souls." Abigail's voice trembled. "My mother was the first to go from breast cancer. My dad died six months later from lung cancer and a broken heart. They weren't much older than I am now."

Marlee handed Abigail a tissue. She longed to brush her lips against the glistening cheek to lick away the tears, but knew it wouldn't be appropriate. She struggled to concentrate on the conversation.

"So that's why you do what you do?" Marlee asked. "Study genetics in hopes of finding a cure?"

"I feel as though we're getting so close." Abigail stood up and moved toward the doorway. "I can't let them win. We have to expose the bloody bastard that's corrupting our work. Let's finish the tour then discuss your plan."

Marlee followed Abigail to the galley, trying to shift her focus to the yacht. She was impressed with its stainless steel appliances, clean countertops, and maple cupboards. "Wow, someone could live on this boat forever. It has everything."

"Thanks," Abigail said. "This is definitely more boat than I need. It's meant to be a world cruising yacht for two people. I bought it because I want Josh to grow up with fond memories of sailing too."

"He certainly seemed comfortable at the controls." Marlee inhaled Abigail's just released breath, the small space of the narrow galley placing them within kissing range, her knees shaking with the sweet gasp. Drowning in the ocean or facing another shark attack seemed less of a threat now as a new reality started to take hold. She was falling hard for a straight woman.

"He needs to know how to operate it if it's just the two of us out here. Josh often spends time on the boat with his dad too, so it's important. I let them use it whenever they want because I really bought it for Josh to enjoy. Keith has always loved sailing."

"So you're still close with your ex?"

"He's a nice man, but I wouldn't say we're close. He's still in my life because of Josh. It's a good thing too because it's best for Josh to be with his dad right now while I deal with this mess in my company."

"How's Josh doing?"

"It's hard to tell for sure, but he seems to be going okay."

"And what about your ex? How's he with the potential charges against you?"

"He's been supportive, both to Josh and to me."

"That's good." Marlee didn't want to hear more about Keith. "Shall we move out of the kitchen and get to work?"

"Yes, let's do."

Marlee led the way back to the dining table, wanting to appear confident. She'd brought her computer and launched her file. "Let's start by talking about Hannah Williams. How well do you know her outside the office?"

"Hannah's been a big help these last few days." Abigail let out a deep breath. "Other than Josh, she's the closest person in my life. There's no way she'd be involved in anything that could sabotage all of our work."

Marlee felt a tinge of jealousy. "Can you be sure? You told me you couldn't trust anyone."

Abigail hesitated, as though struggling to find the right words to describe Hannah. Marlee knew they'd worked together on a number of genetic decoding projects and were very close when it came to their research. Surely Hannah would never betray her, but Marlee's gut told her to keep watch on this woman.

Was it jealousy or was there something more? It didn't matter. Abigail's office had a mole and she couldn't rule anyone out.

"Hannah's been very helpful over the years," Abigail finally said. "I'm sure it's not her, but if I'm to be fair, Hannah has to be investigated like everyone else."

"What exactly do you think is happening?" Marlee was used to tackling crimes with a victim, a body, or at least something concrete like drugs or guns, and she needed more specifics.

Abigail sighed then lowered her head. "I think someone is trying to develop genetic sequencing that would cultivate cancers or mental and physical deformities within a specific DNA profile type."

"As in developing a weapon for biological warfare?" Marlee asked.

"I'm afraid so." Abigail nodded. "A bioweapon could be disastrous. Take me, for example. Any inherent cancer genes in my system could be switched on through a simple environmental change like an allergic reaction to pollen. The tumors could be fast or slow growing, depending on the environmental controls, and entire populations could be targeted or just a few people."

"You're both scaring and losing me," Marlee said. "How could someone do that?"

"By turning genes on or off," Abigail said. "The focus of my research has been about finding a way to switch cancer genes off, to rid the world of this terrible killer, but unfortunately a byproduct of this work has uncovered potential ways to propagate more cancers."

"Can you think of anyone who might have a motive?" Marlee imagined herself back in a patrol car, where crimes seemed simpler and police procedure straightforward.

"No." Abigail shook her head.

"What about an employee who could have links to a terrorist organization or who needs money to support an addiction like gambling or drugs?"

"They're all good people who're passionate about their work," Abigail said. "Those are the only kind of people I hire. My human resources department thoroughly screens every applicant under consideration and I must approve before a hiring takes place."

"Can you trust everyone in your HR department?"

"Obviously not." Abigail groaned. "So how can you help me?"

"By doing more of what I'm doing now." Marlee's confidence was waning, but she kept her voice strong. "I wish I could get into your office. Maybe you could hire me as an internal security expert."

"That wouldn't work." Abigail bumped her knees against the table as she shot to her feet. "I have a fully staffed security team in place and they'd know you were planted. Besides, I need a refuge right now and you fit that role because you don't have anything to do with my company." She lurched away from the table and went to the interior controls where she started fidgeting with the buttons. "It's getting too hot in here. I'm turning on the air conditioner."

"Why don't we take a break?" Marlee closed her laptop and pushed it aside, holding her hands together on the table in front of her. She straightened her spine like an eager student looking for a reward, but in reality felt she'd just failed her first test.

Abigail sighed. "I feel like we're getting nowhere. I wish I knew what to do."

"I know this is a very difficult time for you, but we're just beginning. Investigations, especially complex ones like this, take time." Marlee approached Abigail and stood beside her. "I think we've made some good progress in that we've started the conversation on suspects and motives. Attention to every little detail and never giving up are two strategies that have helped me many times to solve cases. Work with me on this, okay?" Marlee put a hand on Abigail's arm and squeezed.

"I'm sorry." Abigail turned to her. "You're right. I'll have to think of this as if I'm in the lab, focusing on every little molecule and always searching for that next lead that could uncover a breakthrough in research."

"I like that analogy," Marlee said. "The work you do is so above me it's nice to hear you use some of the same strategies I use as a police officer."

"Don't ever think my work is above you." Abigail's face softened. "I need you because your experience and expertise in solving crimes is a skill set I don't have. It's not about being above or beneath one another. It's about working together to bring out the best of our individual strengths."

Marlee wanted to melt in this woman's arms. Instead, she smiled and turned away. "Is there anything to eat in that fridge?"

They spent the rest of the afternoon discussing the work of AbTay Biosystems and key employees in each department, but nothing or nobody stood out as unusual. Exhausted and wanting to rest before their return in the dark, Abigail suggested they have a nap.

"You can sleep with me in my room if you want," Abigail said.

"Are you sure?" Marlee's heart started to race. "You're okay with that?"

"Yes." Abigail led them to the bedroom. "The bed is certainly big enough and I know you're still nervous on the boat. I want you to relax and feel safe."

"That's very thoughtful. Does that mean you now trust me to keep my hands off you?"

"Yes, of course." She smiled. "I'll throw you overboard if you don't."

"Yikes." Marlee gave a nervous laugh.

Abigail got on top of the covers. "Besides, I kind of like the idea of having a police officer by my side. Now let's get some sleep while we can."

Abigail slept for two hours while Marlee savored the tingling brought on by just lying beside this woman and listening to her even breathing. It was far better to focus on that than the fact she was drifting on the ocean and vulnerable to what lay beneath the waves, even if it was on a luxury sailboat with a beautiful woman. She hadn't felt this good in a long time.

CHAPTER NINE

Marlee was back in her apartment for less than an hour when a thud against her door disrupted the tranquil evening. Abigail had dropped her off after their day on the boat and should have been long gone. Adrenaline kicked in.

"Who's there?" She slowly turned the knob. The door burst open and Tyler came crashing in, almost rolling onto her feet. He was curled up on his knees and grasping his stomach.

"Holy shit, Tyler." Marlee slammed the door shut and dropped to the ground. "What happened to you?" She cradled his bloodied head and scanned the rest of his body, noting swelling, scratches, and bruises that were usually signs of a brutal beating.

"Sorry to be a bother." Tyler's words were barely audible. "Can you help me into my flat?"

"We need to get you to the hospital." Marlee reached for her phone.

"No." Tyler raised a hand to stop her. "I've been here before and I'll be okay. I just need to get to my bed."

"Who did this to you?"

"My fucking ex." Tyler struggled to stand up, clutching his stomach. "He must've known I was on the beach. He jumped me."

"That's assault and you need to press charges." Marlee held his arm. "I'm calling the police."

"I don't want the fucking police involved." Tyler jerked away. "There weren't any witnesses and it's not worth the hassle." He held out his keys. "Could you unlock my door? It sticks sometimes and I couldn't get it to open."

Marlee grabbed the keys. "You can't let him get away with this. I think you should go to the hospital."

"Will you just help me get inside?" Tyler's green eyes started to tear up. "Please?"

She jiggled the key until the lock released then pushed the door open. Stale air mixed with his cinnamon aftershave wafted out as they shuffled inside. Marlee turned on the hall light. "Let's have a look at you. I can see some cuts and at least one bruise on your cheek."

"He has a pattern." Tyler dropped on his couch and flopped back. "He likes to go for the face. I'll look like shit tomorrow."

"You look like shit now." Marlee lifted his feet onto the sofa. "How's your stomach? He must've hit you there because you keep clutching it."

"He kicked me, actually." Tyler raised his T-shirt, but there were no obvious signs of trauma.

"What a fuck," Marlee said. "If you don't do anything about it, he'll do it again."

"No, he won't." Tyler's voice was flat. "It's no big deal."

"This is a big deal because next time it could be a lot worse. These things have a way of escalating." Marlee began to gently probe his abdomen. "Does it hurt when you breathe?"

"No. I don't think he broke any ribs this time." Tyler closed his eyes.

"Can you try to sit up so I can see your back?" Marlee tugged at his hands to help.

"I think my back's okay." He struggled up and leaned forward. "It's not hurting anywhere and I don't think I got any blows there."

Marlee lifted his shirt. There were no scrapes or bruises, but she persisted. "I don't understand why you won't go to the hospital or police."

"I don't want the fucking hassle." Tyler eased back down. "It's not happening."

Marlee took a moment of silence to imply disagreement and visually scan his apartment. It was the mirror image of hers with its one bedroom and bathroom, tiny kitchen and cramped living area decorated with imitation artwork, minimal furnishings, and a small television. There were few personal possessions of his beyond clothes, a computer, his cell, and a set of headphones.

"We should get you cleaned up," Marlee said. "Where do you keep your washcloths and towels?"

"There's some in the bathroom." Tyler sighed.

Warm wet cloth and towel in hand, she squished beside him on the couch and began to carefully clean his face. Tyler flinched as she dabbed the fresh cuts and bruises.

"We should really disinfect these," she said. "Do you have anything I can use?"

"No, but don't worry about it. Like I said, this has happened before so it's okay."

"It's not okay." Marlee flung her hands in the air. "Family violence is never okay."

"He's not family."

"He was your partner and could have killed you."

"Well he didn't," Tyler said.

"How did you get away?"

"Someone came along and he ran." Tyler stared into his lap. "He's a big brute of a coward and I hate the bastard." Tears began to dot his beige cotton shorts.

"What if he finds you again?" Marlee handed him a box of tissues, her voice softening. "You can't run away forever."

Tyler took a few minutes before answering. "He's paid me back now so he should leave me alone."

"Paid you back? For what?" Marlee was almost afraid to ask.

"I hacked into his bank account and took some money."

"Like in stole?" Her heart dropped.

"He thinks so." Tyler sniffed. "It was my money too and he tried to steal it first by sticking it in his own account. I only took what belonged to me. I wasn't going to leave him with everything."

"Hacking is a crime. You could have been charged."

"I know."

Marlee had heard enough. She helped Tyler to the shower then tucked him in for the night before going home and climbing into bed. When she turned out the light, her mind kept replaying images of a beaten up Tyler curled against her door. She'd always found the domestic abuse calls some of the hardest on her job and wanted to block those memories out. She needed to focus on something else.

Her thoughts wandered to Abigail. She dared to imagine what it would be like to kiss her. She needed something to help her fall asleep and tallying smooches was much more appealing than counting sheep.

* * *

Marlee woke to the sound of movement in her kitchen. A cupboard door had opened and she heard the clinking of glass. The smell of coffee drifted into her room just as the smoke alarm shrieked.

"Sorry!" She heard Abigail's voice.

"Tay? Is that you?" Marlee jumped out of bed, pulled on a pair of shorts and almost skipped across the floor.

"I can't believe I just did that." Abigail scraped a piece of blackened toast over the sink.

"What are you doing here?" Marlee brushed up against the counter, hardly able to contain her excitement.

"I woke early and wanted to drop off another file before heading to the office." Abigail's cheeks reddened. "I hope you don't mind that I used your key and made myself at home."

"Of course not." Marlee touched Abigail's arm. "I'm glad you feel comfortable to do that."

"I should have picked up something for breakfast, but I didn't think of food until I got here. I hope it's okay I poked around your kitchen to make something to eat."

"You can poke around my kitchen anytime." Marlee grinned, thrilled at the thought.

"I should get going." Abigail avoided Marlee's eyes.

"Let me finish getting dressed while you eat your toast." She wanted Abigail to stay.

When Marlee came back, she found Abigail sitting at the dining table, scanning through an open file. Marlee sat down beside her.

"These are the email addresses of every employee at AbTay Biosystems," Abigail said, pointing at the column of names. "I still think the network has been hacked by an outsider, but the IT department can't prove it. I thought maybe the personal emails would help."

"I wish I was more of a computer geek, but I'm not," Marlee said, feeling inadequate.

"But you're a police officer so you may see something that an IT specialist wouldn't. I'd also like you to look at my email account this evening."

"We can do that." Marlee's heart fluttered at Abigail's belief in her. "We can see how many of these personal email addresses turn up in your contacts."

"Perfect." Abigail got up to leave. "You're already looking for patterns and I think this will be helpful."

Marlee followed her to the door and gave a friendly farewell hug. "I hope you have a good day, or at least one that's tolerable. I'll be thinking about you and sending positive vibes your way."

"Thank you." Abigail seemed to collapse into the embrace. "It means a lot to me because I've felt so alone the last little while. I really appreciate your help."

"I'm glad." Marlee eased back and looked into beautiful, blue, bloodshot eyes.

Abigail stunned her with a kiss. It was a quick one, a dab on the lips before Abigail pulled back. Marlee stared at her, shocked. Then, without thinking, she leaned forward and pressed their lips together to taste Abigail's fuchsia-tinged lipstick. Abigail's lips remained limp so Marlee began to pry them apart with her tongue. A firm tongue began pushing back so Marlee sucked it into her mouth, prompting gasping moans, only some of which were hers.

Abigail tore her tongue out of Marlee's mouth and yanked back. "We can't let this happen again. This is not who I am."

"Are you sure?" Marlee's legs wobbled from the kiss.

"Yes." Abigail turned away and was out the door before Marlee could respond.

CHAPTER TEN

Marlee fought against the wind, sprinting along the boulevard toward the water as she tried to make sense of her feelings, and Abigail's. Her sneakers were wet after stepping in a leftover puddle of the night's rain and the air was salty stagnant with humidity despite the breeze.

Suffocating from smothering lust, she needed to burn off energy and regain control before checking in with Tyler. Marlee longed for the openness of the beach to help clear her head, leaving pavement for sand in one large stride. A few dog walkers, three distant fellow joggers, and a lone pelican fishing in the surf were the only other signs of life on the serene shoreline.

It started to drizzle as she slowed to catch her breath and relive the kiss again. The rain didn't matter because Marlee was already soaked from sweat and aroused beyond belief. She pictured Abigail sitting alone at her desk, legs crossed and trying to ignore the pleasant throbbing in her groin. At least that's what Marlee wanted to believe—that Abigail was feeling it too because there was no way that kiss had gotten things out of her system and the only moving on she wanted to do involved progressing to an orgasm.

When she got home, a lingering shower helped relax Marlee before heading to Tyler's.

Marlee let herself in when he didn't answer the door. The living room was dark and empty. "Hi there, it's me." She called out, going into the bedroom.

"Hey." Tyler was awake, but his eyes remained closed. "What time is it?"

"Ten fifteen. How are you feeling?" Marlee noted his pale face.

"I think I need to go to the hospital." Tyler's eyes fluttered open, his breathing labored. "Can you take me?"

"Of course I can. Are you in pain?" Marlee touched his stomach and he gasped.

"It hurts like hell when I breathe." His eyelids closed and quivered. "I must have broken a rib after all."

"I'll call an ambulance."

"No, please don't." He started to get up. "I don't want all the fuss. Could you just drive me? We can take my car if you like." He pushed himself off the bed and headed to the bathroom.

"I don't know about this," Marlee said. "You could have some serious internal injuries."

"I don't need an ambulance," Tyler stood at the bathroom door. "I just need a ride."

"I'll get my keys."

When they arrived at the hospital emergency department, Tyler hobbled in while Marlee parked. She had forgotten to check her phone and was excited to see a message from Abigail, but her joy was short-lived when she read the four words. *Can't make it tonight.* Marlee trudged across the parking lot, drowning in dejection.

"It's going to be a long wait." Tyler had already been assessed by the triage nurse and was seated along the wall with many others. "You can skip out if you want and I'll take a cab home."

"I'll stay." Marlee sat beside him, opening her laptop and connecting to the free WiFi. She didn't want to be alone.

"Are you stalking her?" Tyler leaned over, the website of AbTay Biosystems obvious on her screen.

Marlee pulled away. "I'm just curious, that's all. I didn't expect to have a snoop sitting beside me."

"It's not looking good for her, especially with the police pulling her in for questioning." Tyler flopped his head back against the wall and closed his eyes. "If it was me, I'd…"

"You'd what? Give up? Let everyone think you're a criminal?"

"Whoa." Tyler's eyes snapped open. "What's going on with you?"

"Nothing. I feel sorry for her, that's all." Marlee felt more rejected than sorry at the moment and didn't want to talk about it. "I'm going to get a coffee. Want one?"

"That'd be nice." Tyler pulled his unzipped hoodie tighter around his chest then leaned back and closed his eyes. "I need something to warm me up."

Marlee knew what she needed as she searched for a coffee shop, but also figured a night of hot sex with Abigail wasn't likely to happen.

* * *

Tyler had two broken ribs and a sprained pelvis. He was prescribed some painkillers and given a doctor's note, as he wouldn't be able to work for at least a few weeks.

By the time they got home, the evening news was already detailing the day's events. Marlee was relieved there weren't any new reports about Abigail, but longed to know how the day had gone, especially since her texts were being ignored.

She offered to make dinner for Tyler, finding an excuse to bake her filet of salmon. A fishy smell in her apartment was the least of her worries, especially as Abigail wouldn't be visiting.

"I don't get it." Tyler chewed a bite of fish as they sat at his dining table. "Abigail Taylor, taking you to get your car the other night?"

"Why are you bringing that up?"

"Don't you think it's weird?" Tyler asked.

"Maybe she's a weird woman."

"Have you heard from her since then?" Tyler put down his fork.

"Would you like some frozen yogurt for dessert?" Marlee wasn't going to divulge anything, even though she was dying to tell him about the kiss to get his opinion.

"No thanks. You didn't answer my question."

"Didn't I?" Marlee stood up. "I should get going. I want to call my friend in Ottawa and it's always awkward with the time difference."

"I bet you have been in touch with Abigail." His eyes lit up. "Sit back down because I want to hear all about it."

"Do you want the rest of the salad?" Marlee rinsed her plate.

"If you don't tell me, I might have to hack into your computer to find out. I can do that, you know."

Marlee swung around, curious. "You can? How?" She remembered the bank account of his ex.

He smirked. "I have my ways. I've always been good with computers and probably should have made it my career, but couldn't stand the thought of uni. I applied to the airlines instead."

"You won't find much on my computer so go ahead and hack all you want." As much as she wanted to know more about his computer skills, Marlee wasn't going to divulge her confidential relationship with Abigail. "See you later."

Back at her place, Marlee poured a glass of chilled chardonnay then parked on the couch, computer in her lap. She tried connecting with Kerry, hoping she was home and available to chat. It looked like there was some interference with the call and she was about to end it to try again when Tyler appeared on her screen.

"How ya going?" He grinned back at her.

"Holy shit, you weren't kidding." Marlee shivered with shock. "How did you do that?"

"It was super easy because we're running off the same network. You won't tell anyone, will you?" He winked. "I'll get out of your face now so you can have your chat with your friend. See you later." He disconnected.

Marlee slammed her laptop shut then began to rationalize bringing Tyler into her confidence. Hacking was against the law and she could get into big trouble. But then again, with Abigail's permission, they wouldn't be breaking any laws if they focused only on the network of AbTay Biosystems.

She stared at the folder of email addresses and feared the hacking would have to go beyond the company and into the personal accounts of employees. Delving into personal bank accounts to track any large deposits would be an essential step in the search for clues, but it would be crossing the line. She finished her wine and had two more glasses before going to bed, her mind percolating ideas but still not made up.

CHAPTER ELEVEN

Breaking news that the police were getting closer to Abigail's arrest headlined media on Monday morning. Speculation was rampant and reporters used words like "possible terrorist-links," "global impacts," "legitimate versus harmful research," "the creation of superbugs," and "deadliest weapons ever."

Despite all the hype, it remained unclear exactly what Abigail would be charged with. Marlee wondered if local police were grappling as much as she was to develop a basic understanding of what they were dealing with.

Marlee had spent a quiet weekend avoiding Tyler and longing to see Abigail. She'd been regularly checking in on Tyler with brief texts, but was beginning to miss his company and felt like chatting. After a jog and shower, she made each of them a cup of coffee and approached his door. Her knocks went unanswered so she used the key he had given her to let herself in.

"Hello?" She hesitated in the dark entrance, waiting for a response. His bedroom door was ajar so she turned on the entry light, put the coffee down, and approached the bed. He was still sleeping, his chest rising and falling. She touched his arm.

He stirred, eyelids fluttering open. "Hey."

"I brought you some coffee. I thought you'd be up by now."

Tyler started to stretch then stopped to rub his side. "Ouch. It still hurts."

"How are you feeling?"

"Tired." He yawned. "I stayed up too late last night."

"What were you doing?" She really didn't want to know.

"Why haven't you called your friend back?" Tyler dropped his feet over the side of the bed, feeling around for his slippers.

"Is that what you've been doing all weekend? Hacking into my computer and spying on me?" Marlee's jaw tightened.

"I told you I would. The coffee smells good. Thanks." Tyler got off the bed and picked up the mug. "Who's Stacy? She sounds like a bitch."

"She is a bitch, but so are you for hacking into my personal life. What else did you find out about me?"

"That you're obsessed with Abigail Taylor."

"I am not!" Marlee raised a fist. She felt like socking him in the ribs for violating her privacy.

"Whoa, please don't hit me." Tyler flinched.

"Then stay out of my space."

"Okay, I will. Your interest in her seems one-sided anyway. I figured you for a stalker."

"You're making it sound like I'm a criminal for wanting to know more about her." Marlee was relieved Tyler hadn't accessed her phone too. "If anyone has committed a crime around here, it's you for hacking into my life."

"I hope you're not planning to get me charged." Tyler's crusted morning eyes widened.

"Then stay the fuck out of my computer. Deal?"

"Okay." Tyler put his mug down and started toward the bathroom. "Besides, I hardly snooped around your account anyway once I hacked into AbTay Biosystems."

"You got into Abigail's company?" Marlee couldn't contain her excitement.

Tyler swung around. "I knew it. You're still in contact. And of course you'd be using your phone instead of email to get in touch with her."

"I wish." Marlee refused to admit to anything. She needed to think before incriminating herself any more. She headed to the door. "I'll see you later."

The local television newscast kept repeating the same video clips about AbTay Biosystems over and over again. It was a mixture of shots from the last few days, but primarily focused on footage of Abigail being led into the police station for questioning, as though she'd already been found guilty.

Marlee felt sick to her stomach and couldn't watch anymore. She longed to hold Abigail and tell her things would be okay. Her texts to Abigail were still being unanswered and it hurt. When she heard a light tap at her door, her heart skipped a beat as she raced toward it, picturing Abigail.

"Hey, mate." Tyler held out his empty mug as she flung the door open. "Thanks for the coffee and looking out for me. I'm feeling heaps better."

"That's good to hear." Marlee sighed as she took the mug and leaned against the doorframe. "Do you think you'll stick around while you're off work?"

"Sure, why not?" His hands were in his pockets and he shuffled his feet. "I don't really have anywhere else to go."

"What about family?" Marlee was trying to decide whether or not to invite him in. She wanted company, but kept hoping Abigail would answer one of her texts.

"They're all in Melbourne, caught up in their own lives. Hey, I'm having a barby for dinner. Want to join me?"

"Thanks for the offer, but shouldn't I be the one cooking for you? Especially since you're the one with the broken ribs."

He smiled. "You can help. Besides, I have some chicken in my fridge that needs cooking up or it'll go bad."

"Sure, why not?" Especially since it didn't look like she'd be hearing from Abigail any time soon. "I'll whip up a salad and pop by later."

Marlee used spiral rice pasta, olive oil, feta cheese, red onions, garlic, and cherry tomatoes for her salad. It was one of her favorite go-to salads back in Canada, especially on hot summer nights. She mixed everything together and adjusted the taste with a hint of salt and pepper, like she'd done many times before.

She'd been restless all afternoon with thoughts of Abigail's kiss and wondering about Tyler's hacking, but kept to herself. She strolled to the grocery store to get some food and tried to relax, but images of Abigail were pictured on newspapers near the checkout line, beckoning attention. Marlee's anxiety wouldn't let up and by the time she knocked on Tyler's door, she'd decided to get drunk.

"Now that's a big bottle of wine." Tyler put the domestic merlot on the kitchen counter. "I wish I could have some too, but I'm sure it'll keep until I'm off my painkillers."

"Don't count on it." Marlee poured herself a large glass. "Cheers."

Dinner was just the distraction Marlee needed. They exchanged coming out stories, talked about their work, and bashed their exes. By dessert, Tyler caved and had a glass of wine while Marlee poured her third.

"Your salad was very good," he said. "Kind of like Greek except without the black olives and cucumbers."

"You can call it my geek salad because I didn't use a recipe." Marlee giggled then took another gulp of wine. "I really like this merlot."

"No kidding." Tyler sniffed his wine then took a small sip and swished it around his mouth before swallowing. "It's not bad, but nothing spectacular. Are you trying to get pissed?"

"It's not like I have to drive anywhere so why not?" Marlee held up her glass then heard the ping of an incoming text. She stood up. "I need to use your facilities."

Thankful that Tyler hadn't seemed to notice she'd received a message, Marlee almost tripped over her feet as she rushed toward the privacy of the bathroom. She closed the door then gaped at her phone. Abigail was in the parking lot, hoping to see her.

CHAPTER TWELVE

Marlee texted Abigail to let her know she was at Tyler's and needed a few minutes.

"I had too much wine," Marlee said as she emerged from Tyler's bathroom. "I'm going to head home now."

"I thought you were just getting started," Tyler said. "You didn't drink that much."

"Well, I can't drink anymore." Marlee faked gagging as she poured her full glass of wine down the kitchen sink. "I think I'm going to be sick."

"Then you'd better hurry home."

Marlee could hardly think as she rushed next door. She wanted to jump for joy, her stomach twirling at the thought of seeing Abigail again. Marlee beamed as she greeted her visitor and let her inside.

"Please, no hugging or touching." Abigail's arms were crossed.

Marlee's heart sank. "For sure."

"Thank you." Abigail made her way to the couch and sat down. "Have you had a chance to look at the list of email addresses?"

"Yes." Marlee's heart wouldn't stop hammering with thoughts of Abigail's kiss. She also wanted to say something about her suspicions over Hannah, but she couldn't bring herself to say anything, for fear of upsetting Abigail. So, she just spent the next hour explaining what she'd done to cross-reference the emails and how she'd made a list of anomalies that required further follow-up.

Abigail reached for Marlee's computer. "Why don't we log in to my account? I don't think we'll get anywhere unless we have access to the company server."

Marlee moved to touch Abigail, but snatched her hand back before contact. "I think it's best if we stay off the Internet for now."

"Why?" Abigail's blue eyes glistened in the soft light of the table lamp. "Have you been having problems with your service provider?"

"No." Marlee hesitated, choosing her words. "Someone hacked into my computer."

"You've been infiltrated too?" Abigail jumped up, hands clenched into fists and eyes watering over.

"It's not what you think." Marlee looked up. "It was Tyler."

"Your neighbour?" Abigail's mouth puckered. "What does he have to do with this?"

"Nothing." Marlee stood, aching to plant a kiss on those inviting lips, but kept her distance. "I think he can help us. He boasted about being able to hack into computers so I dared him to break into mine. It didn't take him long to intercept a call I was trying to make to Kerry. He knows I've been researching your company and told me he hacked into your system."

"That's impossible." Abigail flinched. "My IT security team has been extra vigilant making sure nobody from the outside gets into our system."

"I don't know how he did it, but he surprised the heck out of me last night. I think his skills could be invaluable. I wish I was better at finding my way around computers, but that's not my area of expertise. I've always relied on others to help with that."

"How well do you know Tyler?" Abigail straightened up, crossing her arms.

"Not a lot, but I like him. I can tell he's a good person."

"Here we go again with the soft, intangible feelings that aren't based on any facts." Abigail sighed. "That doesn't work for me."

"The facts are that I've gotten to know him over the last while and I trust him. I also did some research on social media and found nothing out of the ordinary. He has a Twitter account he hardly uses and his Facebook page hasn't been updated in over four months."

"Have you told him about me?" Abigail asked.

"No. I told him you rescued me and he knows I'm sympathetic to your situation…"

"So he does know about me. Fuck." Abigail moved toward the door. "And I don't want your sympathy." She twisted the knob and tried to yank the door open, but it was locked.

Marlee rushed over and slapped a hand over the deadbolt. "Can you just wait a minute and hear me out? I thought you were supposed to trust me?"

Abigail sighed and leaned against the door. "Go ahead. I'm listening."

"I'd never risk jeopardizing our investigation by bringing in someone I didn't believe in."

"You haven't known him long enough to have any kind of confidence."

"We haven't known each other very long either, but I trust you." Marlee held eye contact.

Abigail stared back. "That's different. I risked my life to save yours."

"Yes you did, to save my sorry ass while a shark was trying to bite it off. Wasn't that sympathetic too?" Marlee's head throbbed. "Don't tell me you didn't have sympathy for me, especially after spending the night because I was all alone."

"You're right." Abigail eased off the door, shoulders hunched. She extended a hand. "I'm sorry."

"I'm sorry too." Marlee's hand tingled in the firm, warm shake.

"Why don't you tell me more about Tyler?"

They spent the next two hours discussing the pros and cons of bringing Tyler into their confidence. Abigail was concerned about his trustworthiness, especially since Marlee barely knew him. In the end, she finally agreed to go with Marlee's gut feeling on the merits of involving him because they didn't have any other options.

Tyler could play a vital role in the online investigation of email traffic. Neither Marlee nor Abigail felt competent to spot anomalies or potential entry points for a system-wide breach and agreed it was worth the risk of involving Tyler for his expertise. Marlee was tasked with recruiting him.

"If you don't mind, I'd like to lie down a bit before heading out." Abigail rinsed her empty wineglass. "I shouldn't have had so much wine."

"Of course," Marlee said. "The last thing we'd need to happen is for you to drive under the influence. Go ahead and lay on my bed so you can get some sleep."

Marlee puttered around in the kitchen, unsure of what to do when she heard Abigail get onto the bed. She was tired too, and longed to lie down, especially next to Abigail, but didn't think she could keep her hands to herself if that happened. In the end, she pulled out a blanket and lay on the couch.

Marlee was still awake when Abigail got up to leave. The couch had been uncomfortable and she couldn't stop aching for a kiss. It wasn't like her to pine after a woman who refused to admit any mutual attraction, but something about Abigail made her crave like never before.

"I didn't mean to take your bed from you." Abigail grabbed her purse. "I guess I should have said something to let you know it was okay for you to lie down too. I'm sorry."

Marlee decided it was best to be honest. "It's not okay for us to sleep together anymore. I'm the one who's sorry. It can't happen again because I'm so attracted to you I wouldn't be able to control myself." She waited for a response, but none came. "There, now you have it and I hope you don't hold it against me for telling the truth."

Abigail stood facing the door, her hand on the knob. "Thanks for being honest with me. We can work from my place from now on."

She left without looking back.

CHAPTER THIRTEEN

Marlee slept until noon the next day. The sweet smell of Abigail's coconut shampoo on the pillow caused a release of endorphins that made Marlee forget about everything except how much she wanted the woman. She postponed getting up, stretching and moaning as her body craved more replays of their tongue-touching kiss.

A knock at the door brought her back to reality. Lunging out of bed, she pulled on a pair of shorts and rushed to open it.

"Hey." Tyler stood at her door, his T-shirt wrinkled and his cheeks pale. He wore aviators, as though trying to conceal bloodshot eyes. "How are you going after getting pissed last night?"

"I can't believe I slept so late." Marlee needed to hit the bathroom in a fierce way, the coffee and wine she'd consumed wanting out.

"I'm bored." Tyler leaned against her unit. "Want to take in a movie or something this afternoon?"

Marlee leaned on her hip. "I need to pick up a few groceries. Why don't you walk with me to the store?"

"What do you need?" He scratched his arm.

"A few things." Marlee needed to talk to him, but could hardly think anymore because her bladder was about to burst. "I'll pop by your unit when I'm ready." She didn't give him a chance to respond, closing her door instead and rushing to the toilet.

She finished in the bathroom by tidying up around the sink and wiping the shower door. There wasn't much space and little room for storage in the tiny outdated bathroom that couldn't compete with the luxurious one on Abigail's boat, but she wanted it to at least look clean.

On their short trek to the store, they spoke mostly of trivial items like the weather, the latest movies, and distracted drivers whizzing by. It didn't take Marlee long to get the milk, bread, and fruit she needed.

"How's your Vegemite supply?" Tyler asked.

"Yuck. I have a full bottle you can have if you want. I don't know how you can eat that stuff."

"Are you kidding? Vegemite sandwiches are the best. I grew up on them."

"I thrived on peanut butter sandwiches and there's no comparison."

"You're right," Tyler said. "I'd take Vegemite any day over peanut butter."

Conversation remained superficial during their walk home. Neither Abigail nor Tyler's cyber skills entered the discussion, as though the topics were to be avoided. Marlee was having difficulty deciding how to approach him about it, and finally decided that the best way was the direct way.

"Have you hacked into any more computers lately?" They approached their units.

"Yours, this morning," Tyler said.

"I thought I told you to stay out of my computer." Marlee jammed the key into her lock then kicked the door open.

"Sorry, but I wanted to know what you were up to when you didn't answer any of my messages." He followed her inside.

"Maybe it was none of your business." Marlee began to put her groceries away, tossing food and slamming doors.

Tyler sat on the couch. "You weren't even online. What's the big deal anyway? I can't imagine you'd be into cybersex or anything like that and even if you were, it wouldn't interest me in the least to watch."

"You're violating my personal privacy and it's wrong." She was almost yelling.

"Okay, it won't happen again. I promise."

"Good, because I want to talk to you about the hacking." Marlee swung around to face him.

Tyler put up his hands. "Please don't hit me. I'm injured, remember?"

"I won't hit you, but I should wag a finger." Marlee smiled and sat down on the couch beside him. "The only problem is, I want you to do it again."

"What?" Tyler's eyes widened. "You want me to hack into your account again?"

"Not my account." Marlee straightened up and leaned toward him. "I want you to hack into AbTay Biosystems again."

"You're obsessed." Tyler shook his head. "I don't get it. Sure she's hot and everything, but you'll never break Abigail Taylor."

"I'm not trying to break her. I'm trying to help her."

"How? You think hacking into her company's system will help her? That she'd even give you the time of day if you found something? We're peons to people like her. She may have given you a ride on her boat, but that doesn't make you buddies."

"Are you finished?"

"No, I'm not. You just scolded me for hacking into your computer and now you want me to hack into someone else's system?" Tyler stood up. "I need to put my groceries away."

"You only bought a loaf of bread and it can wait." Marlee patted the couch. "Can you please sit back down and hear me out?"

"This is starting to stress me when I should be healing," Tyler said, but sat down again.

"I'm sure someone inside AbTay Biosystems is manipulating their system to frame Abigail."

"And she told you that?" Tyler scoffed.

"Evidence is mounting to support it." Marlee stared into his green eyes. "She's been back here and we've been working together on this."

"No shit?" Tyler's eyes bulged. "When?"

"She comes at night so no one will see her. We debated about whether or not to tell you because she's afraid to trust anyone, but I convinced her that you'd be okay. I sure hope I was right. Don't let me down."

"Wow." Tyler shook his head. "Abigail Taylor is seeing you. I can't believe it."

"It's not like that." Marlee looked away. "She's not a lesbian."

"And if she was?" Tyler tapped her knee. "Wouldn't you be interested?"

"I can't stop thinking about her." Marlee's head dropped. "She's so fucking hot that I don't know what to do with myself. You'll be a good diversion."

"So you're using me for more than my hacking skills," Tyler said. "I'm touched you trust me enough to risk compromising whatever it is you have with Abigail."

"If you do anything to betray us, I'll break the rest of your ribs." Marlee grinned as she held a fist toward him.

Tyler leaned away. "I don't doubt it. What am I looking for?"

"I don't know yet. Anything unusual."

"What kind of bioweapons are they developing?" Tyler squinted. "It all sounds so foreign and futuristic to me. Like some kind of science fiction story."

"It scares the shit out of me," Marlee said. "I don't understand it. Abigail's devastated her research is being stolen and twisted into something evil. We have to help her."

"We could be putting our lives in danger." Tyler jiggled his knees. "Especially if terrorists are involved."

"A lot more lives than ours are in danger if we don't stop this." Marlee sighed. "Abigail says cancers could be propagated in targeted populations through something as simple as an allergic reaction to pollen. We can't let it happen."

"Why do scientists have to play around with our DNA anyway?"

"To find cures for awful diseases." Marlee stood up and put her hands on her hips. "These aren't scientists we're dealing with. They're criminals, plain and simple, and we have to keep that in mind. Whether or not we understand the science behind what they're doing is irrelevant. My skills in policing and yours in hacking make us capable of bringing them down. And we also have Abigail, who understands the science. I think we make a good team."

"Abigail Taylor. Wow. I still find it hard to believe. You're not shitting me, are you?"

"What is it about trusting me?" Marlee dropped her arms. "It's been so hard to get Abigail to have faith in me and she still seems doubtful at times. Am I too quick to trust others or what?"

"You can't blame me for being a bit skeptical." Tyler stood up and headed to the door. "I think I need to take a nap and process all of this."

Marlee yanked his arm and looked into his eyes. "If this is going to work, we have to believe in each other. You'll work with us, won't you?"

"I guess. What's next?"

"Abigail wants to meet you. She's dropping by later this evening and we can talk more about your role."

"She's coming here?" His eyes bulged again. "Why wouldn't you be meeting at some fancy hotel or at her mansion in Darling Point?"

"You know where she lives?"

"Not exactly, but I'm sure it's somewhere around there. Her house is worth millions and has an impressive swimming pool with an Olympic length lane. I remember reading about it."

"She hasn't told me anything about her home, but I've been back on her boat."

"You have?" Tyler's jaw dropped. "Like when has she had time to go sailing?"

"It wasn't really a day of sailing. We discussed the case and key employees at her company, but so far we don't have any leads. Abigail and I aren't very adept at computer systems and need to do surveillance on the company network without anyone knowing. That's where your skills will be useful."

"I need to lay down." Tyler opened the door. "Message me when she gets here and I'll pop back."

Marlee closed her door and let out a sigh of relief. She sent a text to Abigail letting her know Tyler was on board, made herself a coffee, and then flopped on the couch with her computer. She spent the next few hours surfing websites on genetics, and real estate in Darling Point.

CHAPTER FOURTEEN

A key clicked in the door just as Marlee sent the last of her emails to family and friends in Canada. Abigail let herself in and smiled a heart-warming greeting.

"Hey." Marlee's stomach twirled with excitement at seeing Abigail, and the fact she used the key to let herself in. "How was your day?"

"It's much better now." Abigail kicked off her sandals and joined Marlee on the couch. "I'm anxious to hear about your conversation with Tyler."

"It went well, but at first he didn't believe me when I told him I'm working with you."

"I suppose it would seem strange. Can he meet with us tonight?"

"Yes. I'll let him know you're here." Marlee messaged him. "Can I get you something to drink?"

"A glass of water would be nice, thanks."

Tyler was at her door before Marlee had a chance to get the water. He'd dressed up for the occasion, wearing beige cotton pants and a light blue button-down shirt.

"You forgot to put on a tie." Marlee whispered and winked as she let him in.

Abigail stood up and offered a hand. "Hello, Tyler. I'm Abigail Taylor. It's nice to meet you."

"It's an honor to meet you, Dr. Taylor." Tyler grinned and shook her hand.

"Please, call me Abigail. And the honor is mine. I hear you're somewhat of an expert on computer systems and might be able to help us."

"I hope so." Tyler jiggled keys in his pocket.

"Marlee told me you hacked into my company's internal network. I'd like to see how you did that."

"Sure, but I didn't bring my computer. I'll be right back." He turned to leave.

"You can use mine." Marlee opened her browser and pulled out a chair at the dining table before assuming her position on the couch beside Abigail. "Show us what you can do."

Tyler sat down and began to type. "It'll take me a few minutes."

"Take as long as you need," Abigail said. "In the meantime, I'll get myself a glass of water."

"Oh shoot, I'm sorry. I forgot." Marlee jumped up. "Tyler, can I get something for you?"

He barely shook his head, absorbed in his task.

"I've been getting offers from people all over the world to help preserve the integrity of my research." Abigail leaned against the kitchen sink and sipped her water. "It's nice to know there are people who believe in my work and are cheering for me."

"I think you have a lot of fans." Marlee stood beside Abigail, her voice low so as not to disturb Tyler. "Your clinical trials are giving hope to terminal cancer patients. I've read some of the online comments about your studies and feel so privileged to be working with you. We'll be the perfect trio."

Abigail smiled. "Now that we've included Tyler, I've been thinking about things and want to bring Hannah into this as well. What do you think?"

Marlee stiffened. "Are you sure? I thought you didn't want to involve anyone from your company?"

"Hannah's been a big help and I can't fathom leaving her out now. Four will be better than three and it'll make us an even team."

"Who's Hannah?" Tyler stopped typing and looked up.

"You haven't heard of Hannah?" Abigail returned to the couch. "She's been working close to me for years now. Some of my most important research projects have been facilitated by her and we've jointly published many papers."

"I vaguely remember the tabloids mentioning her." Tyler looked at Marlee. "Have you met Hannah?"

"No, not yet." Marlee didn't want to meet her either. She preferred being the only other woman on this team.

"Are you into my network yet?" Abigail leaned toward the computer.

"Yes." Tyler picked up the laptop to show her. "I assume these internal files on employee data aren't meant for public consumption."

"How did you do that?" Abigail jumped to her feet. "This is outrageous. I pay a ridiculous amount of money to people who are supposed to be the best in network security and you hack into my system in less than fifteen minutes?"

"It actually took me quite a few hours the other night," Tyler said. "Sorry, but it's the way it is."

"You don't need to apologize, and thank you for bringing this to my attention. I'm going to dismiss the whole lot of them tomorrow."

"You can't fire them," Marlee said. "Not yet, anyway. This could be our first big lead where we can monitor network activities. You can do that, can't you Tyler?"

"I should be able to," Tyler said. "I'd need to set up a tracking device through injecting a virus into your system." He looked at Abigail. "I could send it to you in an email attachment and you'd need to open up the file for activation."

"Won't her IT security team be able to see it?" Marlee asked.

"Not if I create a spam email that makes its way to Abigail's account," Tyler said. "I can set something up to make it look like a legitimate marketing email on investing or something like that."

"Do whatever you have to do and I'll open it," Abigail said. "Those bloody bastards aren't going to get away with this."

"Tyler should examine the file of personal emails you gave me," Marlee said.

"Having access to personal email addresses would be helpful," Tyler said. "I could hack into employee bank accounts to see if anyone has been making large deposits."

"No." Abigail swung around to face Tyler, her eyes stern. "I'll let you have whatever access you need to my network, but there is to be no illegal hacking into the personal bank accounts of my employees. Is that clear?"

"Yes," Tyler said.

Over the next hour they examined internal files on the AbTay Biosystems server. Abigail shook her head and snapped her tongue while Tyler opened up secret documents and accessed company data that was supposed to be secure.

"Now that we've established Tyler can hack into your network," Marlee said, "we need to set up a protocol for documenting anomalies. The notes we make could be useful as admissible evidence in court when prosecutions begin."

"You're optimistic," Tyler said. "Just because I'm able to prowl around the system doesn't mean we're going to solve this."

"True," Marlee said, "but this is a big break for us. I'm sure it'll provide more leads."

"How?" Abigail asked. "I've been searching our network for weeks and haven't spotted anything out of the ordinary."

"Hacking into the supposedly secure system of your company is unusual and should be thought of as a lead. It opens up the possibility that maybe this isn't being done from the inside after all."

"Hmmm." Abigail hesitated. "I'd certainly like to believe that because I can't imagine anyone within the company doing something so atrociously disloyal."

"It's getting late." Tyler yawned and fondled his ribs. "I'll have to call it a night. I've cut back on the painkillers, but I need one now."

"What happened?" Abigail asked. "I'm sorry. I didn't realize you were injured or I never would have agreed to asking you to do this."

"I'm okay to work with you," Tyler said. "Really. It's a long story. I have a few broken ribs. I'm off work for now so I'd be playing on my computer anyway to pass the time. I need to do something or I'd go crazy."

"You mean I'd go crazy," Marlee said. "Just this morning he came to my door complaining he was bored."

"It was more like this afternoon," Tyler said, "and someone had just gotten up."

Abigail followed Tyler to the door. "It was very nice meeting you Tyler, and I'm sorry to hear about your injury. I really appreciate you wanting to help, especially with broken ribs. Thank you." They shook hands.

"It's my pleasure."

"See you." Marlee closed her door and turned to Abigail. "I'm not sure about involving Hannah in this. Why don't we wait and see what Tyler comes up with after a few days investigating your internal network?"

"What are you worried about?" Abigail slipped on her sandals and got her purse. "It's hard not to have her involved because we work so closely together. Besides, I think it'll be good for the two of you to meet. She's single right now and has a weakness for attractive women. She'll be a good diversion."

"Excuse me?" Marlee stepped back, anger rising. "You're throwing me a bone? You think I'm that shallow?"

"Of course not," Abigail said. "I'm sorry if I insulted you." She paused then mumbled. "Maybe I'm the one who needs a diversion."

"What's that supposed to mean?"

"Nothing. I have to go." She gave Marlee a quick hug and was out the door before anything more could be said.

CHAPTER FIFTEEN

Marlee endured a long night fighting with her sheets and her emotions over Abigail's parting words. As daylight crept into her room, she gave up trying to sleep, dressed in jogging gear, and headed out for a run while most were still in bed.

Quiet streets and ocean air beckoned her toward the loudening roar of water slapping against shore. That she'd been insulted the night before was an understatement. Her heart sputtered over Abigail's comments about having Hannah as a diversion. The faster she ran, the more certain she became they needed to talk—in private, without Tyler and especially not Hannah. That was going to be a challenge because their exclusive meetings could be rare, if not over, now that Tyler was involved.

By the time she'd raced along the beach and back through the streets, Marlee had resolved to confront Abigail about her remarks. The way she'd slipped out without explaining was unacceptable. If there was one thing Marlee had learned over the years, it was that she was a pretty good judge of mutual attraction. The way Abigail looked at her with glistening eyes, touched her so gently, gave glowing smiles, and kept coming back with an urgency to talk were all the usual clues. As Marlee got home and stepped into her shower, she was determined to broach the subject again with Abigail before Hannah was thrust into the mix.

After dressing, Marlee opened her computer and noticed she'd just missed a call from her brother. She took five minutes to make herself a coffee then tried to connect with him.

"G'day stranger." Gabriel's smile lit up her screen. "I'd just about given up on talking to you tonight because it's past my bedtime."

"I'm glad you didn't." Marlee bit into her toast, Abigail still on her mind. "It's good to see you. How are things?"

"Busy, but great. Between gymnastics and dance, our van is always on the go. How are things down under?"

"Fine, just like the weather here. I could get used to this life."

"Don't get too relaxed, because you'll be coming back soon enough," he said. "We all miss you, especially the girls who are anxious for another sleepover. Stephanie and I can't wait too."

The harsh reality of her limited time in Australia suddenly struck Marlee. "I miss you guys, but I'm really going to miss it here. I'm trying to make my time last as long as possible."

"Have you met someone?" Gabe knew her so well.

"Sort of." Marlee smiled as she imagined another cherry-flavored kiss.

"You're scaring me." His forehead wrinkled. "I hope you're not thinking about staying for some woman."

"She's not just some woman. She's interesting, smart, and I've never met anyone like her before."

"What's her name?" Gabriel yawned.

"It doesn't matter because it's not going to go anywhere." Marlee stared into creamed coffee brimming her mug. "I should let you get to bed. Say hi to everyone for me."

"Take care of yourself and keep in touch. See you."

Morning drifted into afternoon. It was almost two o'clock when Marlee approached Tyler's door. They'd messaged each other a few times to check in, but had kept mainly to themselves until Marlee couldn't handle the restlessness anymore. Her mind anguished over aching for Abigail and the need to return to her job in Canada. She resigned to live for the moment.

"I can't believe we're working with Abigail Taylor." Tyler sat at his computer, a glass of water and half-eaten Vegemite sandwich beside him. "No screwing around with her, that's for sure, unless it's you."

"I wish."

"I thought she was going to bite my head off when I suggested checking out bank accounts."

"Can you blame her? She's under a lot of stress and doesn't want to add breaking the law to her problems."

"She's really getting to you, isn't she?" Tyler swung around. "I saw the way you looked at her with your big lusty eyes. I bet you had to change your knickers after she left."

"Stop it." Marlee crossed her arms and dropped on the sofa. "It's hard enough to cope with my attraction as it is. I don't need you teasing me about it."

"I'd be willing to bet you weren't the only one who had to change your undies last night." Tyler snickered as he turned back to his computer.

"What do you mean by that?" Marlee jumped up and hovered over his shoulder. "What did you notice?"

"Couldn't you see the way she was looking at you?" Tyler tapped a few keys. "Her eyes kept moving from your breasts to your lips and her face lit up every time you got near."

"I didn't notice. What else did you see?"

"How jealous you looked when she talked about including Hannah."

"I wasn't jealous."

"You had me fooled."

"I don't like the idea of involving Hannah because, for all we know, she could be the one trying to frame Abigail."

"I looked her up and they could be sisters," Tyler said. "The fact they each have a long blond ponytail sure makes them look similar, and they're both very attractive. Maybe you could get lucky with Hannah instead. It sounds like she's bi."

"I'm not interested in getting lucky with the bitch."

Tyler laughed. "You're sounding jealous now. This could be fun to watch."

"The only gawking you should be doing is on the company network. I'll see you later." She slammed the door and left, more determined than ever to risk another kiss that evening until Abigail texted to say she'd be dropping by later with Hannah.

Hannah had a private Facebook page and Marlee wanted in, but there was no way in hell she'd send a friend request. She finally broke down and begged Tyler to help her access the page that could provide a lead. It turned out the site hadn't been updated in over a year.

The information on Hannah was scant, with mostly shared sites or videos related to her research, but Marlee didn't like that she'd used an image of Abigail's boat for a cover photo as though it were hers.

Hannah did look a lot like Abigail, could have been a younger sister, and was gorgeous, but her pictures did nothing for Marlee. She ate a quiet dinner of shrimp and rice then arranged her sitting room in preparation for an extra person.

When the knock finally came, she put on her best smile and pulled open the door. Abigail was by herself.

"Hi." Marlee's heart fluttered at Abigail's sexy smile and the fact that she was alone. "I thought you were bringing Hannah."

"She couldn't make it tonight." Abigail put a container of fruit salad on the table. "I'm starving and haven't had a minute to eat yet. I hope you don't mind that I brought my food."

"Not at all." Marlee almost skipped to the kitchen. "Let me get you a proper bowl."

"That would be nice." Abigail brushed against Marlee as she washed her hands at the kitchen sink.

"We need to talk." Marlee set the dish and fork on the table. "I've been thinking about things all day and..." A knock sounded at the door.

"It's Tyler. I'll let him in."

They spent the next hour discussing email traffic and employee connections at AbTay Biosystems. Tyler had tracked thousands of messages and hadn't been able to find a single abnormality in anyone's mailbox.

"What about links to my account?" Abigail asked. "How many employees have had direct email contact with me?"

"They all have," Tyler said.

"Of course." Abigail shook her head. "I send out weekly bulletins." She reached for her purse. "I'm getting tired and should probably head out."

Marlee couldn't let her go before they'd talked, but she had to get rid of Tyler first. She caught his eyes, flashed hers toward the door, and then bulged them when he didn't seem to be getting the hint. He finally nodded.

"I've got to run." Tyler grabbed his computer. "See you later."

"What was that all about?" Abigail slipped into her sandals right after he'd left.

"I'm not sure." Marlee stood in front of the door.

"I haven't told Hannah about you yet." Abigail played with her ponytail. "The timing didn't seem right and when she was busy tonight, I just let it go. We make a good team, the three of us, and I'm going to hold off on including her for now."

"I think that's a wise decision." Marlee looked at the beautiful blond mane. "How long have you been letting it grow?"

"I've always had long hair." Abigail wove her fingers through the tresses. "I've thought about cutting it off and keeping a carefree style like yours, but I just never had the courage."

"I love your hair. It must feel so soft."

Abigail held out her ponytail to Marlee. "You can touch it if you like."

Marlee touched the smooth strands, conscious of how close the back of her hand was to the breast that she ached to caress. "It was the first thing I noticed as you raced to save me from the shark. When I clung to you on the water scooter, it felt so reassuring against my cheek. The way it feels, the way it smells like coconut, and the way you're letting me touch it now are amazing. Like you."

Marlee dabbed a kiss on Abigail's cheek, then another and another as she made her way toward the mouth. Deep, uneven breaths escaped Abigail as her eyes closed and she let go of her ponytail to put a hand on the door. When their lips met, Abigail moaned then shoved back, her eyes avoiding Marlee's.

"What are you afraid of?" Marlee stepped back.

"I don't want to become a lesbian." She looked at the floor.

"You can't just *become* a lesbian. You either are one or you aren't. I thought you, as a geneticist, would know this."

"You're right." Abigail put an arm through her purse handle. "What I meant to say is I don't have the gay gene."

"How can you be so sure? Have you discovered the gay gene?" Marlee's voice was getting louder.

"No, but there's a body of research studying how certain genes can be turned on or off, depending on the environment. It's known as epigenetics and when I'm with you…" Abigail looked at her painted toenails. "I've never felt like this before and I'm not ready to cut my hair."

"What's that supposed to mean?" Marlee's throat was dry. She was hurt by Abigail's comments and afraid she was going to cry. "You don't want to look like a dyke, like me with my short hair?"

"That's not it." Abigail kept looking at her feet.

"Maybe you should just leave for tonight." Marlee opened the door.

"Let's talk tomorrow when we're not so tired and emotional." Abigail squeezed Marlee's arm before heading out.

Marlee toppled into bed, frustrated and demoralized, but not defeated. Geneticist or not, Marlee was determined to unravel whatever genetic love code necessary for a breakthrough with Abigail.

CHAPTER SIXTEEN

"I think I'm onto something." Tyler worked at his computer while Marlee languished on his couch and sipped her breakfast coffee. She had popped over with the intention of talking about her failed attempt at another kiss.

"You are?" Marlee perked up. "What is it?"

"The little tracking device I sent Abigail really worked." Tyler rubbed his hands together. "I was able to scan all activity in her email over the last three years and it seems like Hannah's taken liberty with her proxy of Abigail's account. There were two instances where Hannah accessed Abigail's email to authorize research that had already been denied."

"She did? What kind of research?" Marlee hovered at his shoulder.

"I'm not sure. Something or other to do with genome sequencing, if that means anything to you."

"We need to show this to Abigail." Marlee texted the code word *shark* they'd agreed to use for new leads and said she was at

Tyler's. Abigail responded immediately, saying she was heading over.

"Before she gets here, do tell me what happened last night," Tyler said. "Did you get lucky?" He bit into a banana.

"I wish." Marlee flopped back on his couch. "She let me play with her hair, but when I tried to kiss her she freaked out and told me she didn't want to cut it."

Tyler laughed. "Does she think she has to go butch if she finds her inner dyke?"

"I don't know." Marlee sighed. "What should I do? I can feel it."

"Feel what? Her hair? I don't blame her for not wanting to cut it because it must have taken forever to grow that long."

"I don't want her to cut it," Marlee said.

"Maybe she should cut it to lighten up," Tyler said. "It'd sure make a nice wig for someone."

"I think she wants me. I can feel it in the way she looks at me."

"Then maybe you need to be a little more persuasive," Tyler said. "Why don't you offer to French braid her hair then finish with a French kiss?"

"I wish. We should get back to business before she gets here. Why don't you explain your complicated spreadsheet to me?" Marlee got off the couch and moved to the computer where they discussed Tyler's data then tried to find out more about genome sequencing while waiting for Abigail.

Abigail was dressed in running gear and perspiring when Marlee let her in. Tyler sat at his computer and mocked braiding her long ponytail as she wiped her face with a few tissues. Marlee wanted to clobber him, fearing Abigail would see.

"I parked by the beach and jogged here so my car wouldn't be in your lot during daylight in case someone recognizes it."

"That's smart," Tyler said. "Some of the neighbours are quite nosy—especially the one who lives next to me."

Marlee swatted at him.

Abigail smiled. "What wasn't smart was I forgot my backpack with a change of clothes in the boot of the car. I hope you don't mind that I'm sweaty."

"Of course not," Marlee said, trying not to laugh as Tyler widened his eyes and ballooned his cheeks behind Abigail. "I can loan you some dry clothes if you'd like to change."

"That would be nice, but I can't wait to see what you've found. Maybe later."

Tyler walked her through his data capture and pointed to two specific emails reversing decisions Abigail had made relating to gene therapy. One had a subject line of *Genetic Sequence Study A-11002* and the other was *Genetic Sequence Study A-11003*.

"I remember these two instances." Abigail peered over Tyler's shoulder and studied the screen. "Hannah had convinced our management team that changing the genetic composition of normal genes to include harmful ones would help with our research into the prevention of birth defects. She argued that the hereditary properties of these deformities could only be better understood if we engineered the necessary pathogenic properties to create them. I felt the research was too risky so denied it."

"Your work is mind boggling to me," Marlee said, "but I think we have our first suspect in Hannah."

"It's not her." Abigail shook her head. "She's just as passionate as I am about our work."

"How can you be so sure?" Marlee said. "She violated her proxy of your email at least two times when she reversed your decisions about her research."

"Sometimes her passion gets ahead of her and I'd be willing to bet my life on her innocence."

"I wouldn't bet my life on anyone," Tyler said.

"I already bet my life on the two of you," Abigail said. "If anything happens here to betray my trust, my life could be over."

"Are we in any danger right now?" Tyler asked.

"I don't think so," Abigail said. "At least I hope not."

"The world is a dangerous place," Marlee said. "We should always be vigilant."

"Let me explain about Hannah," Abigail said. "Her younger sister was born with a severe cleft lip. Surgery never completely fixed it and her life was miserable with nonstop bullying and teasing. She ended up committing suicide on her sixteenth birthday. Hannah was eighteen at the time and never got over her sister's death. She has dedicated her life to research around finding ways to eradicate facial abnormalities at birth."

"Pretty heavy stuff," Tyler said. "Where do we go from here if you believe Hannah's innocent?"

"Keep doing what you're doing," Abigail said. "I'm impressed with what you've uncovered so far. Marlee was right to involve you."

"And I think your decision to not involve Hannah at this point is the right one," Marlee said.

"She's going to find out about you soon enough," Abigail said. "I thought we could work from my place this weekend. Hannah comes over every day to use the pool. It'll be good for the two of you to meet her. She's a lovely person."

"What are you going to tell her about us?" Marlee asked, anxious to assess Hannah for herself and giddy at the prospect of going to Abigail's.

"I'll say I hired the two of you to do some maintenance around the yard. It might give you a chance to chat with her. Josh will be there too, so I'll keep him occupied while she's at the pool."

"Won't he tell her about me?" Marlee asked.

"No, I've asked him not to say anything to anyone about our episode out on the water, especially with the shark."

"The shark?" Tyler looked at Marlee. "You didn't say anything about a shark. What really happened to your board?"

"It was nothing really," Abigail said. "We saw a shark out on the water and watched it for a while. I could use a fresh shirt now, if the offer's still open."

Marlee couldn't wait to get Abigail out of there and into her unit. She chose her newest clean T-shirt and left Abigail alone in her bedroom to change. She wanted to help her undress, to seduce her right then and there, but she knew it would be inappropriate. Abigail was obviously struggling with her feelings and Marlee knew it was a bad idea to push her into something she wasn't ready for. Maybe would never be ready for.

When Abigail emerged from the bedroom in Marlee's shirt, a few wrinkles around her eyes highlighted her weariness as she sat down.

"I'm exhausted and need a little rest before heading back to my car," she said. "I hope you don't mind if I park myself on your couch for a bit."

"Of course not." Marlee sat beside her. "I can't imagine how tired you must be with the stuff going on at your company and everything else with me."

"I'm sorry," Abigail said. "I know I said we'd talk today, but I just can't right now. Can we just sit here and enjoy each other's company for a bit?"

"Sure we can." Marlee leaned closer, but didn't touch. "I like that you enjoy being with me. You can relax on my couch for as long as you want and we don't even have to say a word."

Abigail smiled, but kept her eyes away from Marlee. "Thanks. No pressure to do anything sounds nice about now."

"Let me fix us something to eat while you rest. I'll whip up a garden salad and have some leftover pasta. How does that sound?"

"Perfect." Abigail leaned back and closed her eyes. "Let's go to my place after we eat for a glass of wine, okay? You can stay the night, if you'd like. I'll get you set up in your own room so we don't have to worry about driving anywhere or sleeping arrangements."

Marlee could hardly contain her excitement as she prepared the food and thought about spending the night at Abigail's. She sent Tyler a message to let him know what was happening and that she didn't want to be disturbed. He wished her good luck.

CHAPTER SEVENTEEN

Marlee expected Abigail's house to be big, but hadn't anticipated the elegant mansion hidden behind the security gates. It was atop a hill and had a modern façade of terra-cotta stucco and solar panels on the tiled roof. The two-story home sprawled over a private park, had lots of windows, a big balcony that wrapped around the front and an underground garage with enough room for at least four cars.

"Wow, what a place." Marlee felt small in the passenger seat as Abigail parked behind a closing door.

"This is certainly a lot more living space than I need, but I love that it's private and fairly new. I'll give you a tour once we get inside."

"Did you have it built?" Marlee followed Abigail through the massive mudroom and up a few stairs into a large open entryway. The air was fresh with a faint aroma of eucalyptus.

"No. I bought it off a couple whose marriage didn't last much longer than the construction phase." Abigail flipped on more lights to brighten the high ceilings and circular oak staircase that led to the second story. "It was perfect for me because I wanted a new house, but couldn't be bothered with the headaches of having one built."

"It's gorgeous." Marlee was in awe and touched that Abigail didn't seem to mind visiting her one-bedroom rental unit off a busy street.

"You can leave your bag on the bench and I'll give you a tour before showing you upstairs to your room."

Abigail led her into a large bright kitchen with lots of shiny white cupboards, an expansive dark granite countertop, stainless steel appliances, and an oversized island with ample space for eating. Marlee felt privileged to be with Abigail in any locale, let alone a gorgeous mansion. She could hardly contain her fairy-tale notion of being swept off her feet by this beautiful blond princess who had saved her life.

"How do you ever keep all of this so clean?" Marlee ran a hand across the pristine countertop, caressing it with her fingertips.

"Well, for one, I'm hardly here. I also have cleaning staff that takes care of things for me."

"Do you like cooking?" Marlee imagined a chef's delight of pots and pans stowed away in the cupboards.

"Not really, but Hannah loves to cook. She's made some fabulous meals here."

Marlee didn't want to hear about Hannah's skills in the kitchen. "Shall we continue?"

Abigail moved on to the dining room, where a glass banquet table large enough to seat twelve graced the room. A prominent centerpiece of white and red roses, eucalyptus leaves, orange kangaroo paws and mixed greenery, presumably from the gardens on the grounds, highlighted it.

"These are beautiful." Marlee leaned into the table to smell the roses.

Abigail smiled as she bent over the arrangement. "They are and I should take more time to stop and smell them too."

"I'd get lost in a place this big." Marlee gawked at the high ceilings in the glassed-in great room at the back of the house. Their words echoed in the immensity of the room.

"I thought so too, but it's really my work that I tend to get lost in."

An in-ground pool off the living space featured an expansive play area near the front and a lap lane that extended along the back for longer swims. Triple patio doors separated the two spaces and highlighted a breathtaking view of the ocean beyond the pool. The inside air smelt fresh with no lingering dampness from the glistening water nearby. The saltwater pool, with its sizable patio deck area to the left, was fully visible from everywhere in the room. Marlee felt the urge to strip off her clothes and dive in, pulling Abigail along with her.

"This place is like a sanctuary where I can escape my work and spend time with Josh." Abigail brushed up against Marlee to sit on the white-cushioned wicker couch. "I love parking myself here and watching Josh in the pool."

"Don't you swim with him?" Marlee sat beside Abigail, their knees almost touching.

"Of course I do, but he likes to stay in the water a lot longer than I can tolerate, especially since I do laps every morning and have already had my fill." She lowered her head, focusing on her knees. "I've missed him over the last few weeks while he's been staying with his father. I promised to pick him up early tomorrow morning so we can spend the day together."

Marlee was disappointed at the prospect of Abigail being up and gone first thing in the morning, but she was glad it was to see Josh. "Shall we keep moving?"

The second level consisted of six bedrooms, two of which had en suite baths, a huge linen closet, and one main bathroom adorned with a colossal whirlpool tub and grey tiled marble flooring. The master bedroom was bigger than Marlee's entire apartment. A tickle flickered inside Marlee's stomach as she tried to keep her eyes off Abigail's fluffy bed with its inviting duvet that made it look like a cloud of paradise. Marlee trembled as she imagined their naked bodies intertwined in the sheets.

"I can't believe you came to my little apartment when you have such a beautiful house." They were now looking at Abigail's large en suite bath with its own whirlpool tub big enough for four.

"I love your place," Abigail said. "Lately it's felt more like home to me than all of this."

"Really?" Marlee's breath caught.

"Yes. It reminds me of my childhood home with its simple existence. This is more of a house than a home to me."

"Why don't you show me my room?" Marlee had to get herself out of there before her legs gave out.

"There's a private bath for you as well." Abigail led them down the hall to the other side of the house.

"This is nice." Marlee placed her backpack on the floor and fondled the fluffy duvet of woven aquamarine linen on the bed, then wandered around the room. "My own walk-in closet too. I should have brought something to put on a hanger because it's pretty empty."

"There are too many empty spaces in this house." Abigail turned to leave. "How about a glass of wine now?"

They spent the next while discussing Hannah. Abigail refused to believe Hannah could be linked to anything criminal and resisted agreeing to any kind of full-scale investigation into her personal emails. In the end, they agreed to introduce Hannah to Marlee and tell her the truth about how they met on the water.

"I know you have an early morning ahead so I won't keep you up any longer." Marlee put her empty glass in the dishwasher. "I've really enjoyed this and am looking forward to seeing Josh again tomorrow."

"So am I." Abigail sighed. "The poor boy was so distraught with my being questioned by the police. He's really worried about me. I'm glad Keith is taking good care of him."

"Thanks for the tour, the wine and the friendly company." Marlee squeezed Abigail's arm. "I hope you have a good sleep. I'll see you in the morning."

"Good night." Abigail stayed still. "Help yourself to anything you need. There are extra towels in the bathroom and let me know if you want anything else."

Marlee headed up to her room, wondering how she'd ever be able to sleep with her heart pounding the way it was. Of course she wanted something else. Abigail. The house was gigantic and she'd be so far down the hall that nothing would ever happen.

Marlee stripped down and put on a baggy T-shirt before crawling between the soft cotton sheets that caressed her bare legs with their freshness. She turned out the light and listened for Abigail's footsteps mounting the stairs and going into her room. She heard Abigail's door close and then the house was silent, with the exception of the ticking of a clock on her bedroom wall.

An hour later, Marlee still lay awake, her eyes adjusted to the darkened room and scanning the ceiling. Her head pounded from a burning desire so strong she debated dipping into the pool to cool off, but she was a guest in Abigail's house and needed to behave.

A soft tap at her door startled Marlee, her heart starting to race. "Ab…Tay?"

The door eased open, revealing a robed figure silhouetted against the soft light from the hall. "Are you awake?" Abigail's voice was low, almost a whisper.

"Yes." Marlee propped herself up on a wobbly elbow. "You can turn on the light if you like."

"I don't want to turn on the light…I…I want to sleep with you."

Marlee's breath caught, afraid she was dreaming. "Do you know what that would mean?"

"Yes." Abigail's breathing was heavy in the dark. She edged forward.

"I need you to be sure." Marlee suddenly felt protective of Abigail and wanted to be certain that this would be the right thing for her at this time. "Tell me what you want."

"Please touch me." Abigail's robe dropped to the floor, her nakedness shadowed by the darkened room as she stood by the bed.

"You're beautiful." Marlee's elbow rested on a pillow, her head trembling and her voice low. "I want to make love with you so much right now, but I need to know that you're ready."

"If you touch me you'll feel just how ready I am."

That's all it took for Marlee to slip out from under the sheets and slide her T-shirt over her head. She nudged her naked body up against Abigail's and they joined together, heavy breathing in tune with hungry kisses as they toppled onto the bed.

"Oh my God, I can't believe how good this feels." Abigail convulsed, her breathing uneven.

"This is nothing yet." Marlee was on top, planting kisses all over the most beautiful breasts she'd ever tasted. She moved a hand downward, exploring until her fingers slipped between Abigail's legs.

"I think I'm going to explode." Abigail's hips arched upward and she screamed out her orgasm in one long burst.

"Can you touch me now? Please?" Marlee could hardly contain her arousal and was afraid she'd crest on her own.

Abigail's uncertain fingers found that perfect spot just in time as Marlee roared in pleasure then cried in relief.

"I'm sorry." Marlee looked for a tissue and blew her nose. "You're the one who's supposed to cry because it's your first time. Isn't that how it works?"

"It doesn't matter how it works, but I'm going to buy you a toaster tomorrow." Abigail smiled. "Let's do that again."

CHAPTER EIGHTEEN

An early morning swim followed by a shared shower marked a new beginning in their relationship. Abigail dropped Marlee back at her place as she made her way to get Josh. The dark-tinted windows of the car kept their five-minute necking session private as they struggled to break away from each other before they had to go their respective ways.

Marlee couldn't stop smiling as she popped over to Tyler's. She kept pinching herself, sure it was all a dream and she'd wake up soon.

"I can't believe you got lucky with her." Tyler blurted out the words as soon as he saw her.

"How would you know?" Marlee strolled in and flopped on his couch, trying to hide her smile.

He began to peel an orange. "Excuse me, but you're glowing all over. Do tell what happened."

"She wants me to meet Hannah today." Marlee wasn't going to admit anything. She could hardly believe they'd finally made love and wanted to savor the memories on her own.

"So she's going to involve Hannah?"

"No, not yet." Marlee's voice shook with excitement. "I'll be introduced as an unfortunate surfer who needed a ride back to shore. We'll stick to the truth on how we met, especially since Abigail's son will be there to verify the facts."

"Tell her what you want, but she's going to know you're sleeping with Abigail." Tyler bit into a slice of orange and the juice scented the air.

"It's no secret I'm attracted to Abigail. What lesbian wouldn't be?"

"I'd be willing to bet she's beaming this morning too." Tyler rubbed his sticky fingers together. "The two of you in the same room will light up like an animated neon sign flashing the words *just had sex*."

"You're crazy." Marlee got off the couch and headed to the door. "You can do a visual assessment when Abigail gets here. She's picking me up later this morning so I can spend some time with Josh and meet Hannah."

"Let me know when she's here and I'll get the two of you to stand in front of a mirror so you can see for yourself."

* * *

Marlee's legs wobbled as she prepared herself a light snack of cream cheese on quinoa crackers, and fresh strawberries. She'd have to warn Abigail about Tyler's intuitiveness and swear she didn't kiss and tell. When the tap at her door finally came, she wedged it open just enough to pull Abigail into her arms then slammed it shut.

Abigail pushed her up against the wall and began to devour her lips with hungry kisses. Marlee couldn't believe the passion she'd unleashed in this woman and held her own as they staggered to the couch, clawing off clothes and gasping for air.

"We only have a few minutes," Abigail mumbled into Marlee's lips.

"That's all we need for a quickie." Marlee's experienced fingers found Abigail's G-spot and stroked it, bringing on a seismic orgasm followed by little aftershocks of breath-catching tremors.

"Oh my God, that was amazing." Abigail reached down to touch Marlee. "We need to get going, but first help me find the right spot for you."

"This is wonderful. You're beautiful." Marlee kept her fingers intertwined with Abigail's to speed up her own release of an orgasmic shockwave that ended with the sound of a message coming into her computer.

"It's Tyler." Marlee stretched her neck to look at the screen. "He wants to know if it's safe to pop over."

"No, tell him we're just about to leave." Abigail clambered off the couch and rushed into the bathroom.

Marlee popped into the washroom after Abigail was finished then sat topless in front of her computer as she typed a response to Tyler. "I have to tell you he's on to us."

"What do you mean by that?" Abigail reached for her ponytail and took out the elastic, letting blond tresses flow over her shoulders. "I'll have to fix this before we go."

"No, please leave your hair out." Marlee reached for the soft locks. "It looks good on you this way and it's so sexy."

"Maybe later." Abigail put the elastic back in and pulled her hair through the rear of her white ball cap. "Speaking of sexy, your body is more beautiful than I ever imagined." She rubbed her nose against Marlee's cheek.

"So you've been imagining me naked then, eh?" Marlee smiled. "I knew it."

"Have you told Tyler about us?" Abigail turned serious.

"No, of course not." Marlee finished getting dressed. "He knows I'm attracted to you, but that's all I've admitted. There was no sense trying to hide it."

"So if you didn't tell him about last night, how could he know?"

"He knew as soon as he saw me this morning. It's something we'll have to watch out for around Hannah. I wouldn't want her to realize we're sleeping together."

"You're right." Abigail began to fidget with her ponytail at the back of her hat. "She'd never forgive me."

Marlee was taken aback. "What does that mean? This has nothing to do with her."

"I know." Abigail sighed. "I should tell you that we slept together once. It was mostly at her prompting, but I was curious and went along with it."

"Why didn't you say something before?" Marlee's heart dropped.

"I didn't think it was relevant." Abigail put her arms around Marlee. "It was only one time shortly after I'd left Keith and I really didn't enjoy it. Afterward, I thought I was just someone who happened to be born without much of a sex drive. Keith wasn't able to pleasure me in the way a sexual partner should, even though I did love him when we got married. I endured sex for a few years to have a child, but I couldn't take it anymore after Josh was born. With Hannah, I was curious to see if having sex with a woman would somehow turn me on. It didn't and that's why this with you has taken me by surprise. This crisis at my company has made it one of the worst times of my life, but then I met you and all of a sudden I feel so happy and alive. Kind of ironic, isn't it?"

Marlee didn't know what to say. She kissed Abigail. "This is a conversation we need to pick up later. I think we should tell Tyler about us and get him to meet Hannah today too. He can give us a sign if we start ogling each other."

"Whatever you think."

A light knock at the door announced Tyler's arrival. Marlee winked as he entered. His eyes rolled when he noticed Abigail fixing her hair in the mirror.

He leaned into Marlee and whispered. "You need to practice safer sex."

"What's that supposed to mean?" Marlee spoke loud enough for Abigail to hear.

"I noticed one of our neighbours eyeing Abigail's car in the parking lot. It's only a matter of time before you get caught."

"We can't have that." Abigail stepped forward. "It's time we move operations to my place. Tyler, can you pack a few things and come with us?"

"Sure. I just have to grab my computer." Tyler stepped toward the door.

"I mean for the two of you to move into my house for now," Abigail said. "God knows it's big enough and we can have a dedicated war room for this. Would that be okay?"

"Are you kidding?" Tyler beamed. "I'll be right back."

"And don't forget to bring your bathing suit," Marlee said then turned to Abigail. "Why don't you head out now and I'll wait for Tyler. It's best if you're gone before someone else starts studying your car."

"Okay." Abigail wrapped her arms around Marlee. "It'll give me a chance to tell Josh and Hannah about the two of you. I'll say that Tyler's a friend of yours who needs a job and is going to help out with some maintenance around the grounds. I hope he doesn't mind playing along with it."

"I'm sure he won't and it'll be fun." Marlee gave her a kiss and then opened the door. "You should get going now. We'll see you soon."

"One more thing." Abigail spoke in a low voice. "You'll be staying in my room. It'll free up yours for Tyler and he'll be at the other end of the hall."

"I can hardly wait." Marlee watched Abigail trot to her car then disappear behind the darkened windows. A whole new world had just opened up for the two of them.

It didn't take long for Tyler to return to her door, rolling airline suitcase in tow, keys at the ready. "We can take my car. I imagine you'll soon be driving one of Abigail's luxury fleet instead of that tin can rental of yours."

"She has a big garage, but I didn't notice a fleet of luxury cars." Marlee grabbed her backpack and locked the door as they left. "From what I can tell, she only has her car and an SUV so there's lots of space to keep your Beemer indoors."

Tyler raised the trunk of his car. "You can put your bag in the boot with mine. What did you think of her place?"

"It's amazing." Marlee smiled. "She has this beautiful great room that looks out over her pool and the most incredible view of the ocean. I never imagined myself being in that kind of luxury."

Tyler started the car and pulled out of the parking lot. "How are you ever going to leave and go back to Canada? I guess with all of her money, you could always become a kept woman."

"I don't want to think about any of that right now." Marlee played with her seat belt. "The most important thing is to help her catch the fucker who's screwing up her life."

"Well said." Tyler laughed. "You want to catch the fucker while you fuck her."

"I'm not fucking her," Marlee said. "We're fooling around, having sex, or even making love. But I'll never fuck her. Got it?"

"Sure, sorry. Now why don't you tell me exactly where in Darling Point her house is?"

When they arrived at the entrance gate, a car was ahead of them and putting in a code to access the property. The vehicle was the perfect match to Abigail's Golf except it was metallic blue instead of white. Marlee figured it was Hannah as a blond woman worked the security pad.

The gates separated only long enough to let her drive through, shutting out Marlee and Tyler.

"Bitch." Marlee scrambled to find the code, but the gates automatically reopened.

"Take a deep breath." Tyler drove them in. Hannah was out of the car already, embracing Abigail on the front steps. "You don't want to look like a jealous lesbian on top of a horny one."

Marlee nudged him as they came to a stop in front of the garage, apprehension bubbling in her veins as she braced to meet Hannah.

CHAPTER NINETEEN

Abigail raised a hand to signal she needed a few more minutes on her own with Hannah. The two women stood head to head, close enough to kiss, as they engaged in an intimate conversation in front of Abigail's house. Marlee gawked from the open car window, wishing she could hear what was being said and squirming when Hannah put a hand on Abigail's arm.

"You're staring," Tyler said.

"Look at how she's touching her. I wonder what they're saying."

"I'm sure Abigail's telling her how great you are in bed."

"Would you stop?" Marlee swatted his arm then got out of the car.

"Hey." Josh strolled from the garage, hands in the pockets of his grey cargo shorts.

"Josh. Hi." Marlee reached out and pulled him into a hug. "It's great to see you again. How are you doing?"

"I'm good."

"I'd like you to meet my friend Tyler." Marlee led Josh to the other side of the car.

"Hey." Josh shook Tyler's hand. "Mum said you're going to help out with stuff around here."

"That's the plan," Tyler said.

"Tyler lives in my building," Marlee said. "Our place just got flooded out and your mom's been kind enough to let us stay here for a bit."

"How'd you get flooded when it's hardly been raining?" Josh asked.

"There was a faulty sprinkler system in our complex," Marlee said. "It somehow got set off and there was water all over."

"Mum said Tyler likes gardening and is going to help out with the grounds."

"Sort of." Marlee wished they had better planned their cover story. She only hoped Tyler would follow her lead.

"Yeah," Tyler said. "I'll find the weeds and Marlee will help with tending your mother's garden. We make a good team."

"Hey, you two," Abigail said. "I'd like you to meet Hannah."

"Hello, Marlee." Hannah smiled and held out her hand.

"It's nice to meet you." Marlee's fingers felt squeezed as their palms barely met.

Hannah lingered beside Abigail, the similarity of the two women all but gone up close. Hannah's nose was bigger with flared nostrils, and her eyes were a dark brown that didn't match her blond hair.

"I'm shocked Tay didn't tell me about you before this," Hannah said. "She's always so modest, but I can't believe she rescued you from that shark. It must have been so scary." Hannah shook, exaggerating. "I'm trembling just thinking about it."

"I'm glad Josh and Abigail were out on the boat that day," Marlee said. "If it wasn't for them, I wouldn't be here."

"I spotted her with my drone," Josh said. "You should have seen the teeth on that shark. It almost ate Mum too."

"Let's not blow it out of proportion," Abigail said. "Why don't we get your stuff inside? Tyler, you can move your car into the garage and we'll bring the bags in from there."

"Sure." Tyler turned to get back in the car.

"Hello, Tyler. I'm Hannah." Hannah stopped him and extended her hand.

"Nice to meet you Hannah." Tyler exchanged a quick shake.

"I'm so sorry," Abigail said. "With everything going on, I seem to have lost my manners and forgot to introduce the two of you."

"I would've expected you to be driving a ute." Hannah studied his car.

"I'm not a tradie," Tyler said.

"Aren't you here to work on the grounds?" Hannah glanced at Abigail.

"He is," Marlee said. "Our apartment building got flooded so we'll be staying here for a bit."

"Enough chatter for now," Abigail said. "Let's get the two of you settled inside."

Tyler moved his car inside the garage and they brought their luggage into the house. Abigail led them from room to room, acting as though it was also Marlee's first time in her home. They ended their ground floor tour in the kitchen.

"Help yourself to anything in the fridge," Abigail said. "I want you to feel at home while you're staying here."

"She's an amazing host," Hannah said. "The fridge is always full and I love using her kitchen."

"I wish I was into cooking. It seems like such a waste to have a kitchen like this when most nights I just make myself a simple meal like a grilled cheese sandwich or omelet."

"I see you got a new toaster." Hannah ran her fingers along the shiny stainless steel top. "A four-slicer. Nice."

"Yes," Abigail said. "I picked it up this morning for my guest…guests."

"A new toaster. I love it." Marlee beamed at Abigail until Tyler kicked her ankle.

"We should keep moving," Abigail said. "I'll take Tyler and Marlee upstairs to show them their rooms. Hannah, why don't you go out to the pool? I'm sure Josh is waiting for someone to keep him company."

Abigail brought Tyler to his room first. "You can put your things in here."

"Wow, this is so big and my own bathroom too." Tyler left his bag beside the bed and approached the window. "What a great view of the grounds. I'm pleased to see they've been well-managed and won't need much maintenance from me."

"What did you tell Hannah about us?" Marlee asked. "We need to make sure our stories are consistent."

"I know," Abigail said. "She was a bit surprised to see you. She's very protective of me and was confused about you being here, especially since she knows I like my privacy. I'm glad you added the bit about the flooding."

"We'll have to be extra careful," Marlee said. "She'll be watching us."

"What was that about the toaster?" Tyler asked. "You two looked like you were sharing some secret candy or something."

Abigail laughed. "I bought it for Marlee. She's been hoping for one."

"It's perfect." Marlee put her hand on Abigail's arm. "I love it. Thank you."

"Instead of having toast, we should be making a toast to the happy couple." Tyler held up an imaginary glass. "What is it about lesbians and toasters? You two are going to blow our cover with Hannah if you keep that up."

"Hannah doesn't see me as a lesbian," Abigail said.

"Don't kid yourself," Tyler said. "With the way you're drooling over each other, it won't take her long to clue in."

"We can't have that," Abigail said. "Let's hurry up."

"Yes." Marlee picked up her backpack and looked at Tyler. "Shall we go for a swim and try to get to know Hannah?"

"Okay," Tyler said. "I'll change and see you down at the pool whenever you get there, but don't take too long."

"We'll behave," Marlee said. "See you in a few minutes."

"Just a reminder that you're supposed to be my gardener too," Abigail said. "I don't let any of the house staff swim in the pool. Play up the flood at your apartment and your friendship with Marlee."

"Will do, boss."

Abigail led Marlee to the bedroom next to hers. "You can leave your things here." She moved closer and whispered. "We'll move them into my room later."

Marlee smiled, gave her a quick kiss, and then approached the bed with its navy duvet and lime-green pillows. "This is nice, like everything to do with your house. Especially you." She dropped her bag and reached for Abigail. "I'm glad Hannah doesn't know you're a lesbian. I couldn't stand the competition."

Abigail stepped back, glancing toward the hall. "Sorry. Josh's room is next to this one and he often pops up here. I don't want him to see us."

"Are you ashamed of me?"

"Of course not." Abigail edged closer to Marlee, speaking in a low voice. "I don't know how Josh is going to react when he finds out we're sleeping together. He doesn't need to know for now."

"Why do you have such a problem admitting you're a lesbian?" Marlee asked.

"This is all so new to me." Abigail locked eyes with Marlee. "Please bear with me. I'm still having a hard time saying the word lesbian, let alone admitting to being one."

"As long as we have this." Marlee kissed her. "I can let you have all the time you need."

"What are we going to do when it's time for you to return to Canada?" Abigail asked. "I can't bear letting you go."

"Let's not think about that for now." Marlee put her head on Abigail's shoulder. "Look how much has happened in the last few weeks. Who knows what's to come?"

"That's what scares me," Abigail said. "I could lose everything."

"You're not going to lose this battle." Marlee clasped Abigail's arms. "I won't let it happen. And I know you won't either."

"Sometimes things are out of our control."

"Shhh. None of that." Marlee kissed her then opened the door. "Now shoo. We'd better get a move on before people start to wonder. I'll change into my suit and meet you at the pool."

"Yes, it's best that you kick me out before undressing." Abigail winked. "We'll have to keep Tyler between us otherwise I won't be able to keep my eyes off you." She blew a kiss, backed away, and closed the door.

Marlee flopped on the bed, her veins bubbling with disbelief at her good fortune. Abigail was now her lover. Nothing else mattered.

CHAPTER TWENTY

Hannah and Abigail sat side by side on lounge chairs facing the pool, deep in conversation, when Marlee came down. Josh was demonstrating dive bombs into the water while Tyler perched on a floating chair. Marlee dropped her towel and leapt to create a big splash of her own.

"Here I come!" She hit the water, sank to the bottom, and then shot up to the surface with another spray. She'd opted for her one-piece suit, avoiding any embarrassing moments of losing her top or bottoms if she decided to play rough in the pool.

"Show off." Tyler kicked water her way.

"I see you found a throne," Marlee said. "How appropriate. Why don't we play something?"

"Find a ball to toss around," Tyler said.

"There's one over here." Josh got out of the pool and retrieved a water polo ball that had been lodged under one of the chairs. He threw it toward the middle of the pool then jumped back in with a big splash.

"Be careful," Abigail said. "I don't want anyone getting hurt."

"Oh, Mum. Chill, will you?"

"I don't want to be soaked," Hannah said.

"Oh, yeah." Josh swam to the side of the pool and flicked water toward her.

"Argh!" Hannah jumped off her chair and rushed to the door. "I don't have my suit on. You'll get me all wet."

Josh laughed. "So? You'll dry."

"Why don't you get changed and join them in the water?" Abigail said.

"I may as well if I'm getting drenched anyway." Hannah shrugged her shoulders. "I'll be right back, but watch out mister. I'm going to get you."

"Just try." Josh laughed.

"And what about you?" Marlee grabbed the edge of the pool and flashed a smile at Abigail. "Are you afraid of getting wet?"

"I'm already wet." Abigail leaned forward and winked. "Your splash into the pool got me."

"Are you playing or what?" Tyler hurled the ball against Marlee's back.

"Ouch." Marlee swung around and grabbed it. "Here, Josh, let's see if you can catch this." She tossed the ball into the air and down the lap lane.

"Go play with the boys," Abigail said. "Have some fun."

"I am having fun. Aren't you going to join us?"

"No, although I'd like to." Abigail rubbed her forehead. "I have work to do. Hannah asked me to review and approve a study related to genome editing so her team can move forward with one of their trials."

"Where's your suit, Tay?" Hannah dropped her towel on a chair. She wore a skimpy two-piece that highlighted a tanned and toned body. Her long ponytail was curled up into a bun.

"Unfortunately my suit's buried under a research report I have to look at." Abigail stood up.

"Oh Tay, you can look at it tonight." Hannah eased into the water. "Have a few minutes of fun while you can."

"Maybe later. I'll see." Abigail went inside.

"Hey, Joshy, throw the ball over here." Hannah swam to the centre of the pool.

"What are we playing?" Marlee joined the others, studying Hannah's attractive features and toned body. She wondered why Abigail had chosen her instead.

"Let's play water polo," Josh said. "Two against two."

"I choose Joshy," Hannah said. "He's the best."

"We only have one net," Josh said, "so whoever gets the ball in scores a goal for their team." He got out of the pool. "I'll set it up over here."

"I'll play from my chair," Tyler said.

"Tay told me about your broken ribs," Hannah said. "How are you feeling?"

"Okay as long as I don't move too much."

"I thought you were supposed to be doing some work around the grounds. Won't that be too difficult right now?"

"I'm going to do the heavy lifting," Marlee said.

"I can't believe I haven't met the two of you before." Hannah treaded water. "You both seem so relaxed here. Who lets their gardener play with their kid in their pool?"

"I'm not her gardener," Tyler said.

"Then who are you?" She lowered her sunglasses.

"He's my friend." Marlee gripped Tyler's chair, but tried to sound charming. "Our place got flooded. Abigail has been so good looking out for me ever since the rescue. I can't thank her enough."

"So the two of you live together?" Hannah raised her chin.

"Sort of," Marlee said.

"Did you know each other when you were in Canada?" Hannah straightened her sunglasses.

"No," Marlee said. "It was kind of a coincidence we hooked up. We both needed short-term rental and that's how we met. It's worked out well, until the flood, of course."

"Where do you live?" Hannah kicked in the water.

"Down by the beach," Marlee said.

"Which beach? We have a lot of beaches around Sydney."

"We're closest to Manly."

"Ready?" Josh jumped back into the pool. Marlee grabbed the ball and threw it into the net.

"Yay," Tyler said. "We got the first goal."

"That doesn't count," Josh said. "The game hasn't even started yet so it's not fair."

"Why not?" Marlee smiled. "I have an injured player so how's that fair?"

"Life's not fair." Hannah retrieved the ball and threw it back into the net. "Score. There Josh, we tied it up and they're going to lose big-time."

They spent the next hour thrashing through the water and fighting for the ball. Marlee was proud she was able to keep the score fairly even. Tyler hung out in front of the net and waved his hands when the ball got close, but Marlee was mostly on her own.

Hannah was very competitive and wouldn't let up, even after Josh complained she wasn't passing the ball. Marlee and Hannah thrashed through the water in a battle to control the ball. Splashes, grunts, and gasps followed the opponents through the waves. It became a game between the two women that abruptly ended when Abigail got into the pool.

"Don't let me stop you." Abigail floated on her chest. "I just want to watch."

Marlee drifted toward Abigail. "Why don't you join me? I've been playing by myself."

"Let's call it a game." Hannah kicked her legs, reaching Abigail before Marlee. "I've had enough. We won, Josh. Ten to eight."

"Sounds like a good game." Abigail lowered her legs and bobbed.

"It was great," Marlee said, "but more like two to one. I didn't get much help from my teammate."

"I'm glad you decided to join us, Tay." Hannah rubbed Abigail's arm. "You're looking more relaxed than you have in a while. Has something good happened that I don't know about?"

"No." Abigail coughed.

"I'm hungry," Josh said.

"I have some sausages in the fridge," Abigail said, "but they need to be grilled."

"Tyler can do that," Marlee said. "He's good with a barbecue, or barby, as you Aussies call it."

"That would be nice." Abigail started a front crawl. "I'll get them ready."

"I'll help you." Hannah followed.

"I'm getting changed," Josh said. "The pool's all yours."

Marlee and Tyler stayed in the water while the others went inside.

"You have to be more careful around Abigail," Tyler said. "I couldn't believe the way you were flirting with her at the side of the pool."

"I can't help myself," Marlee said.

"You needed a good slap to bring you back to reality." He laughed.

"Why don't we act as though we're a couple? Hannah thinks we live together anyway."

"Don't kid yourself." Tyler slid off his chair into the water. "I saw her looking you up and down. You scream dyke and I'm not exactly a bundle of masculinity. Flat mates would be more like it. She was sizing you up. Don't be surprised if she hits on you."

"Don't scare me. Besides, I didn't feel any vibes from her." Marlee got out of the pool.

"Maybe she wasn't interested." Tyler laughed as he followed Marlee out of the pool to get ready for lunch.

CHAPTER TWENTY-ONE

The water polo ball drifted in the pool while food was served. Playtime over, it was down to the serious business of adorning buns with condiments and coleslaw for barbecued pork or vegetarian sausages.

"Who's ready for a snag?" Tyler stood at the grill, shuffling a mound of white onion slices on the heat so they didn't burn.

"I'm ready for two." Josh hovered beside Tyler and held out his plate. "And make sure they're meat."

"None of that vegetarian crap for you?" Tyler laughed.

"Hey." Hannah barged over. "The vegetarian ones are the best. That's all Tay and I eat when it comes to snags."

"I wondered who ate them." Tyler put one on her plate. "Where's your bun?"

"I'm not having a bun," Hannah said. "I'll take a second snag to go with my slaw, but no onions."

"Sure thing." Tyler placed another on her plate.

"Thanks heaps. You're good with the barby. Have you ever worked in a restaurant?"

"Nope. Can't say I have. Who's next?"

"I'll try one of each on my bun and some onions too please." Marlee bumped into Hannah as she held out her plate. "Whoops, sorry."

"No worries." Hannah moved to the table. "I have to leave soon and pop by the office to do a few things this arvo."

"Oh?" Abigail asked. "What things?"

"I promised my team I'd look at some data this weekend. Since I asked you to review work, I'd better do some of my own."

"What data is that?" Abigail held out her plate to Tyler. "I'll just have one vegetarian please."

"It's from one of our small trials on gene editing for leukemia." Hannah chewed as she spoke.

"I'm sure it can wait until Monday."

"I won't be available Monday. Remember? I'm going to the office in Canberra for a few days."

"I thought that was next week." Abigail sighed as she sat at the patio table. "It means I'm behind more than I thought. Maybe I should go into the office too."

"I think you should stay here and enjoy your time with Josh and your house guests," Hannah said. "I hope you don't mind if I finish eating on my way out. It was nice meeting you both. I hope we'll see each other again." She leaned over and pecked Abigail on the cheek. "Ta, Tay."

"Let's touch base in the morning," Abigail said. "We should go over a few things before you head to Canberra."

"Sure. See you later Joshy." Hannah waved as she disappeared into the house.

"Maybe she didn't like my grilling," Tyler said.

"Hannah's like that," Abigail said. "When she decides to do something, she gets on it right away. That's why she's such a good leader on my team."

"I'm going to finish eating in my room," Josh said.

"In your room?" Abigail said. "Why don't you stay with us until you finish your food?"

"I want my computer. See you." He went inside.

"Poor Josh." Abigail wiped her mouth with a napkin. "I've hardly seen him lately, but right now I'm glad the three of us have a chance to talk. We have to tell Hannah what we're doing."

"Why?" Marlee stopped chewing. "She doesn't need to know."

"She knows something's up," Abigail said. "We talked a bit in the kitchen. I told her you're a police officer."

Marlee's throat tightened. "What else does she know?"

"That's all I told her for now," Abigail said. "She's worried about me and doesn't understand why the two of you are here. I can't blame her. I promised to tell her what's going on. I want to do it tomorrow."

"I thought you agreed to limit this to the three of us." Marlee almost rolled her eyes in exasperation.

"We could wait until she comes back from Canberra," Tyler said.

Abigail shook her head. "I can't keep this from Hannah. She's worried about me and has a right to know."

"Then do what you have to do and tell her." Marlee stood up and grabbed a few dishes. "I'll clean up."

Abigail reached over to Marlee. "I didn't mean to put it like that. We can certainly wait until she returns from Canberra if you prefer."

"I think I'll go for a little nap and leave the two of you to sort it out." Tyler got up.

Marlee dropped back into her chair as he went inside. "I feel like I'm going to explode. I'm so excited and worried about you at the same time. I can't believe what happened last night and how good I feel inside, but I don't want to lose sight of the fact I'm responsible for protecting you."

"No, you're not." Abigail straightened her shoulders. "I can look after myself. Just because you're a police officer back in Canada doesn't mean you have that responsibility here."

Marlee leaned forward and lowered her voice. "I consider myself responsible for protecting you because I'm your lover now and that's what lovers do for each other."

Abigail smiled. "You're right. I want to kiss you, but Josh might see us. I'm not ready for that yet."

"I'll take a rain check then, which I plan to cash in on tonight." Marlee tapped Abigail's knee then stood. "I'll clean up out here. Why don't you get whatever work you need to do out of the way now?"

"Thanks. That'll be helpful. I'm hoping you and Tyler can work with me a bit later."

"Sure, but won't you want to put that aside while Josh is here?"

"Yes, but he's not staying overnight. Keith is taking him to a net ball game this evening. I'm thinking once he leaves we can get our workroom set up in the den. If there's time, I'll give you and Tyler a tour of the grounds you're supposed to be looking after."

"Sounds like a plan," Marlee said. "Now go get your work done. I don't want it interfering when it's time for bed."

Abigail pecked her lips toward Marlee then went inside.

They spent the rest of the day apart, with Marlee tidying up and strategizing next steps for the investigation into AbTay Biosystems. Now that her primal hunger for Abigail was satisfied, she could focus on finding out who was messing with Abigail and her company.

* * *

Later in the evening, after Josh had gone and they'd set up a common workspace with a table and chairs, Abigail gave Tyler and Marlee a tour of the grounds. A few cockatoos squawked as they flew between power lines, bushes, and grass in the big block of land. Mature deciduous trees interspersed with a variety of evergreen shrubs, including ones projecting dark yellow flowering spikes, surrounded Abigail's property.

"These remind me of corn on the cob," Marlee said, fondling the flowers.

Abigail laughed. "I never thought of corn on the cob, but they do kind of look like it."

"What are they?" Marlee asked.

"Banksia. They're endemic to Australia and a member of the protea family, with a genus of about seventy-five species."

"What about these over here." Marlee touched a deep pink spike flowering on another shrub. "They're gorgeous."

"They are, aren't they?" Abigail said. "We call them bottlebrush. Don't you think they look like one?"

"They do," Marlee said.

"They're another Australian genus belonging to the myrtle family." Abigail ran her fingers over the soft flowers.

"I hope I'm not expected to remember all this," Tyler said. "I know you're a geneticist, but I didn't realize you're a botanist too."

Abigail laughed. "I'm not, but I wanted to give some context. I expect your focus to be on my network rather than my garden."

"Whew, that's good," he said.

"I smell eucalyptus." Marlee inhaled. "I have some cuttings in my place back in Ottawa. I love the scent."

"Doesn't it smell heavenly?" Abigail fondled a bluish-leaved shrub. "They're also from the myrtle family and native to Australia." She smiled at Marlee. "I'm glad they make you feel at home."

"Me too." Marlee snuggled up to her.

"Would you like me to leave the two of you alone?" Tyler asked.

Marlee and Abigail giggled.

"Sorry," Abigail said. "I'm behaving like a teenager. It's a good thing you're around, Tyler. Hannah and Josh could pick up on this and we can't have that right now."

"I think I have a bruise on my back from Tyler's slap with the ball," Marlee said.

"You were getting out of hand so I had to take drastic measures," Tyler said.

"Why don't we call it a day?" Abigail said. "It's been a long one and we need to get some rest so we can get to work first thing in the morning."

"Sounds good to me." Tyler chuckled as he turned toward the house, "I don't imagine the two of you'll get much rest tonight though. Toodle-oo."

CHAPTER TWENTY-TWO

Marlee trembled with anticipation as she slipped into Abigail's inviting bed, naked and about to make love with the woman she could only fantasize about the day before. There was no hesitation on either part, the joining of their bodies a perfect fit as though a long lost puzzle piece had finally been found and put into place to complete the picture.

"I just want to hold you for a minute," Abigail said.

"A minute?" Marlee said. "I want to hold you forever. Will you move to Canada with me?"

"What have we started?" Abigail brushed her lips against Marlee's. Their tongues met for a devouring kiss.

"This can't be real." Marlee spoke through their smooches. "I'm afraid to wake up from this dream."

"I was so nervous last night when I stood outside your door," Abigail said. "I raised my hand three times before finally knocking."

"Are you kidding?" Marlee said. "With the way I've been lusting after you? What were you afraid of?"

"Me." Abigail shifted. "I've never felt this way about another person. It doesn't make sense. I never thought of myself as a lesbian."

"And how do you feel about being one now?" Marlee caressed Abigail's ponytail.

"It seems so natural with you," Abigail said. "I've spent my life studying genetics, mapping DNA profiles related to cancers and disease, and looking for cures to make life better. I've never given any credence to the genetics of love and claims of love at first sight."

"I'm a big believer in love at first sight," Marlee said. "I call it chemistry and think it has everything to do with how we're made up as individuals. I know my chemistry matches yours."

"How can you be so sure without comparing our DNA profiles?"

"I don't need some DNA test to tell me when it feels right," Marlee said. "I either have chemistry with someone or I don't. Take Hannah. The two of you could be sisters. You're both beautiful, smart, and sexy, but I don't have any chemistry whatsoever with her."

"That's because you met her under different circumstances," Abigail said. "Hannah's a lovely woman."

"So why aren't you lovers?"

Abigail snorted. "I'm not attracted to her in that way."

Marlee chuckled. "Now do you understand? There are lots of gorgeous women I like, but am not attracted to. They just don't turn my crank."

"What do I have that turns your crank?"

"Chemistry." Marlee rolled onto Abigail. "Think of a beaker with sizzling vinegar and baking soda that's about to overflow. You turn me on like that."

"I didn't know you were an expert in chemistry." Abigail reached between Marlee's legs and fluttered her fingers. "You're so wet. You must have already overflowed."

"Please don't stop." Marlee moaned. "I'm about to explode. It's time to get my beaker off the burner."

"Like this?" Abigail quickened her pace.

"Yes." Marlee stifled her gasp as an orgasm erupted and her body convulsed.

Their lovemaking overtook conversation and they finally fell asleep in each other's arms, exhausted and satisfied, but not satiated.

* * *

Marlee heard the knock at the bedroom door first. She tugged at Abigail then slid under the covers.

"Who's there?" Abigail called out, her voice groggy.

"It's me, Tay," Hannah whispered as she opened the door and leaned in. "I just wanted to make sure you're okay."

Marlee held her breath and squeezed onto Abigail's waist while hoping Hannah didn't notice the extra mound under the covers.

"Of course I'm okay. It's the middle of the night. What time is it?"

"Sorry, it's just after three."

"What are you doing here?"

"I'm worried about you, Tay. I know something's going on and I don't like being kept out of the loop."

"There's no need to be worried. Go home and get some sleep."

Marlee stayed still, her head resting on Abigail's stomach as she snuck a breath and strained to hear over her thumping heart.

"Let me turn on the light so we can talk," Hannah said.

"No." Abigail raised her voice. "Don't turn it on. It's too bright for my eyes. I'll get up and meet you downstairs. Just give me a minute."

"Sure, okay." Hannah closed the door.

Marlee stayed still. She heard Hannah's footsteps move away and waited for Abigail to make the first move.

"Oh my God," Abigail whispered as she pulled back the covers. "I feel like I've just been caught doing something naughty."

"That's nonsense. This is your house, your bedroom, and you shouldn't feel like that." Marlee sat up and wrapped the sheet around her. "Who the hell does she think she is, coming here in the middle of the night?"

"She's my concerned friend and I don't blame her." Abigail put on a robe. "Letting you and Tyler stay here doesn't seem rational. Now of all times is not the time for me to act irrationally."

"But to come to your bedroom in the middle of the night? Has she done that before?"

"No. There's never been a need to," Abigail said. "She's always respected boundaries and only used her key to let herself in when I'm not here. I'll have a chat and try to ease her mind."

"What are you going to tell her?"

"Shhh. I won't tell her anything tonight. I just need to make sure she leaves and it doesn't happen again." Abigail pecked Marlee's lips. "I'll be right back."

Marlee listened to the scuffle of Abigail's feet disappear down the hallway. She felt defenseless, as though back in the water with a shark readying to attack. Hannah was now the menace, circling in the kitchen for Abigail to fight off on her own. Marlee had to help. She snuck to the bedroom next to Abigail's, tousled the bed sheets to make it look like she'd been sleeping in it, pulled on shorts and a T-shirt, and went downstairs.

Hannah and Abigail stood close together near the kitchen counter, quietly talking, casting shadows on the floor in the low lighting of the range hood. They both looked up as Marlee entered. Hannah snapped her tongue, turned away, and wouldn't face her.

"I thought I heard noise down here," Marlee said. "What's going on?"

"It's nothing," Abigail said. "Why don't you go back to bed?"

"Okay, but don't hesitate to wake me if there's anything I can do to help."

Marlee retreated upstairs and into the room she was supposed to be sleeping in. She got into the bed, turned out the light, and waited. When Abigail finally climbed the stairs, Marlee lurched to the door and met her in the hallway.

"Is she gone?"

"Yes." Abigail sighed. "Let's get some sleep."

"Should I stay here instead of your room?"

"Of course not." Abigail reached for Marlee and ushered them back to her bedroom. "I want you beside me."

"What if Hannah comes back?"

"She won't."

"How do you know?" Marlee undressed and crawled into bed.

"She told me she wouldn't and I trust her." Abigail switched off the light then wrapped her body around Marlee's. Can we try to get some sleep now and talk more in the morning?"

"Sure." Marlee snuggled against Abigail, rattled about Hannah's visit and concerned about her lover's unwavering trust for the annoying woman. As hard as she tried, she couldn't get back to sleep and lay awake in the dark for a long time afterward.

CHAPTER TWENTY-THREE

Tyler sat hunched at his computer as Abigail and Marlee entered the workroom, coffee in hand and ready to work. It was only nine o'clock on Sunday morning, but they'd already shared a swim, shower, and healthy breakfast of fresh strawberries mixed with granola, cereal, and yogurt.

"We heard movement and figured you were already in here." Marlee handed him the mug.

"Thanks." Tyler took a sip without moving his gaze from the computer screen.

"How are you going Tyler?" Abigail asked.

He glanced at her. "Hannah was on the network late last night, snooping around your email account."

"I know." Abigail sat down. "She told me, but good on you for spotting it."

"What was she doing?"

"Hannah's concerned about us staying here," Marlee said. "She came back late last night and told Abigail she was looking through her email to see if she could find out more about us. You didn't hear anything?"

"No." Tyler rolled his chair back to face them. "What time was that?"

"Around three in the morning," Marlee said. "She came right up to Abigail's room and knocked on the door."

"No shit?" Tyler shook his head. "That must have been stressful. Did the two of you get caught?"

"Caught doing what?" Abigail asked, her face straight.

"Nothing." Tyler's cheeks reddened.

"I take it you had a good night then if you didn't hear anything?" Abigail winked at Marlee. "I hope the room was fine."

"Perfect," he said. "I had a really good sleep."

"It's a wonderful room, isn't it?" Marlee said. "I had the best night of my life in that bed."

"I didn't know you slept in it," he said.

"Who said anything about sleeping?"

Abigail cleared her throat. "I, uh, think it's time to get to work. Where should we start?"

"Let's take stock of what we know," Marlee said. "I find it useful jotting information down and then taking a step back to examine the notes."

"I'll open up a new file and be your scribe." Tyler swung back around to his computer.

"Perfect," Abigail said. "Maybe we should get Hannah over here now to help us."

"You filled her in last night?" Tyler looked back over his shoulder.

"No," Abigail said, "but I'm thinking this would be a good time to include her. I'm sure she'd come over now if I asked."

"I don't like the fact that she was snooping around your email last night," Marlee said.

"She was just concerned about me. Hannah's a good friend. I appreciate that she's looking out for me."

Marlee tried to ignore her feelings of jealousy and get back to the job. "Let's jot our thoughts down now that we're here. We need to get moving on this and she can always add to the document later."

"Whatever you think," Abigail said. "Where do we start?"

"With the facts." Marlee turned to Abigail. "Why don't you start by telling us what you know for sure?"

"Company research is being tampered with," Abigail said. "I found proof of it in one of our experiments related to chromosome mutations in birth defects. Instead of preventing embryonic flaws, the research had been modified to propagate physical deformities affecting the face in fetal development. Hannah was devastated when this was discovered because it was one of her research projects. She was totally opposed to the modifications."

"Let's get this down," Marlee said. "One of Hannah's research projects was tampered with to promote birth defects. There are no suspects. Got that Tyler?"

"I do now."

"Who would've had access to this research?" Marlee asked.

"No one," Abigail said. "Hannah likes to work alone on studies in the lab so she can be in complete control of inputs."

Marlee resisted the urge to scoff at Hannah wanting to work alone. She believed research should be based on sharing and suspected Hannah was somehow undermining Abigail's authority by doing this. "Who discovered the tampering?"

"I did," Abigail said. "I monitor company studies and offer support wherever I can."

"How was the research impacted?" Marlee didn't like this.

"I spotted microscopic genetic abnormalities in the specimens right away."

"Could it have been done, perhaps erroneously, by Hannah?" Marlee struggled to give her the benefit of the doubt.

"No." Abigail's nostrils flared ever so slightly. "Hannah doesn't make mistakes like that."

"But who else could have accessed the lab to alter the research?" Marlee asked.

"It could have been anyone." Abigail frowned, as though trying to convince herself it was someone else. "Unfortunately there was a malfunction in some of our security cameras in the building so nothing was recorded for a few hours the night it happened."

"Someone must have shut down the cameras through your network," Tyler said. "Another fact I'll add is that the company has been hacked by me so therefore could be hacked by somebody else."

"Good." Marlee stood up to get a closer look at the notes, wanting to ensure that all of Hannah's suspicious behaviors were included. "Did you document the times when Hannah accessed Abigail's email account to reverse decisions?"

"I have notes in my spreadsheet," Tyler said, "but I'll add it to this list as well."

"Hannah left in a bit of a hurry yesterday afternoon, don't you think?" Marlee folded her arms as she stood behind Tyler.

"And she snuck back in the middle of the night," he said.

"She didn't sneak back." Abigail stood up. "She let herself in and came to my room because she was concerned about me."

She also slept with you once. Marlee mentally added it to the list, jealousy or not.

"Why don't we review our notes?" Marlee backed up so Abigail could study the screen.

"Hannah's name sure does appear a lot," Tyler said.

"It does, doesn't it?" Abigail reviewed the list, her head shaking. "Maybe we should hold off on involving her."

"It sounds like we might have a suspect," Tyler said.

"No, we don't have a suspect," Abigail said. "Just because I want to wait a bit longer before involving Hannah with us doesn't mean I believe it could be her. It's more that I want to be cautious because her name is so prominent in our list. I'd like to think about it for a bit before I make a final decision on whether or not to involve her."

"That's a good idea." Marlee touched Abigail's arm. "I want you to feel comfortable with what we're doing and trust in your own gut about this. We'll do whatever you want."

"Thanks." Abigail put a hand on Tyler's shoulder and grasped Marlee's arm with the other. "I really appreciate the effort you two are putting into this. I want you to know how grateful I am."

"No problem," Tyler said. "I never would have believed I'd be doing something like this. I'm enjoying it."

"I'm glad to hear that." Abigail smiled as she stepped back toward the door. "I think I'll leave you two for now while I deal with a few things from the office."

"Do you have to go in?" Marlee asked.

"No, but I need to finish reviewing Hannah's data. And I also need to think about what I'm going to tell her when she comes over later this morning, expecting an explanation."

"Blame it on me," Marlee said. "Your police officer advises against involving her."

"I might have to," Abigail said. "She can be very persistent when she wants something."

"I can talk to her if you like." Marlee didn't really want to. "Let me know."

"I will." Abigail's footsteps faded into the distance.

"Hannah's overstepping her boundaries," Marlee said. "We need to zero in on the little bitch."

Tyler chuckled as he twirled in his chair to face Marlee. "What happened last night?"

"She at least had the good sense to knock on the closed door first," Marlee said. "I hid under the sheets while Abigail chased her away."

"And she didn't notice a big bulge under the blankets?"

"Abigail wouldn't let her turn on the light," Marlee said, impressed with her lover. "I went downstairs a few minutes later and asked them what was going on. Hannah wouldn't look at me."

"I bet. One wrong look and the two of you could've ended up in a catfight. Two pussies fighting over Abigail." Tyler laughed. "It would have been fun to watch."

"You're disgusting." Marlee scowled.

"Don't let jealousy cloud your perspective on Hannah. Abigail believes she's innocent. We should trust her judgment and not waste a lot of time zeroing in on the wrong person."

"I'm not jealous of Hannah," Marlee said. "I'm watching out for Abigail."

"The way she calls your lover Tay and touches her whenever she can. 'Ta Tay.' Don't tell me that doesn't get you going."

"Look at the evidence," Marlee said. "Hannah's implicated in everything. Her research was fucked with. She abused her proxy of Abigail's email. She left in a hurry yesterday and snuck back in the middle of the night."

"What are you going to say to Hannah if she wants to talk to you?"

"I don't know yet, but I'll think of something. I can't let her know she's my main suspect."

"You're that sure?"

"No, but she's the only suspect we have right now. I have a hunch about her. Something's off with the way she acts around Abigail. It's like she's trying to imitate her. They have the same ponytail, drive the same car, do the same research, and Hannah has a picture of Abigail's boat for her Facebook profile. I don't like it."

"Go figure," Tyler said. "What do you suggest we do now?"

"I want you to track every move she makes on the network. What time she's logged in, who she's sending emails to, what sites she's visiting, when she proxies into Abigail's account, when she's badged into the building, when she's working remotely, and anything else worth noting. Can you do that?"

"I have my ways," he said. "I'll get on it right away."

"Perfect," Marlee said. "I need to check in on a few things back home."

"Like returning to work in a few weeks? How are you ever going to go home?"

"I'm going to request an extension on my work leave. I can't return now. This is starting to feel like home."

"I could get used to this being my home too." Tyler motioned around the room. "Who wouldn't in a place like this?"

"I meant Australia and with Abigail," Marlee said. "I found the love of my life here."

"Love is a pretty strong word," Tyler said. "You don't really know that much about her and how this is all going to turn out."

"I think she loves me too." Marlee smiled.

"You can't be serious," Tyler said. "You may be infatuated with each other, but love? I don't think so. It hasn't been long enough for that."

"Long enough for what?" Abigail came into the room.

"Is Hannah here yet?" Marlee's patience with the woman was waning.

"Yes. She's out by the pool and wants to talk to you." Abigail fidgeted with her ponytail. "I feel so terrible. I didn't know what else to say to her other than you, as the police officer, advised me against telling anything."

Marlee's heart drummed and her mouth suddenly dried. "You didn't tell her I was working with the Australian police, did you?"

"No." Abigail shook her head. "All she knows is that we met by chance and now you're helping me. She doesn't understand why the two of you are staying here and I couldn't think of what to say so I suggested she speak to you."

"Does she suspect anything going on between us?" Marlee's stomach churned.

"No. She knows I'm not a lesbian." Abigail put a hand on Marlee's arm. "Sorry. I didn't mean for it to sound like that."

"I know," Marlee said. "Let's get this over with. I'll think of what I'm going to say while we head to the pool."

"I was hoping you'd go on your own." Abigail pulled her hand back. "I need some space by myself to think and can't deal with this right now. I'm picking up Josh this afternoon and we're taking the boat out for a few hours."

"Is she okay with that?" Marlee asked. "Talking to me on my own?"

"Yes." Abigail backed away. "She insisted on speaking with you, actually. I promised to say good-bye before I go. She's expecting you now on your own."

Marlee took a deep breath as she watched Abigail rush out of view then approached the doorway. "Here goes nothing."

"Good luck," Tyler said.

"Thanks. I'll need it." Marlee's tongue stuck to the roof of her mouth as she headed to the pool. She didn't know what was worse—facing off against Hannah with no prepared words, or her disappointment at not being invited on the boat.

CHAPTER TWENTY-FOUR

Hannah's fingers hammered against the patio tabletop as Marlee trudged toward her. She sat cross-legged in one of the chairs and her face was hidden by unruly hair sticking out of a black ball cap that matched one of Abigail's.

"Good morning, Hannah." Marlee held out a hand. "Thanks so much for agreeing to talk with me."

"What are you doing here?" Hannah swung her head to face Marlee, enlarged black pupils glaring through glassy eyes, her body rigid. "Abigail is vulnerable right now and I won't have strangers taking advantage of her."

"I'm sorry you feel that way." Marlee spoke in a soft voice as she pulled up a chair and sat down. "I understand the two of you are close friends and can appreciate your concern."

"You haven't answered my question." Hannah crossed her arms and looked at the pool.

"She saved my life." Marlee struggled to keep calm. "I owe her and will do whatever is necessary to catch the scum who's trying to hijack the good work of her company. I'm staying here because it's convenient and I don't want anyone but Abigail to know about my investigation."

"Then who the fuck is Tyler?" Hannah twisted around with such fury that she almost overturned the table.

"He's my friend and I'm helping him too." Marlee stayed still. "His ribs were broken by an angry ex and he needs a safe place to stay right now. I couldn't leave him alone and Abigail graciously allowed him to come here with me."

"Sounds pretty contrived to me. Are you working with the Australian police?" A spray of spittle followed Hannah's words.

"No, of course not." Marlee wiped her cheek. "This has nothing to do with my position as a sergeant in the Ottawa police. I'm on leave at the moment and working for Abigail."

"How convenient," Hannah said. "She's not a lesbian, in case you haven't noticed."

"What's that supposed to mean?" Marlee stifled a flinch.

"She's a very rich, attractive, vulnerable woman." Hannah leaned toward Marlee and tapped on the table to the beat of her next words. "Don't kid yourself into thinking she can be seduced by a loud dyke like you."

Marlee's patience was gone. "That's not what I'm trying to do. How would you know what she likes anyway?"

"I'm her best friend and know everything about her."

"No you don't or we wouldn't be having this conversation." Marlee gripped the arms of her chair.

Hannah bent closer, her mouth slightly open to reveal shiny white teeth. "Abigail is susceptible right now. I'll do whatever is necessary to protect her from anyone who tries to take advantage of the situation. I expect to be included in your investigation. Got that?"

"For sure." Marlee stood, her jaw tight. "You, like everyone else in the company, will certainly be included in my investigation. Got that?"

Marlee swung around to retreat and almost knocked Abigail over. They grabbed onto each other as Abigail gasped then quickly let go and stepped away to put a chair between them.

"I'm heading out now," Abigail said. "I'll have my phone if anything urgent comes up, but please don't contact me if it can wait. I want to focus on Josh for the afternoon and have some time to clear my head."

Hannah stood up and pulled Abigail into an embrace. "I'm worried about you, Tay. Please be careful."

"I will." Abigail returned the hug and pecked her cheek. "Try not to worry about me, okay?"

Hannah kept her grip. "You're my best friend, Tay. Of course I'm going to worry about you."

Abigail pulled out of the embrace, turned to Marlee, and nodded. "Enjoy the rest of the day."

"You too." Marlee's throat constricted as she watched Abigail disappear inside. She resisted the urge to follow and stomped into the yard to calm down, conscious of Hannah's spiteful gaze on her back. She strolled around the perimeter of trees, touching the foliage, inhaling the eucalyptus, and made it to the front of the house just in time to see Abigail backing her vehicle out of the garage. She waved and was about to approach the rolling SUV when Hannah's car started. All she could do was watch as the two women drove away. Dejected, she went into the house in search of Tyler. He was still seated at his computer.

"They're both gone." Marlee flopped into a chair. "We have the house to ourselves. Yippee."

"They left together?" Tyler's eyes widened.

"No. They went at the same time, but not together. That bitch better not follow her to the boat."

"I take it your little chat didn't go very well." Tyler leaned back. "What did you say?"

"It doesn't matter what I said to her, we don't trust each other." Marlee's body shook with anger. "I can tell Abigail feels caught in the middle. She's probably going to insist we include Hannah."

"You don't know that," Tyler said. "Abigail's a smart, rational woman and she'll think things through."

"She thinks the world of Hannah. She even kissed her good-bye—on the cheek. All I got was a nod."

"What did you expect?" Tyler laughed. "You of all people should have recognized that Abigail was on the ball by not divulging your illicit affair."

"It's not an illicit affair." Marlee punched her knee. "We love each other."

"So you've told me. If I was Hannah, I'd be nervous too. Think of it. Abigail has been her best friend for years and all of a sudden two strangers move into her house. Wouldn't you be freaking out too?"

"This is getting complicated." Marlee sighed. "It's so much easier when I'm not personally involved in a case. I know what you mean, but it doesn't matter. I can't empathize with that woman and especially not when Abigail's future is at risk."

"How did things get left between the two of you?"

"She's going to think about things." Marlee sighed.

"What things? Did you give her some kind of ultimatum?"

"Of course not," Marlee said. "I'd never ask her to choose between Hannah and me."

"I meant Hannah." Tyler chuckled. "How did you leave things with her?"

"This is some kind of game for you, isn't it? Laughing when things aren't so funny."

"It's easier for me because I'm not personally involved," Tyler said. "I'm just your IT hacker guy along for the ride."

Marlee's phone buzzed with a text. "Abigail's spending the night on the boat with Josh. Shit. I was hoping to talk to her tonight."

"As in pillow talk?" Tyler said.

Marlee swatted at him. "We need to go to the marina to make sure Hannah's not there too. Abigail's picking up Josh so we should be able to get there before they head out to ensure they're left alone. I don't trust that woman."

*　*　*

Tyler eased his car into a parking space behind a white minivan in the marina car park. Marlee watched Abigail and Josh load a few bags onto the boat. There was no sign of Hannah or her car.

"Wow, nice boat," Tyler said. "I wouldn't mind sailing on that. Are you going to get out and let her know you're here?"

"No. She asked not to be disturbed unless it was an emergency."

"I thought it *was* an emergency," Tyler said. "You, a police officer, even ordered me to run three yellow lights."

"It's not like they were red," Marlee said. "We had lots of time to clear the intersections. Besides, we were in hot pursuit and didn't have a second to waste at lights."

"The only hot pursuit was in your pants," Tyler said.

Marlee folded her arms and lowered her chin. "I had to make sure Hannah wasn't anywhere near that boat before they left."

"Oh, come on. You couldn't stand the thought of Hannah spending the night on the yacht instead of you."

"Abigail said she needed some time to herself to think," Marlee said. "I want to make sure she gets that. Otherwise I'd be over there now myself, weaseling my way in."

"Like you expected Hannah to be doing?"

"Yes. I'm feeling more encouraged about Hannah now that it looks like she's giving Abigail some space."

"It's a good thing because after a night of thinking on her own, Abigail could insist we include her," Tyler said.

"I know." Marlee put down her window and watched as the impressive boat navigated out to open water then disappeared from view. She longed to be on it. "Let's go."

CHAPTER TWENTY-FIVE

When Abigail returned the next morning, Marlee and Tyler were in the workroom sipping on coffee. Marlee was tired and adjusting to the new day after a restless night of brooding and longing. She hoped the caffeine would reverse her blah mood after Abigail hadn't invited her on the boat. Tyler, on the other hand, was humming away at his computer when Abigail burst into the room and almost made Marlee spill her mug.

"Good morning." Abigail was perky and dressed for the office. She looked stunning in her fitted navy skirt with matching blazer and a light floral patterned cotton blouse underneath. "How are you going?"

Marlee's jaw trembled at the sight of Abigail. Her eyes begged Tyler to answer.

"Hard at it, but nothing new to report," he said after a pause.

"I hope you didn't work all night." Abigail hovered over his shoulder to look at the screen.

"Nah," Tyler said. "We were out and about a bit yesterday after you left."

"I'm glad to hear that." Abigail turned to Marlee. "I was wondering if I could have a few words alone with you?"

"Sure." Marlee's knees shook as she followed Abigail out of the room, afraid of what was coming.

Abigail led them out by the pool and stopped at the edge.

"I hope you're not going to push me in," Marlee said.

"Should I?" Abigail's tone was serious.

"It depends." Marlee's mouth was dry. "If you're going to tell me you've thought about things and want us to be over then yes, push me in."

Abigail smiled and pulled Marlee into her arms. "Oh, Marlee, that's not it at all. I spent a lot time thinking about you last night. I can't seem to ever get you off my mind and you make me feel so good. I want you in my life. This is so crazy, but I don't care what Hannah says. I love you."

"Oh, Ab, I love you too." Marlee gave a kiss then clung to her with relief and joy. "I was so terrified of what you were going to say. When you led me out here instead of to your room, I was sure you were going to dump me."

"I didn't know what you were thinking of me anymore," Abigail said. "I left in such a hurry yesterday, expecting you to deal with Hannah on your own, and put you in an awkward spot. I imagined you being furious and thought it more appropriate to talk out here instead of in my room."

"You did, did you?" Marlee squirmed in delight as she began to tug at Abigail's blouse. "How appropriate would it be for me to rip your clothes off right here and now?"

"Not very. I'm already late for a meeting at the office." Abigail giggled as she tried to stop Marlee's hands. "As much as I'd love to let you strip me naked and jump in the pool with you, unfortunately I have to go to work now."

"Oh come on, you're the boss." Marlee slid her hands under Abigail's blouse and cupped her breasts. "Skip the meeting and let's have some fun."

"I can't." Abigail wriggled away. "I need to meet with Hannah before she leaves for Canberra this afternoon. She's waiting for me at the office."

"Oh." Marlee stepped back. "Are we going to have to include her?"

"No." Abigail shook her head. "Not when she tried contacting me three times yesterday after I asked to be left alone." She embraced Marlee. "It meant a lot to me that you respected my request for some personal space last night. I've decided to keep our little team the way it is for now."

"I'm glad." Marlee kissed her. "I was preparing myself to include her if you insisted, but I much prefer the status quo."

"She's quite upset with me right now." Abigail rested her forehead against Marlee's. "A week away at our Canberra office will be good for her. She's been carrying a lot of the workload lately and really has been a big help."

"I'm sure she has. Do what you have to do, but be careful. Okay?"

"I will. You were my first priority this morning and I'm so happy we talked." Abigail gave her a lingering kiss then moved away. "I'd better go now."

"Hurry home."

Marlee practically skipped back to the workroom, smiling and breathing a sigh of relief as she plopped into a chair beside Tyler.

"All's good with the two of you?" He kept his eyes on the computer screen.

"Yes. She had to hurry into the office, but wanted to let me know Hannah won't be joining our team for now. Thank God."

"I was afraid we were in shit or something." Tyler looked up. "Did she notice us spying on her at the marina yesterday?"

"No." Marlee checked an email that had just come in and gasped. "Fuck. They won't extend my leave from work."

"Oh shit. When do you have to go back?"

"In less than three weeks." She stared at the message, ears ringing from the sudden throbbing in her head. "I can't leave now."

"Then quit and apply for your Australian citizenship," Tyler said. "You could try to get on with the New South Wales Police Force."

"I can't quit my job right now," Marlee said. "That was the deal on my leave. I have to go back for at least three months. What am I going to do?"

"Don't worry about it for now," Tyler said. "Focus on helping Abigail. A lot can happen between now and then. Look at the last few weeks and how much your life has changed since you met her. Live for the moment and whatever's meant to be will be."

"I wish it was that easy," Marlee said. "I just met the love of my life and can't leave our future up to chance."

"Yes you can." Tyler tapped her knee. "Look how fast the two of you supposedly fell in love. In three weeks from now you'll probably be planning a family together and you'll become a stay-at-home wife to a multimillionaire."

"You're forgetting one critical detail," Marlee said. "Abigail and her company are being exploited by criminals trying to engineer bioweapons. In three weeks from now we could all be in jail or, worse yet, dead."

"I doubt it." Tyler shook his head. "We're not breaking any laws, so jail is out of the question, and I don't see someone like Hannah being capable of murder."

"Don't kid yourself about Hannah," Marlee said. "If she's behind this, killing us would be minor compared to the mass murders bioweapons could cause in the hands of terrorists. And if you think you can't be tossed into jail over this, think again. Just being associated with anything related to terrorism can get you thrown in prison these days."

"You're scaring me." Tyler's eyes widened. "What have I got myself into?"

"The chance of a lifetime to use your illegal hacking skills for something good and help save the world."

"You're so dramatic," Tyler said. "Seriously, how dangerous do you think this is?"

"Dangerous enough that we need to be extra vigilant with everything we do." Marlee ran a hand through her hair.

"Do you think our lives are at risk right now?"

"Everybody's lives are always at risk." Marlee met his gaze. "Just crossing the street can put a person at risk. Will somebody try to kill us over this? Maybe."

"Do you have access to a gun?" Tyler paled.

"No." Marlee shook her head. "I don't want to complicate my life any more than it already is by trying to get a gun in a foreign country."

"We're dealing with criminals who probably have guns," Tyler said. "We need to protect ourselves."

"Do you know how to use one?"

"No, but you do. I could help you get one."

"How? Through some illegal Internet connections?" Marlee rolled her eyes.

"No. My ex has one and I still have a key to his place."

"Forget it." Marlee didn't want any part of a stolen firearm.

"Why not? He legally owns it and keeps it hidden in the back of his closet. We could get it while he's at work and he'd never know it was missing."

"I'm not going to steal a gun," Marlee said. "What kind of police officer do you think I am?"

"One who can't protect us," Tyler said as he began to rock back and forth in his chair. "What good is a police officer who doesn't have a gun?"

"I rely on my brain a lot more than my gun when I'm working. My police experience is going to protect us more than any gun would."

"How? By talking a terrorist out of shooting us? I doubt that."

"By calling the police for assistance with guns if it's needed," Marlee said. "The last thing I want is to get arrested in Australia for having a stolen gun."

"At least you wouldn't have to worry about going back to your job in Canada."

"I will not break the law." Marlee stood up and moved to the door. "I'm going for a swim to clear my head and think about our next steps."

"What if I steal the gun?" Tyler asked.

Marlee swung around. "It'd be a dumbass thing to do. You'd be putting your life at risk if you got caught and breaking the law if you didn't. I don't want to hear anything more about it. Is that clear?"

"Yes, Abigail. I mean Marlee." Tyler saluted as she left the room.

CHAPTER TWENTY-SIX

Marlee was in bed when Abigail got home from the office late that evening. It had been a long day for both of them. They clung to each other.

"I hope you don't mind I didn't wait up," Marlee said. "I had a headache and needed to lie down."

Abigail kissed her forehead. "Of course not. Too bad about the headache."

"I think I got too much sun today."

"And here I thought you were cooped up inside, hard at work with Tyler. What did you get up to?"

"I spent the day outside, doing a security check around the house and tidying up the bushes so Hannah can see a difference when she gets back from Canberra."

"Good on you. Thanks. Any headway on your work with Tyler?"

"No." Marlee sighed. "There's not much we can do right now but monitor activity on the network to see if anything unusual pops up."

"Unusual like what?"

"Any kind of a blip, something that looks out of place," Marlee said. "That's what makes it hard. We don't know what we're looking for. Yet. Now tell me about your day. How was it?"

Abigail sighed. "Long, but not long enough. Hannah wanted to cancel her trip to Canberra, but I finally convinced her to stick with her plans. She left this afternoon. She didn't want to leave me alone right now and is so upset I won't tell her what's going on with the two of you staying here."

"I'm glad she's gone." Marlee kissed Abigail's forehead. "I don't want any more knocks on your bedroom door in the middle of the night."

"There shouldn't be any tonight," Abigail said. "How's that headache of yours?"

"It's gone." Marlee rolled on top, ran her fingers through the blond tresses, and began to rub her knee between Abigail's legs. "I'm glad you came to bed prepared."

"Prepared?" Abigail cuddled closer.

"Yes. Naked and wet."

* * *

Instead of a knock on the bedroom door, the ping of a text to Marlee's phone woke her. Abigail was in a deep sleep, their two bodies entwined. Marlee carefully dislodged herself and grabbed her cell. Tyler wanted to know if she was awake and able to come to the den.

She slipped out of bed, pulled on a pair of shorts and a T-shirt then rushed to the room. "What is it?"

"Something strange is going on with the network." Tyler's hair was disheveled. He squinted as he stared at the computer screen. "There's lots of online activity for the middle of the night. It looks like files are being downloaded to an external source."

"Let me see." Marlee leaned over his shoulder to look at the display of filenames flashing across the screen. "I'll get Abigail."

Marlee raced back to their bedroom and nudged Abigail awake. "We need you to see something on the network. It looks like someone is downloading a bunch of company files."

"What files?" Abigail sprang out of bed and threw on a robe.

"I don't know. That's why we want you to have a look."

Tyler stood up when they walked into the den. "Take my seat, Abigail."

Abigail gasped when she saw the screen. "Those are some of our most confidential research files. Can we stop it from completing the download?"

"I can try," Tyler said.

"Then do it." Abigail moved out of the way.

"Where is this being orchestrated from?" Marlee asked.

"It could be anywhere," Tyler said, "but if I had to guess, I'd say somewhere here in Sydney."

"Someone could be doing it from the office?" Abigail asked. "Right now?"

"It's possible." Tyler pounded on the keyboard.

"Alert your building security," Marlee said. "If anyone's there, they should be able to see who badged in and catch them."

"I'll call right now." Abigail hurried from the room.

"Good work." Marlee tapped Tyler's shoulder. "How did you notice? Surely you haven't been up working all this time."

"No. I created an app for my phone that alerts me to any unusual activity on the network, such as the downloading of internal files. Yay." Tyler leaned back. "I crashed the system so the transfer has stopped."

"Perfect. We should wait for Abigail to get back to see what she says before doing anything else."

"Sure thing, boss."

"Okay, thanks." Abigail clutched her phone as she returned to the room. "Security's going to do a complete building check, but no one's badged in right now."

"Someone could have launched the download before leaving today," Tyler said. "I'm beginning to doubt a big file transfer like this could have been initiated from anywhere else except at the main server."

Marlee turned to Abigail. "Ask security to check on who was last to badge out."

"That would have been me," Abigail said. "I turned out the lights when I left."

"Then get them to check to see who else worked late," Marlee said.

"Okay." Abigail typed a message on her phone. "I'm relieved Hannah left for Canberra this afternoon. It couldn't have been her at the office. She was long gone by the time I left for the day."

"Tyler crashed your system and stopped the download," Marlee said.

"Brilliant, Tyler." Abigail patted his shoulder. "You'd think I'd be able to rely on my highly paid IT team to prevent something like this, but for all I know, they could be involved."

"Whoever was doing this will know we aborted the download," Tyler said.

"They'll be desperate to find another way to get the files." Marlee turned to Abigail and took her hands. "You could be at risk and need protection."

"What about Hannah?" Abigail's eyes widened. "She's by herself right now in Canberra and could be in danger."

"I think it's time to involve the police," Marlee said.

"Wait." Abigail tensed as she read a message on her phone.

"What is it?" Marlee tried to see the words.

"I don't believe it." Abigail shook her head. "Hannah was the last one to badge out tonight, an hour after me. She told me she was leaving in the afternoon."

"Caught in the act," Tyler said. "Let's call the police and have her charged."

"We can't do that." Abigail snapped her tongue. "There has to be some other explanation. I won't have her picked up for questioning. I know how humiliating that is."

"I agree," Marlee said. "Let's wait a bit and keep an eye on her to see what else we might find out."

"We can watch her," Abigail said, "but I'm still not convinced Hannah's behind this. I want to talk to her first thing in the morning to see why she was in the office when she should have been in Canberra."

"We might as well go back to bed," Marlee said. "I'll double-check the house's security system then try to get more sleep. There's not much else we can do right now."

When Marlee crawled back into bed, Abigail held on to her. "I can't fathom the thought of Hannah betraying me like this. I've done so much for her over the years and it hurts." Her voice started to shake. "It's so sad to think of being betrayed by a close friend."

"Let's not jump to conclusions." Marlee rubbed Abigail's back. "I'm sure she has a good explanation. Try to get some sleep and you can talk to her in the morning to see if you can sort things out."

"You're right." Abigail wiped a tear and they kissed. "I love you."

"I love you too. Good night."

CHAPTER TWENTY-SEVEN

"Hannah says she lost her company security pass." Abigail lay on her stomach in bed, naked and straddling elbows as she read the message on her phone. It was early morning and they had just woken up. "Someone must have stolen it to use last night."

"Is she in Canberra?" Marlee reclined on her back and tickled her nose with Abigail's flowing hair.

"Yes. She's at her hotel and about to head to the office, but can't find her pass."

"Ask what time she checked into her hotel yesterday."

"Okay." Abigail keyed in the question. "I think she's afraid I'll be upset over her losing the pass, but this is such a relief because it proves it couldn't have been her in the building last night."

"Did she drive or fly?" Marlee asked, her suspicions not so easily dropped.

"She took her car."

"How long would it have taken her to drive to Canberra?"

"Around four hours, maybe less if she didn't stop and traffic was good. Here we go." Abigail read the reply. "Hannah said she checked into the hotel about six yesterday then went out for dinner. It would have been impossible for her to be at the Sydney office last night."

"Sounds like it," Marlee said. "Has she ever lost her company badge before?"

"No." Abigail rolled over and started to get up. "I lost mine once, though. It can happen to anyone."

"Did you ever find it?" Marlee sat up.

"Yes. I found it about two months later when I was reorganizing supplies underneath one of the seats on the boat. It must have slipped off and I never noticed."

"It's good to know it wasn't stolen," Marlee said. "Maybe Hannah's wasn't stolen, either."

"Of course it was stolen." Abigail slipped on her robe. "Who else would have used it to enter the building?"

"You're right." Marlee decided to drop it for now. "Are you having a swim this morning?"

"No, there's no time. I have to get to the office, but go ahead. I'll have my shower now and pop by the pool to say good-bye before I leave."

Marlee put on her one-piece bathing suit and stopped by the den on her way to the pool to find Tyler hunched over his computer.

"Didn't you go back to bed last night?"

"I couldn't sleep after that," Tyler said. "I've been trying to source where the files were going."

"Any luck?"

"Not really." He straightened up and stretched his neck. "All I know is that the destination server is somewhere outside the country, most likely in the Middle East, maybe Russia, but that's all I can decipher."

"Probably some terrorist group," Marlee said. "Thank God you stopped the download."

"This is a lot bigger than Hannah," Tyler said. "We're not equipped to deal with terrorists."

"I know, but hopefully the Australian Police Force is on top of that one."

"Don't count on it," Tyler said. "They didn't even bring in the right suspect from AbTay Biosystems for questioning when they pulled in Abigail instead of Hannah."

"Hannah told Abigail she lost her security badge yesterday," Marlee said. "She apparently checked in to her hotel around six last night then went for dinner. It would have been impossible for her to be in the Sydney office last night."

"Nothing's impossible these days," Tyler said. "It's just a short hop between the two cities and there's a commuter flight almost every hour."

"I was wondering about that." Marlee wrapped her towel around her neck and tugged the ends. "She could have easily driven to Canberra, checked in to her hotel for an alibi, then jumped on a plane back to Sydney for a few hours. There'd be a flight record of course, but even then, she might have used a false name."

"It's so tempting to check out Hannah's banking information," Tyler said. "Do you think we should make one small exception to Abigail's order to stay out of personal accounts?"

"As much as I'd like to, we can't." Marlee sighed. "We gave our word and I won't betray her confidence in us. I'm heading for a swim now. You should get some sleep."

Marlee was looking forward to a good workout in the water. She put her towel on one of the chairs by the pool then performed some stretches. She bent over to touch her toes and held the position for a few seconds when a small piece of paper beside one of the large planters bordering the deck caught the corner of her eye. She reached over and picked it up. The paper had been torn, one little piece of a bigger page, and had a few handwritten numbers that didn't mean anything to her.

"I thought you'd be in the water by now." Abigail approached with car keys dangling. She had on a light blue business suit with a silky yellow blouse and low-heeled pumps.

"You look gorgeous in that skirt." Marlee smiled. "Makes me want to put my hand up it."

"Maybe later."

"Do you know what this is?" Marlee held out the slip of paper. "I found it under one of the planters."

"Let me see." Abigail brushed up against her. "It looks like my security code to override the hidden cameras around the house. I had them tested and reset last month to make sure everything was in order. One of the workers must have written down the password then ripped up the paper."

"Okay, that makes sense. Just thought I'd check. Too bad you can't join me for a swim."

"I know." Abigail hugged Marlee. "It's going to be another long day and I'm so glad I have you here to come home to."

"Life sure has changed a lot in the last few days." Marlee peered into warm blue eyes. "I can't imagine mine without you now. What are we going to do when it's time for me to go back to Canada?"

"Let's not think about that for now." Abigail pecked her on the lips. "I have to go. Try not to get too much sun today. Keep me posted on anything new that might crop up."

"I will." Marlee watched Abigail rush away and wondered what the day would bring.

Tyler was still at his computer when Marlee popped into the den following a rigorous swim and long shower. His head reclined on a hand and he stared at the screen. "Hannah's bank accounts and credit card statements look normal."

"What are you doing in her accounts?" Marlee gasped. "I told you not to do that. Abigail will be furious."

"She doesn't have to know," Tyler said. "We're just looking out for her anyway."

"We're betraying her confidence and I don't like it," Marlee said, feeling like she'd just let Abigail down. "I'm going to have to tell her"

"Should we also tell her that Hannah might go by another name?"

"She does? What is it?"

"Taylor Williams," Tyler said. "Abigail's last name combined with hers to create a new identity."

"Are you sure?" Marlee moved closer. "How did you find it?"

"I said she might use another name." Tyler leaned back and folded his arms. "I didn't say it was for sure. I stumbled on it when I was in her document of usernames and passwords. It was identified as a username, but there was no account or password attached to it."

"It could be anything then," Marlee said. "She has the hots for Abigail, so who knows, maybe it was just wishful doodling on her part."

"On her computer and in an important file like that? I doubt it."

"So then figure it out," Marlee said. "Do what you do and find out for sure."

"I can't. You just told me to stay out of her personal stuff and without more trolling around, we'll never know."

"Argh." Marlee backed away, feeling tortured at the thought of betraying Abigail's trust again. "Okay, see what you can learn and I'll tell Abigail about it tonight."

"Blame it on me because I'm the one who broke the rules first," Tyler said. "You're just telling me to keep breaking them."

"What am I doing?" Marlee grabbed her hair and pulled as she struggled with her guilt. "Abigail trusts me and I shouldn't be letting you do this."

"You're doing everything you can to protect her," Tyler said. "Sometimes you have to break the rules to get ahead."

"It's not about breaking the rules," Marlee said. "It's about breaking her trust and it makes me feel like shit."

"You'd feel worse if Hannah does something to hurt Abigail."

"True." Marlee pulled out the scrap of paper she'd found earlier and handed it to him. "There's one other thing. I found this lodged underneath one of the planters by the pool this morning. I showed it to Abigail and it wasn't hers, but she recognized the numbers as being the access code for her security cameras."

"It is," Tyler said. "The system was one of the first things I checked when we got here. Everything's working." He brought the video images to his screen. External cameras were installed around the perimeter of the building, including the pool area, the garage, and main entrance.

Marlee leaned over his shoulder and studied the images. "Are you sure? Something doesn't seem right. The pool is empty and I'm sure the water polo ball was floating on the surface when I got out just awhile ago."

"Let me have a look." Tyler tapped a few keys and followed the feed from the camera. "It seems to be working. I see the ball now. It's lodged in a corner, up against the tile and bobbing."

"That's funny because it wasn't there a minute ago," Marlee said. "At least I don't think it was.

"Your guilty conscience is getting to you," Tyler said. "I need to get some sleep now. Toodle-oo."

CHAPTER TWENTY-EIGHT

"He did what?" Abigail swung around and glared at Marlee. "I told him not to do that. I won't invade anyone's private life and especially Hannah's."

"I know." Marlee sighed. She stood at the kitchen counter preparing a quinoa and feta salad with roasted tomatoes and squash for a late dinner with Abigail. The recipe was one of her favorites that always made her feel better after a long day. She hoped Abigail would appreciate it. "I'm really sorry, but we couldn't resist digging into her personal affairs after her pass was used to access the building last night."

"We?" Abigail's face and neck reddened. "You were involved too? How could you have done this to me? I trusted you."

Marlee dropped her utensils and rushed to Abigail's side. "I know and I feel so bad, but we couldn't help it."

"You couldn't help yourselves." Abigail pushed away. "I'm disappointed in you Marlee."

Marlee stumbled back as though she'd been slapped. She knew that Abigail was right and felt awful about breaking her trust, even though she had Abigail's best interests at heart. "I'm sorry, Ab, but I'll stop at nothing to protect you."

"You make it sound like I'm some pathetic little creature. Just because I'm not a police officer like you doesn't mean I can't look after myself."

"I know you can." Marlee took Abigail's hands. "You're a strong woman, my hero, and I wouldn't be alive today if it wasn't for you. You're all about protecting others, just like you're protecting Hannah right now, and I love that about you."

"Hannah's my best friend and I won't compromise her right to personal privacy."

"Tyler uncovered a few things about her that I think you should know," Marlee said.

"I don't want to hear about it." Abigail pulled her hands back.

"So you're going to just bury your head in the sand and hope for the best?"

"Is that what I've been doing with you?"

"Of course not," Marlee said. "I expect you looked into my background and gathered whatever information available about me. Like when you interrogated me at the beginning. A smart businesswoman like you wouldn't have just accepted me into your circle without checking up on me."

"I was upfront with you the entire time," Abigail said. "Yes, I did my research, but I didn't hack into your bank accounts to see whether you were a broke, money-hungry predator."

Marlee's eyes watered with disappointment and dejection. "Is that what you think of me? That I'm just after your money?"

"Of course not." Abigail sighed. "It's what Hannah thinks. She's begging me to get away from you."

"Then why aren't you listening to her?" Marlee's voice shook. "I thought she was your best friend."

"She is my best friend, but you're my lover now." Abigail dropped into a chair. "Why does this have to be so complicated?"

"Because your best friend is my main and only suspect right now," Marlee said. "I need to find out if I'm on to something and the only way I know how to do that is to let Tyler go through her personal accounts. Please trust me on this."

"Trust." Abigail scoffed. "I don't know what that word means anymore. Look at me. I'm betraying the confidence of my best friend by letting my lover get away with violating her right to privacy."

"This has nothing to do with betrayal." Marlee put a hand on Abigail's shoulder and squeezed. "It's about finding out if your friend is the one double-crossing you."

"I don't like this." Abigail got up, shaking her head. "I'm hungry and want to eat. Let's have dinner. It'll give me time to think."

"Good idea," Marlee said. "I just need a few minutes to finish the salad."

"Fine. While you're doing that, I'll run up and change out of these work clothes."

"Can we hug and make up first?" Marlee took Abigail into her arms. "I missed you today. I don't want to go to bed mad at each other. Let's never do that, okay?"

"Okay." Abigail relaxed into a kiss.

Tyler walked into the kitchen just as Marlee's hand was reaching up Abigail's skirt. They jumped apart and Abigail headed to the stairs. Marlee felt her cheeks flush.

"Hello, Tyler." Abigail smiled as she passed him. "I'll be right back as soon as I change."

"I'm almost finished making a quinoa salad," Marlee said. "We're just about to eat. Will you join us?"

"Is it safe?" Tyler asked. "I heard the two of you arguing with my name thrown into the mix and next thing I know you have your hand up her skirt. What's going on?"

"Obviously she's upset with us." Marlee's hands went to her hips. "I don't blame her. From now on, we have to make sure she knows about everything we're doing."

"Did you tell her Hannah might be going by another name?"

"No, not yet." Marlee turned back to her salad. "Let's eat by the pool since it's so nice outside. Grab a few plates and I'll bring out the rest."

Marlee and Tyler were seated at the patio table when Abigail came back down, dressed in khaki poplin shorts and a white fitted T-shirt.

"I'm famished," Abigail said, taking a seat next to Marlee. "I didn't have time for lunch today."

"Oh, Ab, you have to eat and keep yourself healthy."

"I know, but things are so busy this week with Hannah in Canberra."

"Here, dig in." Marlee struggled to keep her eyes off that beckoning bosom as she pushed the salad toward Abigail.

"This looks delicious." Abigail smiled as she dished up her plate. "I'm being spoiled coming home to a healthy dinner like this."

"I'm feeling pampered too," Tyler said. "I could get used to a life like this."

"I really appreciate the work both of you are doing for me," Abigail said. "Hannah is also a big help right now. I felt lost without her at the office today. I don't know what I'd do without her."

Marlee's knife clanged against her plate in frustration. How could Abigail be *praising* Hannah? "Have you ever heard of a Taylor Williams?"

"No." Abigail's full fork stopped midway to her mouth. "Who is she?"

"Nobody really," Marlee said. "We stumbled across the name today. Just thought I'd ask in case it sounds familiar."

"Of course it's familiar." Abigail eased her fork back to her plate. "It's my last name with Hannah's. Where did you see it?"

"It was referenced in one of Hannah's documents." Marlee sipped her water.

"I see." Abigail picked up her fork. "Your salad is delicious."

They finished their meal while watching a few squawking cockatoos fly amongst the trees and land on the fence. Conversation was light, concentrating on mundane things like the weather and grocery items needed for the next week.

"I want to check the video feed on the camera by the pool." Tyler had gotten his laptop when he helped clear the table. They were having a light dessert of vanilla ice cream topped with fresh strawberries.

"Is there something wrong with it?" Abigail asked.

"I don't know," Tyler said. "I've been tracking it all day and things seem to be okay, but thought I'd verify the feeds while we're by the pool."

"We've been monitoring the video cameras all day," Marlee said. "I know you said they were checked and reset last month, but I wanted to double-check after finding the slip of paper with the code on it this morning."

"Okay," Abigail said. "What do you mean by verifying the feeds while we're here?"

"The pool camera acted a bit strange this morning," Tyler said. "Marlee thought there was a ball in the water, then there wasn't and all of a sudden it appeared. It must have been the wind, but I just want to have a look while we're sitting here. Marlee, can you walk toward the steps at the pool and stand still for a minute?"

"Sure." Marlee sauntered over and put her hand on the rail. "How's this?"

"It looks fine," Tyler said. "Now jump up and down."

"Are you trying to get me to fall in?" Marlee bounced a few times.

"There," Tyler said. "Did you see it?"

"See what?" Abigail leaned toward the screen for a better look.

"Jump again," Tyler said.

"What is it?" Marlee hopped up and down, anxious to know what was happening.

"There," Tyler said. "Marlee's not jumping on the video, but look at her jumping by the pool. There's a delay in the camera."

Marlee rushed to the screen just in time to see herself in the video for another second. "We need to get your security company back here as soon as possible to make sure the surveillance cameras are working properly."

"I'll contact them right now." Abigail stood up. "They'll have to come tonight and fix it right away. This is unacceptable to be paying for the best in video surveillance only to find out it's not working properly." She stormed inside.

"I don't like this," Marlee said. "Do you think someone's tampered with the system?"

"Hard to say," Tyler said, "but we'll know more when the technician comes."

The service agent arrived within the hour and Abigail led him out to the pool, where Marlee and Tyler were waiting.

"We noticed a slight delay in the camera by the pool," Abigail said. "I want it fixed. Marlee and Tyler can show you. "

"Hi." Marlee shook his hand, noticing *Bob* on his company nametag. "We can start with this camera, but I'd like all of them checked. Okay, Bob?"

"Sure, no problem," he said. "Let's have a look."

"I have some work to do tonight," Abigail said, "so I'll leave you to it." She went into the house.

Tyler and Marlee demonstrated the time delay, but when Bob used his own computer to monitor the system, everything was functioning in real time.

"Seems to be working fine," Bob said.

"It wasn't fine about an hour ago," Marlee said. "Something's not functioning properly and we need to fix it. Any suggestions?"

"I can try one more thing." Bob connected some wires to the camera and read the output on a handheld device. "Hmmm. The readings are a bit off. Must be something wrong with the camera. I'll replace it and see if that helps."

It took him fifteen minutes to install a new camera and recalibrate the system. When they tried it, the camera seemed to be working okay, but the readings on his device were still off.

"I don't understand it," he said. "It's a brand-new camera so the readings should be precise. Can one of you go in front of the pool and move around?"

Marlee went over and began to bounce. "I feel like a kangaroo."

"There it is," Tyler said. "See?"

Bob shook his head. "You're right, there is a delay. This shouldn't be happening." He rubbed his chin. "I don't know what to suggest other than having someone come back tomorrow to check all the wiring."

"Could someone have tampered with the system?" Marlee asked. "As in being able to control it from somewhere else?"

"Nope," Bob said. "You can't do it with our system. It's very secure. It'll be a loose wire somewhere. We'll get it fixed tomorrow."

"I'll let Abigail know," Marlee said.

"I'm right here." Abigail stepped outside and approached. "What's the status?"

"It looks like there's a loose wire somewhere in the system," Marlee said.

"We'll get it fixed for you," Bob said.

"I want the entire system replaced tomorrow." Abigail spoke with authority. "Please ensure someone is here first thing in the morning to do the work."

"That won't be necessary." Bob shook his head. "We'll fix the wire and you'll be good as new."

"It will be new." Abigail emphasized each word as she glared at Bob. "The entire system must be ripped out and replaced tomorrow."

Bob grabbed his ball cap by the peak and used the back of his fist to wipe his sweating forehead. "I'll see what I can do."

"It's to be done tomorrow," Abigail said. "If you can't do it, I'll get another company."

"I'll have a crew here by eight o'clock in the morning." He put his cap back on. "How's that?"

"That will be fine," Abigail said. "Until then, I want my system closely monitored tonight and to be notified immediately if the least little thing doesn't seem right. Am I clear?"

"Yes," Bob said. "I'm on it."

"Good." Abigail started to head back inside. "I'll see you in the morning."

Tyler and Marlee escorted Bob to his vehicle, watched him leave, and then went inside for the night. Marlee was impressed with the way Abigail stood up to Bob and demanded that the security system be replaced in the morning. She also kept thinking about Abigail's reaction to the name of Taylor Williams when mentioned over dinner. Marlee hoped Abigail was finally starting to suspect Hannah too.

CHAPTER TWENTY-NINE

Marlee and Tyler oversaw the installation of a new security system over the next few days, ensuring the existing setup was completely removed and the new cameras worked seamlessly. Marlee worried that they'd been spied on and was convinced of Hannah's involvement with the malfunctioning security camera.

She examined the torn scrap of paper over and over again, studying the handwritten security code for any identifying characteristics. The ink was purple, the writing cramped, and the numbers jotted in an uneven line. As far as Marlee could tell, Hannah tended to use red ink when commenting on documents, while Abigail's notes were primarily purple or blue.

Marlee liked that Abigail avoided red ink with its harsh implications of error. Abigail's comments focused on praise, questions, or suggestive feedback, whereas Hannah's were blunt and often involved deleting entire sections in the documents Marlee had flipped through.

It was in the characteristics of the writing, however, that Marlee concentrated. Abigail's handwriting consisted of well-formed letters that were easy to understand whereas Hannah's notes were scribbled and hard to follow. It was a small clue, especially since she was comparing numbers to text, but enough to keep Marlee centered on Hannah and anxious about Abigail's safety.

While the new security system was being installed, Abigail spent long days at the office. She came home just in time to crawl into bed and sleep snuggled up with Marlee, too tired for anything else. It was eleven o'clock on the evening that the installation of the new system was complete, and the two were cuddled in bed. Abigail fought to stay awake while Marlee luxuriated in their entwined naked bodies.

"Thank God Hannah will be back tomorrow." Abigail stifled a yawn.

Marlee stiffened. "I've really missed you over the last few days. I worry when you come home so late."

"I've missed you too." Abigail clung to Marlee and spoke with her eyes closed. "One of the nicest things about coming home in the dark is crawling right into bed with you and falling asleep in your arms."

"Starting tomorrow," Marlee said, "I want to drive you back and forth to the office. I don't like you coming home alone in the dark. I can be your personal bodyguard."

Abigail opened her eyes. "Won't that be a conflict because you're also my lover?"

Marlee smiled. "No wonder you're such a good businesswoman. Always thinking about best practices. I'm not on your payroll, so of course there's no conflict."

"Okay, you can be my chauffeur." Abigail kissed Marlee then took a deep breath, closing her eyes again as she exhaled. "Love you. Have a good sleep."

"Love you too." Marlee buried her nose in Abigail's hair as she lay awake in the dark and began to plan her approach to narrowing in on Hannah.

* * *

Marlee manoeuvred Abigail's dark Prado to badge open the underground parking security gate then drive into the bowels of AbTay Biosystems headquarters. The large SUV with its black-tinted windows felt appropriate for a chauffeur-driven vehicle, especially since it was an automatic and Marlee wasn't ready to tackle the manual transmission on Abigail's car. She stopped in Abigail's reserved parking spot near the elevator and turned off the engine. It was six thirty and her vehicle was the first of the morning.

"I hope I get to see your office someday," Marlee said.

"Me too." Abigail gathered her purse and computer bag.

"I imagine you have a beautiful view of the harbor. You must be so proud of what you've accomplished."

"I'm not feeling very proud at the moment." Abigail sighed. "I'd love to take you up there right now and show you around, but…" Tears began to flow down her cheeks as she reached for a tissue. "I'm sorry. This is not like me to cry and I hate it."

"Oh Ab, you don't ever need to apologize to me for crying." Marlee leaned over and hugged her. "I'm so proud to be with you. I'd love to waltz in there right now and go up to your penthouse office, where I'd spend the day watching you work. I read some of your comments to staff and you're so good at what you do. Your words of encouragement on those documents, like telling people they're on the right track and repeatedly thanking them, should make you feel proud."

"My lover, confidante, chauffeur, and now therapist." Abigail wiped her tears and smiled. "I don't know what I'd have done if I hadn't met you." She balled up her tissue.

"You should go up to your office before everyone else starts coming in," Marlee straightened up, humbled by Abigail's words and wanting to jump her right there in the parking lot. She couldn't let that happen.

"I noticed you've been calling me Ab." Abigail's hand was on the door. "What's that all about?"

"You being special," Marlee said. "I know you don't like Abby and I just can't bring myself to call you Tay anymore.

Abigail's far too formal for how I feel about you. I've never taken to names like 'honey' or 'sweetie' for lovers."

"What's wrong with Tay?"

"That's Hannah's name for you. It doesn't work for me. Besides, Ab comes first in your company name, and I want to be number one." Marlee smiled.

Abigail grinned back. "In my mind, there's no competition between Hannah and you. Your roles in my life are entirely different. Hannah is a close friend and colleague; you're my lover." Abigail leaned over for a peck on the lips then opened the door. "I've got to go. I'll call you later."

"Take care of yourself and have a good day." Marlee lowered the window and blew a kiss as the elevator doors closed.

When Marlee got back to Abigail's, Tyler's car was gone. He hadn't said anything about going out so she checked to see if he'd left a note by his computer. There was none so she decided to do some laps in the pool while contemplating her next steps with Hannah.

Marlee knew there was competition with Hannah for Abigail's trust, and she needed to win that battle. Hannah would be back at the office, trying to convince Abigail to dump her. It made Marlee swim harder.

By the time she'd finished her laps and showered, Tyler was waiting for her in the workroom and anxious to talk.

"I have something for you." He held out a plastic bag, his hands trembling as she reached for it.

"What's this?" She was afraid to look at the heavy object inside.

"Something you need."

Marlee saw a brown fabric gun case and gasped. "Tyler, where did you get this?"

"It doesn't matter. Take it out and see what you think."

"I told you I don't want a gun." She shoved the bag back at him.

"Aren't you at least going to look at it?" He folded his arms.

"You stole this from your ex, didn't you?"

"I borrowed it. He won't even know it's gone, and I'll return it as soon as we're done with it."

"I don't like this." She sat with the plastic bag on her knees until finally reaching in to open up the zippered pouch and have a peek. "A nine millimeter Smith and Wesson. How nice. There's even a box of bullets." Marlee didn't want to touch the weapon. She closed the case. "You need to return it."

"I told you I would. Aren't you going to have a closer look?"

"I don't want my fingerprints all over it," Marlee said. "If anything were to happen with this, I could be deported and not allowed back into the country."

"Here, take these." Tyler pulled a pair of latex gloves from his pocket. "It's not like you're going to use it for anything criminal and Abigail's life could depend on you having it."

Marlee accepted the gloves and fondled the bag. "I don't know. It's stealing."

"It's about safeguarding," Tyler said. "Defending Abigail and protecting the next poor sucker to get hooked up with my ex. The fucker held it to my head once and pulled the trigger. He'd left one bullet in the cartridge. I thought I was going to die."

"Oh Tyler, poor you." Marlee put a hand on his shoulder.

"I'm glad I took the gun. He doesn't deserve to get it back. If you don't want it, I'll keep the thing under my mattress for now."

"We should at least check to make sure it's not loaded."

"Good idea," Tyler said. "I wouldn't want it going off while I'm sleeping."

Marlee slid the gloves on then carefully took the weapon out of its case. She removed the cartridge, verified that it was empty, and put it back in. She held the pistol, feeling its weight and familiar form, and studied its black stainless steel barrel before putting it near her nose for a faint oily metallic whiff. She'd never report for duty as a police officer without her gun, but this wasn't legal and she couldn't bring herself to keep the weapon.

"Have you ever shot anyone?" Tyler asked.

"No." She put the gun back in its case and handed it to Tyler. "Lock this up somewhere for now until we figure out what to do with it."

CHAPTER THIRTY

Abigail called Marlee to pick her up from work just after lunch, exhaustion and agitation in her voice. Marlee met her at the front entrance to the AbTay Biosystems office tower.

"Let's head to the boat." Abigail got into the SUV and fastened her seat belt. "It's a beautiful afternoon and I need to think."

"Sure," Marlee said. "I'll stop at a store to get something for a salad so we can have supper on the water. I'll even grab a few things for breakfast in case you want to spend the night."

"That would be nice." Abigail leaned back against the headrest as Marlee drove.

"Are you okay? You look a bit frazzled."

"Hannah asked me to go to Canberra with her over the weekend. She wants us to search the office while everyone's away to verify employee behaviors."

"How are you supposed to do that?" Marlee couldn't believe the nerve of the woman.

"She suggested we sit at each desk to see if there's anything unusual like a disturbing photo, joke, saying, or something written in Arabic."

"And then what?" Marlee didn't expect anyone would leave incriminating evidence out in the open. Besides, the police would have been on the lookout for things like that.

"I don't know. She expects us to leave Saturday morning and doesn't want you or Tyler coming along."

"Well, that's not happening," Marlee said. "She's trying to get you away from us. I'm starting to get concerned for your safety around her."

"She said the same thing about you." Abigail sighed. "I need some time on the water to clear my head."

"Does she know you're heading to the boat?"

"No. I told her I wasn't feeling well and was going home. I left her in charge so she'll be too busy to think about anything else."

"Why search the Canberra office?" Marlee asked. "Did she discover something while she was there?"

"No. She said it was just a hunch and an opportunity for the two of us to spend time together."

"What's that supposed to mean? She's with you all day at work." Marlee jerked the vehicle to a stop in a grocery car park.

"It's not the same." Abigail closed her eyes. "She wants to spend some one-on-one time with me.

"How do you feel about that?" Marlee tried to control her breathing as she lowered the windows then shut the engine.

"I don't know." Abigail shook her head. "I'll wait here for you."

"I won't be long. Is there anything special you'd like?"

"Yes, a bottle of red merlot, please. I think there's one on the boat, but I want to be sure we have some."

Marlee hurried into the store, pondering what had happened at the office to make Abigail want to leave early and head to the boat. Not that she minded spending time with the woman of her dreams on the boat.

She wondered what Abigail was thinking about Hannah. Had the woman been pressuring Abigail to get rid of her and

Tyler? Marlee imagined Hannah breaking down in fake tears trying to convince Abigail to get them out of her house.

When Marlee got back to the vehicle, she'd decided that afternoon sex on the boat would be good for Abigail. Marlee watched as Abigail fidgeted with her seat belt, her legs jumping. Sex would help to relax her. And hopefully keep Abigail's mind off Hannah. Something didn't seem right with the proposed surveillance trip to Canberra and Marlee hoped Abigail would refuse to go.

By the time they were out on the water, Marlee sensed that Abigail wanted to make love with her too. The way she gave lingering touches, brushed up against Marlee at every opportunity, and kept locking eyes was a clear sign. Marlee had almost forgotten about Hannah.

"I've decided to go to Canberra with Hannah this weekend," Abigail said. They had put some cushions on the front deck of the boat and were seating themselves for a bit of fresh air.

"Okay." Marlee sprawled out beside Abigail, taking time to choose her next words. "I haven't been to Canberra yet. I'll tag along."

"I thought you'd insist, considering you're my bodyguard." Abigail grinned as she sipped her wine.

"So I've been promoted from chauffeur to bodyguard?" Marlee ran a hand up Abigail's leg until her fingers brushed the damp crotch of tight bikini bottoms.

"Yes." Abigail's breath caught. "But right now I want you to be my lover."

"Did you bring me out here to seduce me?" Marlee tapped her fingers against the firm fabric, increasing the pressure and motion with each touch.

"No." Abigail panted, her hips swaying. "I brought you out here so you'd seduce me. Oh, that feels so good."

"I think you should put your wine down before you spill it," Marlee said. "And then I want you to relax while my fingers do the rest."

"You're going to give me an orgasm right here on the deck of the boat? Someone will see." She put her glass down and braced.

"No they won't because we're just going to keep sitting here as if we're having a conversation." Marlee slipped her fingers under the suit and began to massage the silky wet folds. "Once I get you off, we're heading to that nice big bed of yours where I'm going to devour you."

Abigail flung her head back and moaned out her release.

* * *

"I'd like to take you to Merimbula," Abigail said. They were in bed on the boat, caressing each other in the afterglow of fulfilling sex.

"What and where is Merimbula?"

"It's a quiet, touristy town with a beautiful beach on the Sapphire Coast of New South Wales. Hannah suggested I spend a few days there next week to reenergize before coming back from Canberra."

"Is she going too?" Marlee stiffened.

"No. She'll fly back to Sydney and I'll drive down to the coast. Of course she didn't mean for me to bring you, but if I'm going to reenergize I need you to help."

"I'm so happy you think that about me." Marlee snuggled into Abigail's shoulder. "It's as if we've known each other forever."

"You're a very special woman," Abigail said. "One who's smart, caring, considerate, easy-going, sexy, and a fabulous lover. I can't fathom life without you now, but we live on two different continents. World's apart."

Marlee's throat tightened. "You could always move to Canada with me."

"And do what? My life is here. I could never leave Josh."

"You're right." Marlee sighed. "I didn't know how to tell you, but I've been denied an extension to my leave of absence from my job. I have to report back to work in two weeks."

"I see," Abigail said. "And if you don't?"

"I could lose my job."

"We can't have that." Abigail stared at the ceiling and put an arm on her forehead.

"Why not?" Marlee sniffed.

"You'd give up your job for me?" Abigail turned to her.

"Oh Ab, of course I would." Marlee rolled into her and squeezed, burying her face in Abigail's hair. "I love you. I'd do anything for you."

"What about your family and friends? We're so far away. You'd be giving them up too."

"No, I wouldn't. I'd visit and bring you with me. They'd come here too. I'm sure of it. I wouldn't be giving them up at all, but going back to Canada would mean giving you up. I need to hold you and make love with you and see you every day. You're part of me now."

"What if I go to jail? Or lose my business?"

"That's not going to happen, but if anything like that ever did we'd figure it out together. I don't want to leave you."

Abigail gave her a lingering kiss. "I love having you here. Maybe you could get on with the New South Wales Police Force."

"Perhaps," Marlee said, "but things have happened so fast I haven't had time to think about it. All I've been able to think about is you and now that I've managed to get into your bed, I'm sure we can sort out the rest."

CHAPTER THIRTY-ONE

"A night on the boat was such a good idea." Abigail beamed as they sat parked at her office tower in the early hours of the next morning. "I can hardly wait until our little holiday on the coast after this weekend."

"What are you going to say if anyone asks about your wobbly legs this morning?" Marlee smirked.

"I'll tell them they're sea legs after spending a night on the boat." Abigail tapped Marlee's arm. "Only I'll know they're oversexed legs from multiple orgasms at sea."

"You're glowing." Marlee giggled as she rubbed Abigail's arm. "We better talk business or something to prepare you for the office."

"I love the fact that we had a night off from talking about any strategic thinking or planning, but managed to make one crucial decision about you staying in Australia. How are you feeling about it this morning?"

"I'm so happy." Marlee leaned over and kissed Abigail. "I know it hasn't been that long, but now I can't imagine a life without you in it. What about you? Any second thoughts?"

"No way." Abigail's lips met Marlee's. "I'd better get to work before we get carried away."

* * *

Tyler was eating breakfast by the pool when Marlee got home. He bit into a slice of toast slathered in Vegemite and her stomach retracted at the thought of eating the foul-smelling spread.

"I didn't expect to see you up so early." She sat down and grinned at him.

"Please," Tyler said. "Do you have to be so obvious about your night of hot sex?"

"You know I don't kiss and tell. I'm feeling refreshed from that nice sea air after a good rest on the boat. I hope you had a relaxing night too."

"Hardly." Tyler took another bite of toast. "Hannah came looking for Abigail last night. And she wanted to know where you were too."

Marlee's grin turned into a scowl at the thought of that woman stalking them. "I hope you didn't say anything to the bitch. It's none of her business where I am and she needs to leave Abigail alone. What did you tell her?"

"That you were out with a friend. She wanted to know who and where, but I said I didn't know because it was none of my business."

"Good answer. What did you say about Abigail?"

"I said I didn't know where she was either. That really pissed her off. Especially when I told her that Abigail's whereabouts was also none of my business."

"I'm sure she loved that." Marlee chuckled.

"She accused me of lying then stomped away." Tyler brushed crumbs from the tabletop. "I'm glad Abigail insisted on replacing the security system. I hardly slept at all because Hannah makes me nervous."

"She's really starting to get on my nerves." Marlee rubbed a stress spot on her neck. "I wish I could talk to someone who works for her."

"Why don't you get Abigail to give you a job at her company? That's the only way you'll find out what employees really think about Hannah."

Marlee was losing patience with the whole Hannah situation. "She doesn't want me working there. Maybe I can figure out a way to question staff at the Canberra office. We're going there this weekend."

"Who? You and Abigail?"

"And Hannah." Marlee wanted to gag.

"That sounds like fun." Tyler snickered.

"Don't laugh—you're expected to tag along." Marlee gave a big-toothed grin.

"What are we supposed to do there?"

"You're going to keep me company while Abigail's busy with Hannah." Marlee was relieved to have Tyler along as a distraction during the day. "The bitch doesn't know I'm coming. Abigail wants us to drive down on our own while she and Hannah travel together."

"I see." Tyler nodded his head. "Abigail wants to bring her sex toy, but doesn't want Hannah to know."

Marlee resented Tyler trivializing their relationship. "I'm not her sex toy. I'm her lover, and partner. She's asked me to stay in Australia with her. I won't be going back to my job in Ottawa."

"Good on you." Tyler smiled and patted her arm.

"Thanks." She frowned, feeling slightly patronized by his reaction.

Tyler seemed to sense her annoyance and leaned over to squeeze her shoulder. "I'm really happy for you, Marlee. That's a big deal, but I thought you had to go back to your job for at least three months."

"I'm supposed to, but it's not going to happen." Marlee knew her life was here now. "My boss isn't happy with me. I sent an email this morning saying I wasn't ready to come back and he responded immediately asking if I was planning to resign. So I did. It feels strange to be quitting after fifteen years with the force."

"Wow, that's a big deal." Tyler piled his breakfast dishes. "Good thing you won't need to work anymore now that you're with Abigail. You're lucky to retire at your age."

"I'm not retiring." Marlee swatted his arm, irked by the tease. "I have a job to do right now and I'll figure things out after that. What about you? When are you supposed to go back to your job? Those ribs of yours seem much better."

"My doctor's slip gives me another seven days off then I'll be reassessed to see if I'm ready to go back." Tyler fondled the front of his shirt. "They do still hurt sometimes, especially when I try to sleep. Why do you think I've been up working late so often?"

"I thought it was because you wanted to help Abigail." Marlee raised her eyebrows.

"Of course I do, but sore ribs are also keeping me up. You, on the other hand, aren't getting much sleep either, but if anything's sore on you, it certainly wouldn't be your ribs."

"Are you ribbing me?" Marlee chuckled then turned serious. "Did you come across anything on the system last night?"

"Nothing. I'm sure they've figured out we have a tracker on the network so I don't expect much will be happening from now on." Tyler stood up and grabbed his dishes. "I'm going to head in for a little nap. You could probably use one too."

"If my Ab can be working hard at the office, I won't let myself sleep on the job."

"Your Ab. How nice. Dare you to call her that in front of Hannah. And by the way, when are we leaving for Canberra?"

"Tomorrow." Marlee led the way back into the house. "We'll leave in the morning and I hope you don't mind taking your car. I'll pay for your gas, of course."

"You mean Abigail will pay now that you've relegated yourself to becoming a kept woman."

"Go have your nap and we'll finalize plans later." Marlee continued up the stairs to the bedroom where she'd left her laptop. She saw Kerry was trying to contact her so prepared for a video chat with her best friend back in Ottawa.

"What's going on?" Kerry glared into the screen, furrows in her forehead. "We heard you're not coming back."

"News sure travels fast." Marlee braced herself. "What did Diane hear?" Kerry's partner, Diane, was a First Class Constable with the Ottawa Police.

"How could you quit your job with over fifteen years of pensionable service?"

Marlee smiled as she thought of Abigail kissing her earlier this morning. "I've fallen in love with someone here and I won't leave her."

"You can't be giving up your career for some woman you hardly know?" Kerry's voice was strained. "You haven't been there long enough for that and please tell me it's not that Abby person you were sleeping with."

Marlee ran a hand through her hair, wishing she could say more. "She's not who you think she is. I know it sounds crazy, but I've met the most beautiful woman. She's amazing, my other half, and I can't leave her."

"Look at me." Kerry leaned into the screen, eyes wide and focused on Marlee. "This is not you. Who is this dyke and what has she done to you?"

"She saved my life." Marlee shuddered at the thought of how close she came to dying out on the water.

"She saved your life? How?" Kerry raised a corner of her mouth as though in disbelief.

"I got stupid with my surfboard and Ab came to my rescue."

Kerry flung back in her chair and crossed her arms. "So it is that Abby woman. I figured she was a surf bum the way she flaunted about being naked with you."

Marlee resented her friend's characterization of Abigail. "She didn't flaunt and she's not a surf bum. She's a wonderful woman and wants me as much as I want her. I've never met anyone like her before, Kerry." Marlee began to tear up. "Look at me. When have you ever seen me cry like this over a woman?"

"So tell me about Abby, then." Kerry rested her elbows on the table and put her head into her hands. "Why doesn't she move to Ottawa with you? Why do you have to be the one to give up your career?"

"It's complicated. I'd like to say more, but I can't right now." She wiped her tears.

"I thought I was your best friend. We tell each other everything."

"I'm sorry." Marlee looked down, realizing her conversation with Kerry was probably not much different than Abigail's with Hannah. Her eyes went back to the screen. "Can you just trust me for a bit on this? I'll tell you everything as soon as I can. When you hear the story of events, you're going to understand. My life has taken this amazing twist that's hard to imagine."

"Does Gabe know you're quitting your job and not coming back to Ottawa?"

"No. I haven't figured out what I'm going to say. This is all so new."

"He's going to be so disappointed." Kerry shook her head. "I ran into him last week and all he talked about was how anxious he was to see you."

"I feel bad enough as it is, do you have to make it worse by laying on guilt?"

"If you're that miserable, you'd be getting your butt back to your friends, family, and job. Our hockey team's just not the same without you on it. I thought we'd at least make it up with a few more golf games next summer. Now that's never going to happen."

"I'll visit and hope you will too. Australia's a beautiful country—you'll love it." Marlee wanted to reach out and hug her friend. "Once things get sorted out, I'll fill you in and you'll be so excited for me."

"Oh Marlee." Kerry started to cry. "Please think about this long and hard before you do something drastic. I have to go now and cry myself to sleep."

"You can do it in Diane's arms, like you have for the past twenty years. No wonder I never settled into a stable relationship. My other half's been here all along and I'm so excited for you to meet her one day soon. Love you." Marlee ended the call with mixed feelings. While she felt guilty about not saying more to her best friend, Marlee was so excited for the day Kerry could meet Abigail. She knew they'd love each other.

CHAPTER THIRTY-TWO

"I think I understand Hannah a bit more." Marlee clung to Abigail's inviting body while they lay naked in bed after a long day apart.

"She's getting on my nerves," Abigail said. "I feel like I can't breathe when she won't let up on you."

"I had a video chat this morning with my best friend Kerry. She was upset with me for staying here and I felt scolded. She thinks I've lost my senses over some woman. I'm sure Hannah feels the same about you."

"Hannah doesn't know we're lovers," Abigail said. "I don't like being treated as if I'm an idiot who can't make decisions on my own. The more I think about her getting into my email and reversing my decisions, the madder it's making me."

Marlee massaged stress lumps between Abigail's shoulder blades. "Kerry says she misses me and wants me back in Ottawa. I miss her too, but I'd long for you way more if I left."

"I need you in my life and Hannah has to get over it." Abigail's breathing was uneven as Marlee worked the knots. "It's time I let her know how much you mean to me."

"I think it is too." Marlee ended her massage with a kiss to Abigail's neck. "Do you still trust her?"

"I don't know." Abigail rolled over and smiled. "Thank you for the massage."

"My pleasure."

Abigail sighed. "She's been my best friend for years. I should confide in her. My priorities have changed and lately it feels like she's getting in the way. I'm thinking of telling her about us tomorrow."

"Can you wait until next week, after our little holiday? I don't want her picturing us together in Merimbula. It's our special time and I'd like to take our lovemaking to the next level."

"Ooh, sounds exciting." Abigail nudged her nose against Marlee's cheek. "Of course I can postpone it. What do you have in mind for us?"

"Dirty stuff." Marlee chuckled. "You'll see. Now we'd better get some rest."

* * *

After a hurried breakfast of fresh fruit and yogurt, Abigail left home to meet Hannah for a quiet Saturday morning at the office. They planned to clear up a few things before their drive to Canberra later in the day. Following their stint in the Canberra office on Sunday, Hannah was to fly back to Sydney in the evening and Abigail would continue on to Merimbula Monday morning. It was the perfect plan.

Marlee had a lot to do to get ready for the weekend in Canberra then tryst in Merimbula, but her first priority was to tell Gabe about her decision to stay in Australia before he heard it from someone else.

"Hey, what a nice surprise." Her brother smiled into the screen from the desk in his study. "I'll let Stephanie and the girls know you're online. They'd love to chat too."

"No, wait." Marlee was nervous and took a moment to clear her throat. "I need to talk to you first."

"About what?" His smile faded.

Marlee took a deep breath. "There's no easy way to say this so I'm just going to blurt it out. I'm staying in Australia and won't be coming home."

"Oh Marlee. Don't tell me." He sighed. "I was afraid of this when you mentioned someone the last time we spoke. Who is she?"

"Her name is Abigail." Marlee's eyes watered, her emotions taking over. "This is it, Gabe. She's the one."

"Then bring her back to Canada." He rubbed his forehead as though trying to relieve a stress headache. "You have a good job and can help her get established here."

"I'll bring her to meet everyone soon, but I can't right now." Marlee couldn't wait for the day when she could take Abigail to Ottawa. "You'll love her, Gabe. She's amazing and makes me so happy."

He leaned back and folded his arms as though a figure of authority. "What about your work? How are you going to manage that?"

"I quit my job." Marlee held her breath.

"You can't do that."

She wasn't going to let him dictate to her. "I already have."

"Why do you have to be so drastic?" His voice escalated. "Can't you just come home and think about things first?"

"I won't leave her now." Marlee glared into the screen, her breathing heavy with anger.

"There has to be another way other than just quitting your job." Gabe looked away, as though searching for solutions.

"They wouldn't give me an extension on my leave. I had no choice but to quit."

"Christ, Marlee, you shouldn't have to quit. Why didn't you talk to your union rep first?"

"It doesn't matter. I'm not moving back to Ottawa."

"This isn't you, Marlee. What's going on?" His voice shook. "You always wanted to be a cop so why can't she move here?"

"Because she can't." Marlee stared into his bloodshot eyes and felt awful for hurting him. "I know it sounds strange, but there's stuff going on and I can't explain it to you right now."

"That's not acceptable." His voice became harsher. "Am I going to have to come over there to find out for myself?"

"Please don't." Marlee sighed. "I know you're concerned and I love you for that, but I know what I'm doing. Please trust me on this, Gabe."

"You're not making any sense. Does Kerry know?"

"Yes, but only because Diane heard I quit the force."

"I want to talk to Abigail. Put her on now." He was almost yelling as he jabbed a finger at his screen.

"You can't." Marlee knew that bullying was out of character for Gabe and she felt sick at bringing out the bad behavior. "She's at the office then heading to Canberra for the weekend."

"Where does she work and what's her last name? I have a right to know."

"I'll tell you everything soon." Marlee sniffed, knowing that Gabe had every right to be upset. "I have lots to do and should let you get on with your evening."

"For fuck's sake, Marlee. I'm your brother. I care about you. Tell me what's going on."

"I will, but not today. Just trust me on this."

Marlee felt like throwing up when she ended the call. Her best friend and then her brother were being left out of her life. She'd never excluded them like this before and the hurt in their eyes was excruciating to see. The tissue was still crumpled in her hand as she approached Tyler in the workroom while he packed up his laptop.

"I know you'd rather be driving to Canberra with Abigail this afternoon," he said, "but can't you at least fake a smile about being stuck with me?"

Marlee flopped into a chair. "That's not it. I hate keeping things from people who care about me. I just finished a call with my brother." She sighed. "I've always confided in him, but not this time."

"I reckon he wasn't happy."

"No kidding. He threatened to come over and find out for himself what's going on."

"You're lucky to have a brother who cares about you." Tyler dropped into the chair at his desk and folded his arms. "I haven't spoken to mine in years."

"I didn't know you have a brother. How many siblings do you have?"

"Only the one brother, but he disowned me and we've lost touch."

"That's too bad. What happened?"

"I was born gay into a homophobic family." He waved a hand through the air, as though swatting a fly. "I left home when I was eighteen and haven't looked back since."

"What about your parents? Don't you ever see them?"

"Nope. My brother was always the favorite and my folks told me to move out shortly after I came out. My being gay apparently made them sick." Tyler's knee banged the corner of the desk as he got up. "As far as I'm concerned, I don't have a family."

"You've got me. I'll be your sister."

"Sweet." Tyler smiled. "Maybe you could get Abigail to adopt me too."

"You're on your own for that." Marlee stood up and gave him an awkward hug. "I'm here if you ever want to talk more about this."

"Thanks. You're a good friend."

"So are you." Marlee moved toward the door. "I'm just lucky my straighter than straight brother isn't the least bit homophobic."

"It sounds like he really cares about you."

"He does." Marlee sighed. "I hope you'll get to meet him one day."

"I'd like to. Shall we head out?"

CHAPTER THIRTY-THREE

Heavy traffic snarled vehicles as Tyler drove across the Sydney Harbor Bridge on their way to Canberra. Marlee felt small and claustrophobic while trying to peer through the large beams and chain-link fencing for a glimpse of the Opera House.

"You can't see much from here," she said.

"You'll have to climb the bridge if you want a good view. Lots of tourists do it and you can even get a T-shirt afterward to say you did. I can stop if you like."

"No thanks. I've heard it's pretty expensive."

"Like you have to worry about that now," Tyler said.

"Yes I do, especially since I'm unemployed."

"Have you been to the Opera House yet?"

"No." Marlee groaned. "I was hoping to at least see it today."

"How could you have not visited the Opera House by now? What kind of tourist are you anyway?"

"One who came here to surf and enjoy the beaches," Marlee said. "Besides, I'm not into opera."

"Liking opera is irrelevant. Our Opera House is world-renowned and a must-see for anyone visiting Sydney. I'll make a quick detour and park somewhere nearby so we can go for a short walk and have lunch at Circular Quay."

After lunch, Marlee offered to drive because Tyler was feeling a bit tired. When she got into the driver's seat, she pulled on the lever to move it forward, but something kept preventing it from sliding. She reached underneath and felt a plastic bag. She tugged on it, but the object inside was jammed and wouldn't budge.

"What's under here?" A piece of plastic ripped off. "I can't adjust the seat."

"Let me fix it." Tyler lunged through the rear door and began to shift things. "There, try now."

"What the fuck?" Instead of reaching for the lever, Marlee pulled out a bag with the gun nestled at the bottom.

"You weren't supposed to see that." Tyler slipped back into the passenger seat and refastened his belt.

"Fuck, Tyler, if we get caught with this we could be in big trouble."

"We'll be in worse trouble if we get caught without it. Give it to me." He took the bag. "I'll put it under my seat and you can forget it's there. I'll take responsibility."

"Yeah, right, and they'll believe I didn't know about it." Marlee groaned. "Let's take it back to your ex's."

"We can't. It's his birthday today and he'll be at home because he always takes it off work. I'll return it next week. We'll be fine for now. Let's go."

"I don't like this." Marlee reluctantly gave in and headed out toward Canberra.

Traffic was steady, flowing and manageable as Marlee drove them out of the city. She was upset about the gun and didn't feel much like talking so was happy to let Tyler nap while she cruised the open highway. When they got to Canberra nearly four hours later, rush hour traffic was at its peak.

Marlee let Tyler take over the wheel to navigate through the city streets and roundabouts that were confusing enough let alone driving on the wrong side of the road. She was exhausted.

They checked in to separate rooms and agreed to meet in the lobby at six for dinner. Marlee flopped on the bed and sent a text to Abigail to tell her they'd arrived. They were booked into different hotels, but Abigail promised to drop by after dark and spend most of the night. She just had to be back at her room in time to meet Hannah for breakfast.

Marlee stressed about the gun. If they were caught with a stolen firearm, it wouldn't look good for anyone. But if things got dangerous, it could come in handy.

By the time she met Tyler in the lobby for dinner, she was content he'd brought the gun along. The more she thought about it, the better she felt. She wouldn't use the gun unless she had to, but somehow it felt good to know it was there. She'd always carried a gun on duty and would surely use this one if it meant protecting Abigail.

They left the hotel to explore a few blocks of businesses and restaurants before deciding on a grill house that served steak and seafood.

"Did you leave it in the car?" Marlee cut a corner off Tyler's grilled sirloin after he'd offered her a taste. She'd opted for fish and chips.

"Maybe. The less you know about it the better."

"Why did you bring it if you don't want me to know anything?"

"Don't worry. If it's needed you'll know about it."

"I already know about it."

"How's the steak?"

"It's good." She swallowed. "Why do you think Hannah really wanted Abigail in Canberra this weekend?"

"To get her away from us, no doubt. Mind if I snag a few chips?"

"Sure, have the rest if you want." Marlee pushed her half-eaten plate toward him. "I'm not very hungry. I have this feeling that whoever's been messing with Abigail is going to strike soon."

"Strike as in what way?"

"I don't know, but the fact that someone tampered with her home security system worries me. I'll be glad when Abigail gets to my room tonight. I don't trust Hannah."

"She has reason not to trust you as well." Tyler bit into a fry. "If she knew her Tay was sneaking off to see you tonight, she'd freak."

"If Abigail's not here by midnight, I'm going to her hotel and if she's not in her room, I'll break down every door until I find her."

"Sounds pretty dramatic. Is that how the police in Canada do things? Break down doors?"

"No, but I'm not a cop in Canada anymore and don't have to follow any rules if it comes to that."

"We have laws here, so you'd better calm down. Abigail was wise to insist I come along to keep you company."

After dinner, they returned to the hotel and went into their own rooms for an early night. Marlee had brought a bottle of Abigail's favorite red merlot and two wineglasses in preparation for a relaxing nightcap. She showered then spent the next few hours surfing television channels, her mind too distracted to focus on anything other than Abigail's arrival.

CHAPTER THIRTY-FOUR

Marlee leapt off the bed to answer the light knock at her hotel room door. She viewed a tired Abigail through the peephole then opened it with a smile.

"You made it." Marlee was relieved to see Abigail and let her inside. Once the door was locked, they fell into each other's arms and kissed.

"I'm so glad you're here," Marlee said as they pulled apart.

"Me too." Abigail sat on the edge of the bed and kicked off her sandals. "It's been a long day."

"It's great you got here before ten." Marlee opened the wine. "I wasn't expecting you for at least another hour."

"I told Hannah I was tired and wanted an early night. Surprisingly she agreed and even offered to pay the bill at the restaurant so I could get on my way. She said she had plans to meet a friend for a few drinks and wouldn't be back until later." Abigail let out her ponytail and fluffed her hair. "How was your day with Tyler?"

"Great." Marlee poured them each a glass of merlot as she spoke. "I finally got to see the Sydney Opera House. We even ate lunch on the front steps with all the other tourists. It was amazing and a nice start to our afternoon drive here."

"I'm glad to hear that." Abigail's feet were on the bed and she reclined against some pillows.

Marlee handed Abigail her wine then sat down in a chair opposite the bed, clutching her own glass. She needed to exercise restraint against the seductive tresses until they'd talked, and the best way to do it was to keep that hair out of reach. "How did the rest of your day go?"

"Okay, but strange." Abigail sighed as she tucked hair behind her left ear. "We didn't leave the Sydney office until later in the day and Hannah seemed distracted for most of the ride."

"I hope she wasn't driving."

"I was happy to be behind the wheel and let my mind wander." Abigail patted the bed and caught Marlee's gaze. "Why don't you sit here?"

"I will, but first tell me what happened today with Hannah." Marlee fidgeted with the bottom of her shorts. She was losing her resolve for self-discipline.

"There's nothing much more to say." Abigail put her glass of wine down on the side table and held out her hands. "Come here. I've been waiting all day for this and want you beside me."

"Sounds like an order." Marlee was melting. "Are you trying to be my boss?"

Abigail grinned. "If anyone's in control right now, it's you. All I could think about during the drive was you and the dirty stuff you've planned for our little vacation in Merimbula. I was so turned on that it was rather awkward sharing space in the car with Hannah."

Marlee laughed as she put her wine down and climbed into Abigail's lap. She eased Abigail back onto the pillows and sprawled on top. "I think we should take some of the edge off now."

"Before we get too carried away, there's one more thing I need to tell you," Abigail said, as Marlee began to cover her with kisses.

"And what's that?" Marlee unbuttoned Abigail's blouse and slid her tongue between two inviting breasts beneath a mauve lace bra.

Abigail's breathing hastened as she caressed the back of Marlee's head. "Hannah's asked me to give her the passcode to my new security system."

Marlee's head jerked back in anger. "She can't have it."

"She said she wants it in case something happens at the house while I'm in Merimbula."

"Doesn't she think Tyler and I are staying behind?" Marlee's voice almost screeched from frustration.

"I told her you're going to Tasmania for a few days." Abigail rubbed her hands along Marlee's rigid arms. "I didn't want her to expect you to be there."

"I haven't been to Tasmania and wouldn't know what to say if she asked me about it." Marlee hated this.

"I know. She caught me off guard when asking about using the pool and I spoke without thinking. Sorry. Someone in the office mentioned a seat sale to Hobart, Tasmania so that's what came to mind. I owe you a trip there after this."

"What about the code? Did you give it to her?" Marlee sure hoped not.

"Of course not. I said I didn't have it with me and the security company could deal with anything that happens to set it off."

Marlee relaxed, a slight tinge of guilt for doubting Abigail. "That's my girl." She slid off her T-shirt and rubbed her naked breasts against Abigail. "Now where did we leave off?"

"The way you turn me on is unreal." Abigail wriggled out of her blouse.

"Just wait 'til we get to Merimbula." Marlee unhooked Abigail's bra and began to ravish the woman who made her feel so complete. How could she ever live again without this woman?

* * *

Marlee woke to Abigail's goodbye kiss. "What time is it?" The room was dark.

"It's just before five. I have to go." Abigail had on navy cotton slacks and a tailored yellow T-shirt, appropriate for a casual day at the office. She sat on the edge of the bed, fingering Marlee's scalp.

"I wish you didn't." Marlee switched on the lamp and sat up.

"Hannah's an early riser and she knows I am too." Abigail sighed. "I can't wait for this hiding to be over with. It's getting on my nerves. I'm going to tell Hannah about you the moment we get back from Merimbula."

"That's a good idea. We shouldn't be hiding our love from anyone, least of all our best friends. I'd like you to meet Kerry and Gabe after Merimbula."

Abigail took Marlee's hand. "I'm so looking forward to having a few private days with you to walk along the beach and talk about us. We haven't had time to think about our future and what it'll mean, especially with you giving up your job and moving here. What do you want to do with the rest of your life?"

"Spend it with you." Marlee kissed her. "That I know for sure."

"I don't want your life here to be just about me. I want you to have a life of your own too."

"I will." Marlee stroked Abigail's ponytail. "At least you won't be stuck with a surf bum because I'll never do that again."

"You can do whatever you want as long as you're happy and fulfilled while we grow old together."

"I like hearing that, especially the part about growing old together." Marlee kissed Abigail's fingers then locked eyes with the woman she was born to love. "I love you, Abigail Taylor, and am so looking forward to spending the rest of my life with you."

"And I you, Marlee Nevins." Abigail kissed her then sighed. "I should get going. I don't think we'll find anything at the office and it's going to be a long day. I'm not looking forward to it."

"Please be careful and keep in touch." Marlee squeezed Abigail's hands and feared for her safety. "I know you'll be with Hannah, but if anything doesn't feel right, get yourself out of there."

"I'll be fine." Abigail entwined their fingers. "What are you and Tyler up to today?"

"We'll be hanging out here in case you need us." Marlee wanted to be near Abigail.

Abigail began to flip through messages on her phone. "Don't waste your day like that. Get Tyler to tour you around our capital city. It's quite beautiful and you have to at least see Parliament House."

Marlee didn't detect any concern from Abigail and was starting to wonder if she was being overly paranoid about Hannah. "He did say there were kangaroos here. I haven't seen one yet."

"You need to get out into the country." Abigail's eyes stayed on her phone. "Tyler can take you to the Tidbinbilla Nature Reserve. It'll make for a nice day and you'll even see some koalas there."

Marlee rubbed Abigail's arm as she tried to alleviate her unease. "I can't go traipsing around looking for kangaroos and koalas while you're trying to find a suspect. My holiday will begin when we hit the road for Merimbula tomorrow morning."

Abigail smiled. "My holiday will begin as soon as Hannah leaves for the airport this afternoon."

"Isn't she supposed to be your best friend?" Marlee nudged her, relieved that Abigail was happy to be rid of Hannah too.

"Let's not talk about that for now." Abigail gave her another kiss then stood. "I have to go. I'll let you know as soon as Hannah heads out. Her flight is for five o'clock so she should be gone by four at the latest."

"I can hardly wait." Marlee pulled on a T-shirt and followed Abigail to the door. "Have a good day, my love."

"You too." Abigail kissed Marlee again then slipped into the hallway.

CHAPTER THIRTY-FIVE

"Want to go inside for a tour?" Tyler stood in front of Australia's Parliament House.

Marlee remained in a state of distracted quiet on this sunny Sunday morning in Canberra. While other tourists awed at the surroundings, Marlee's exhilaration focused on the brief conversation she'd had earlier that morning with Abigail about their future together. A fresh start in a new country with an amazing woman she loved and who loved her back. Maybe she really had died out on the water and was now in Heaven because that's what her future with Abigail felt like.

"Hello." Tyler waved a hand in front of her.

"Sorry." She gave her head a shake. "What did you say?"

"That I heard you and Abigail making out all night."

"Stop it. You weren't even in the room next to mine."

Tyler laughed. "Your poor neighbours."

"You seem obsessed with our sex life." Marlee put her hands on her hips and glared at him. "I wouldn't have expected that from a gay man."

"Whoa." He stepped back. "I was just teasing. Sometimes it's so obvious where your mind is. Just like now when you were in gaga land."

"Well you're wrong. Just because you can hack into my computer and listen to my chats doesn't mean you can do the same with my brain."

"You were zoned out." He shook his head.

"No, I wasn't. We need to keep focused on helping Abigail and I can't help it if I'm on cloud nine whenever I think about her."

"You must feel like you won the lottery." Tyler winked.

"Winning the lottery doesn't begin to compare to how I feel about her." Marlee was getting annoyed. "You, on the other hand, hit the jackpot when we met and I brought you into Abigail's world."

"Yeah, right." Tyler flopped onto a bench and looked up at her. "It's a jackpot with an empty bottom because I'll be moving out of her mansion soon while you get to stay. I can't imagine going back to my stuffy stinky little flat. How am I ever going to serve coffee on an airplane after all this?"

"Then do something else with your life. Maybe Abigail can give you a position in her company."

"I don't want to work in her IT unit and she wouldn't hire me anyway because I already checked and you need a degree to work there."

"Then go back to school and get it. You're too brilliant with computers to not use those skills in some work capacity."

"I don't know." He sighed. "What are you going to do with your days once things settle down? Do you still want to be a cop?"

Marlee was feeling a bit overwhelmed. "I haven't thought that far ahead. All I know for sure is I'm spending the rest of my life with Abigail."

"Keep your options open because there's no guarantees with the future." Tyler frowned.

"Maybe so, but my destiny's with Abigail. That I'm sure of." Marlee tapped Tyler's knee then stood up. "Let's see if we can find some kangaroos."

"You've hardly even looked around here." He stood and put his hands in his pockets. "We should go inside for a tour so you can understand how things work in your newfound homeland."

"I will, but not today." Marlee knew she'd never be able to concentrate.

"Well then how about a walk by the lake since we're close and it's so nice out? We can hike around it to the National Museum of Australia and you can make a note of another building you need to visit next time you're here." Tyler stretched his shoulders. "Who knows, we could get lucky and spot a kangaroo or two on our stroll."

They spent the next two hours exploring on foot, meandering along the pathway to the museum. Ducks swam near the shoreline, magpies and cockatoos flew around the path, joggers and cyclists whizzed by, but no kangaroos were in sight. A lunch of toasted sandwiches in the museum cafeteria offered a pleasant refueling before heading back to the car and driving to a local nature reserve where Marlee finally spotted some kangaroos.

"They're such strange animals," she said as they watched six kangaroos lying, eating, and hopping around the landscape. Two mothers stood upright, balancing on their thick tails as they fed joeys from their pouches.

"They're not strange and you'd better get used to them." Tyler took a few pictures. "I think they're cute and I adored my stuffed kangaroo when I was a kid."

"I loved my black teddy bear and took it everywhere." Marlee posed up against the fence. "Can you get a picture of me with the kangaroos in the background? I want to send it to my brother and get him thinking about bringing the family over for a visit."

"Does Abigail know you're inviting them?" Tyler held up his phone and clicked.

"I'm talking about later, when things are more settled." Marlee got excited just thinking about it until her thoughts came back to the present. "I haven't heard anything from Abigail since this morning. I hate to text her in case Hannah sees it."

"Hannah." Tyler rolled his eyes. "She's probably hard at it right now trying to convince Abigail to get rid of us, and especially you."

"She's wasting her time then because Abigail's just as committed to me as I am to her." Marlee could feel it in her heart. "Let's head back to the hotel because I want to be there if she manages to escape early."

* * *

"Hey, how's it going?" Marlee could hardly contain her excitement as she answered Abigail's call.

"We're done, thank God, and I'll be heading your way shortly." Abigail's voice was low.

"Yes! I can't wait to see you." Marlee teetered on the edge of her hotel room bed while Tyler sat in a chair flipping channels on the muted television. "Did you find anything unusual or suspicious?"

"Nothing." Abigail sighed. "We can talk more when I see you, but it was a frustrating day. I couldn't get away from Hannah even for a minute to text you."

"I figured as much." Marlee struggled to keep her voice calm. "Hannah still believes you're heading to Merimbula on your own?"

"Yes and I'm glad for that because she seems anxious for me to go. She'll be here any second to say good-bye."

Marlee heard a knock on Abigail's door. "Let me know as soon as she leaves. Love you."

CHAPTER THIRTY-SIX

Marlee noticed a slight tremor and subdued aura as soon as she greeted Abigail at their hotel room door. Something was wrong. The three of them were in the room, discussing the touristy events of the day.

"Here's a picture of Marlee with some kangaroos." Tyler handed his phone to Abigail. "It's a good thing you have a big house. She wants to use this snapshot to lure her family here for a visit."

"That's not true," Marlee said. "They know I've never seen a kangaroo in the wild and I wanted to show them."

"Nice photo." Abigail said, her voice flat as she returned the phone. "I'm pleased the two of you enjoyed yourselves today."

"How was your day?" Marlee straightened the pillows behind her back. She reclined on the bed, facing Abigail and Tyler who occupied two padded chairs by the window.

"I'm glad it's over." Abigail sighed.

"Was it that bad?"

"It was a waste of time and I hate wasting time." Abigail's legs were crossed and her right foot rocked back and forth. "I don't know what Hannah was thinking."

"I take it you didn't discover anything unusual in your Canberra office then," Marlee said.

"Not in the office, no." Abigail bit her lower lip.

"What happened, Ab?" Marlee got off the bed and approached Abigail's chair, squatting at the side to drape an arm over her shoulders.

"Hannah kissed me." Abigail almost spat out the words.

"She kissed you?" Marlee stumbled back and had to grab the chair.

"I pushed her away as soon as I felt her tongue."

"Her tongue. That fucking bitch." Marlee jumped up and swung a fist through the air.

"She knows I don't like her that way." Abigail shook her head. "It was so unexpected."

"Did she hurt you?" Marlee's throat was throbbing.

"I'm fine." Abigail reached for one of Marlee's hands. "It's okay. She stopped and left right after."

"What the hell was she thinking?" Marlee's jaw was tight.

"I don't know because I've never…" Abigail's voice faded.

"The security cameras," Tyler said. "She must have seen the two of you together."

"That's got to be it." Marlee's mind was racing to find an answer.

"There's no way," Abigail said. "We've been very discreet."

"Except for by the pool. She knows we're lovers."

"She would have asked me about it."

"Not if she didn't want you to know she knows."

"Especially if she spied on you through your security cameras," Tyler said.

"Thank God I didn't give her the code to the new system." Abigail shook her head.

"Maybe it's time to involve the police," Tyler said.

"And say what? That she kissed me?" Abigail got up from her chair and began to pace, wringing her hands.

"Let me get you something else to drink." Marlee reached for Abigail's glass. "Would you like some wine now?"

"How about the whole bottle?" Abigail flopped on the side of the bed. "I'd better stick to water, but please have the wine if you or Tyler would like something stronger."

"Not for me, thanks." Tyler groaned as he stood up. "I think I'll pop back to my room for a little nap before dinner."

"I hope you'll join us at the restaurant downstairs," Abigail said.

"Sure." Tyler was at the door. "Let me know when you're ready to go."

"Probably in an hour or so," Marlee said. "I'll send you a text."

"Perfect. See you then." Tyler left.

Marlee sat on the bed beside Abigail and pulled her into an embrace. "I'm so sorry this happened to you."

"Me too." Abigail kept her head down.

"What's wrong, Ab? You're agitated and I get the feeling it's more than a yucky kiss from Hannah that's thrown you off."

Abigail started to cry. "I hate feeling like this."

"Like what?" Marlee used a finger to lift Abigail's chin so their eyes could meet. "Did she do anything else?"

"No." Abigail reached for a tissue and wiped her nose. "I feel so cheap and dirty."

"You shouldn't. You've done nothing wrong." Marlee hugged her.

"I hated snooping through the personal workspaces of my staff. I felt dirty enough with that, but when Hannah tried to stick her tongue into my mouth, it was like my feelings were inconsequential."

"I'd love to get my hands on that fucking bitch." Marlee shook with anger.

"Please calm down." Abigail straightened. "It's my own fault."

"Don't blame yourself. You were duped and this is going to stop as soon as we get back to Sydney."

"You're so worked up over this." Abigail stroked Marlee's arm.

"I'll never accept anyone else kissing you on the lips." Marlee took a deep breath.

"Good, because neither will I." Abigail gave a lingering kiss.

"You deserve the best in friends, especially since you now have the best in lovers." Marlee pushed Abigail back against the pillows. "Let's forget about Hannah for now and think about us as we start our holiday."

"I like that." Abigail let out a sigh of relief. "You know, Marl, you always make me feel so great and I know you have my best interests at heart."

"Marl. I kind of like that." Marlee kissed Abigail and grinned. "Ab and Marl. We sound like an old lesbian couple."

Abigail laughed. "We're certainly on our way to becoming one."

"I'm so looking forward to talking about our future together as we stroll along the beach in Merimbula. We'll have to catch a sunset to walk into."

"Yes, we will." Abigail rolled on top of Marlee. "There'll be lots of sunsets for us to experience together and I hope there'll be some Canadian ones too."

"For sure. I can't wait to take you there." Marlee wrapped her legs around Abigail. "How much time do we have left before dinner?"

"Not enough, considering we'll be eating with Tyler and he doesn't miss a thing." Abigail kissed Marlee's nose. "Let's save it for dessert and just cuddle for a bit now."

"I can do that. Why don't you put your head on my chest and listen to my heart beating for you?"

"You're such a romantic." Abigail lowered onto Marlee and closed her eyes. "I feel like I'm lying on a cloud."

"Now who's the romantic?" Marlee took a deep breath and realized Hannah knew that she, as Abigail's lover, would also be going to Merimbula. If Hannah was indeed the guilty one, that bold kiss could have been the start of her closing in on Abigail. It was a good thing Tyler had brought the gun along.

Marlee knew she would stop at nothing to protect the woman she loved.

CHAPTER THIRTY-SEVEN

"I need the gun," Marlee told Tyler.

They were in the hotel dining room. Abigail had left the table to sign for the dinner bill and ask about driving directions to Merimbula.

"Now?" Tyler's eyes bulged as he scanned the room.

"Not right now, but before we head back to our rooms."

"What's up with that? You didn't want it a while ago."

"I'm worried we might have company in Merimbula. I don't trust Hannah. She could be dangerous."

"The police should be involved. You don't know what you might be dealing with."

"That's the thing," Marlee said. "I don't know anything for sure and I won't risk embarrassing Abigail by coming across like some jealous lover."

"Abigail could be compromising your safety."

"Shhh. Here she comes. We'll chat later." Marlee watched Abigail meander back to the table.

"Ready?" Abigail stayed standing, obviously anxious to get back to the room and plan their early morning departure.

Marlee stood up. "Yep. I have to get a few things from Tyler's car first."

"Do you need a hand?" Abigail asked as they headed to the lobby.

"We're fine. Go ahead to the room and relax. I'll be up in a minute."

"Thanks for the dinner and everything." Tyler held out his hand to Abigail.

"I'm the one who should be thanking you." Abigail took his hand and held it between her two. "I really appreciate how you've been helping out. I won't forget it."

"It's been my pleasure. Have fun in Merimbula." Tyler beamed as he and Abigail exchanged a quick hug.

"No big parties at the house now." Abigail smiled as she stepped into the up elevator. "See you soon." The doors slid shut and she was gone.

"I'm not giving it to you," Tyler said. "It was a mistake taking it and I'm going to return it as soon as I get back to Sydney."

"Maybe you're right." Marlee stepped into an empty down elevator, wondering if jealousy over Hannah kissing Abigail was clouding her judgment. "I shouldn't jeopardize Abigail's reputation by being caught with it."

"Or yours either, especially now that you need to keep it squeaky clean to stay in the country," Tyler said as they descended to the parking garage. "Don't you have everything out of my car?"

"I do but I need to bring something up to the room now. What can you give me?"

"You were going to carry it up on its own? How were you planning to do that?"

"It's in a plastic bag. I'd just say it was a book or something if she asked."

"You should be ashamed of yourself." Tyler wagged his finger at her. "That's lying and the last thing Abigail needs right now is for you to betray her trust."

"I want to protect her." Marlee plopped against the car, her throat tightening. "This is starting to get to me in a bad way."

"You're in love and have lost your senses."

"Yeah, and now's not the time to lose my better judgment." Marlee folded her arms and stared at the dirty cement floor. "How am I going to keep her safe?"

"By trusting in your gut and dialing triple zero if you need the police. Come on. Let's head back upstairs and I'll leave you two alone for the rest of the night while I check out a few clubs."

When Marlee got back to her room, Abigail was propped on the bed, computer on her lap, and typing away. She barely looked up as Marlee entered.

"I was hoping you wouldn't have to work tonight." Marlee slid onto the bed. She could see that Abigail's email inbox was full of new messages.

"I wasn't planning to, but thought I'd respond to a few quick messages before you got back. Did you get everything?" Abigail closed her laptop, put it on the night table, and then snuggled up to Marlee.

"Everything I need is right here." Marlee kissed her. "I'm so excited about the next few days. This'll be our first trip together. I hope we don't have any fights."

"Why would we?" Abigail's eyebrows furrowed.

"I was just joking." Marlee chuckled. "Travelling with someone, and especially me, can be a challenging test of a new relationship."

"I think we're beyond that test." Abigail giggled. "After all, what bigger challenge than rescuing you from a shark could I ever face?"

"I can be annoying sometimes, especially when I travel. You might trip over my shoes or get frustrated with my indecision over where to eat."

Abigail tapped Marlee's shoulder. "Are you afraid of vacationing with me?"

"Not at all, but you've been under a lot of stress and I want to make sure you're okay. If you'd rather relax at home, I'd be fine with that."

"Would you now?" Abigail straightened up and looked at Marlee. "What's going on?"

"Nothing. I'm just being crazy because I'm so madly in love with you." Marlee pulled Abigail into an embrace and squeezed her. "Call it my second sense, intuition, or whatever, but I'm a bit apprehensive about going to Merimbula. If anything were to happen to you, I'd never forgive myself."

"What could possibly happen to me there?"

Marlee hesitated before responding. "I'm afraid Hannah's going to follow us there."

"Hannah? Don't tell me you're going to let her ruin our vacation. The only way she'll follow us there is if you let her. Can't you just forget about her for a few days?"

"I'm not the jealous type."

"Good, because Hannah's been a big part of my life up until now and I haven't given up on her yet."

"I wouldn't dream of giving up my friendship with Kerry and I don't expect you to do that with Hannah."

"Then what exactly do you expect me to do about her?"

"I don't know and that's the problem." Marlee wished she had some concrete evidence one way or another.

"I know you don't like her, but I believe she's not a threat to us in Merimbula. Trust me on this, will you?"

"Okay, but only if we can kiss and make up." Marlee ceded to Abigail, against her better judgment.

Abigail pulled her into a hug. "We weren't fighting. There's no need to make up, but there's a growing need to make out."

"Nice play on words." Marlee fell into Abigail. "It's fun making up though, and I believe it's time for dessert. What would you like for yours?"

"I'll take a piece of that orgasmic pie you've been feeding me." Abigail giggled as she nibbled Marlee's neck. "I've been saving room for at least two pieces, maybe more."

"Are you sure you can handle it? I wouldn't want you getting too much sugar, especially if we'll be going for a long walk along the beach tomorrow."

"I'm sure." Abigail fondled Marlee's breasts. "Your pie is the best ever. It's full of sweetness that burns off calories and lightens the load. I could eat it forever."

"Ooh, I can hardly wait for you to taste the orgasmic cake I'm keeping for Merimbula."

"Cake has always been my favorite, but I can't imagine it topping your pie."

"I think it will," Marlee said, "but for now I want to enjoy tonight's dessert."

Abigail moaned in pleasure as Marlee's fingers stirred the silky wet ingredients of her orgasmic pie.

CHAPTER THIRTY-EIGHT

Abigail yawned as she finished her morning coffee. "Do you know how to drive a manual?"

"I do in Canada, but not here on the wrong side of the road." Marlee zipped her backpack and took one last look around the room, her nerves a bit jittery.

"I'd like you to drive my car today. There are some challenging hairpin turns on the road to Merimbula and they'll help accustom you to driving a manual on the other side of the road."

"I've never shifted with my left hand before." Marlee didn't need more stress.

"I'm sure you'll figure it out, considering how talented you are with those hands of yours."

Marlee slung the backpack over her shoulder. "I'll have to look into buying a car. My rental has to go back at the end of next week and I don't want to have to rely on you for my wheels."

"We shouldn't need more than two vehicles between us." Abigail opened the door into the hallway and motioned for Marlee to exit first.

"I don't expect you to provide me with a car." Marlee kissed Abigail, touched by her casual response.

"I know, but I want to." Abigail followed Marlee down the corridor toward the elevator.

"It's not necessary." All that Marlee cared about was having this wonderful woman in her life.

"What's not necessary?" Tyler was at the elevator, as though he'd been waiting for them.

"Fancy meeting you here," Marlee said, a bit confused. "I thought you'd still be in bed after going out last night."

"I want to get back to Sydney before rush hour." Tyler's hands fidgeted in his pockets.

"I forgot to mention the cleaning staff will be coming to the house tomorrow morning," Abigail said. "I coordinate everything on the same day so the pool specialists and grounds workers will also be there. My head cleaning woman has a key and lets everyone else in. I'll let her know you'll be there."

"Actually, I won't be there." Tyler's hands settled. "I'm staying at a friend's for a few days."

"Really?" Marlee squinted at him. "You haven't mentioned anyone to me."

"Well I do have some friends," Tyler said as the elevator arrived. "I'll be around though, so text if you need me."

A couple shuffled to the back of the elevator as they stepped inside and everyone rode in silence to the underground parking area.

"Have fun in Merimbula, as I know the two of you will." Tyler's car was beside theirs.

"We will and thanks," Marlee opened the rear hatch of the Golf and placed her bag inside.

"Have a safe trip back to Sydney." Abigail put her luggage next to Marlee's then went to the passenger side. "We'll be back on Thursday afternoon."

"What about you?" Marlee stood beside the driver's door of the vehicle. "How long will you be away?"

"Probably just a day or two." He winked and snickered. "Lucky you. In the driver's seat now."

"Abigail is giving me a driving lesson on shifting gears with my left hand, if you must know." She just wanted to get going.

"Never mind your left hand," Tyler said. "Your whole life is shifting gears. I'm jealous."

"We'll talk more when I get back about how you should be changing your life too. Catch you later." Marlee got in the car and closed her door.

"What was that all about?" Abigail asked as Marlee buckled herself in, engaged the clutch and practiced shifting through the gears.

"I want to help Tyler sort out his life." Marlee started the car engine. "His computer skills are far too good for him to be waiting on airline passengers for a living."

"I agree, but first we have to sort out our own lives." Abigail massaged Marlee's bare knee.

Marlee was good on the clutch, changing gears smoothly as she drove around the underground garage to get a feel for shifting. After building confidence, she headed to the exit ramp and they were on their way. Traffic flow was smooth and she felt comfortable behind the wheel until entering her first roundabout. She cursed while struggling to signal and shift gears with her left hand at the same time.

"Sorry," Abigail said. "I forgot to warn you about downshifting and signaling in the roundabouts. You'll get the hang of it, but this will be good practice for when we get back to Sydney where the traffic is much heavier."

Marlee looked over her shoulder as a car sped up beside them and honked as she swerved to avoid a collision while trying to exit. She let out a sigh of relief as they merged onto a straight road again. "You're optimistic we'll make it back in one piece with me behind the wheel."

"Of course we will," Abigail said. "I have every confidence in your driving abilities. What else could go wrong on what's beginning to feel like a perfect little getaway?"

"It does feel perfect, doesn't it?"

"I'm going to find the right moment to tell Josh about us," Abigail said. "I want him to know how much you mean to me and that you're a big part of my life now."

"How do you think he'll take it?" She suddenly felt insecure, wondering what would happen if he resented their relationship.

"He wants me to be happy so he should be fine with us." Abigail lowered her window. "I wish this was a convertible because I'd like to wave my arms in the air and let the breeze blow through my hair. I feel so good right now and want to enjoy the moment."

"Me too." Marlee reached over to caress Abigail's bare knees.

"You're a fast learner." Abigail closed her eyes and reclined against the headrest. "You've not only mastered the gear stick and indicate switch with your left hand, but also how to relax your passenger."

"That's good because I want you to unwind and rest for the next few days."

"Rest? I thought you were going to take our sex to the next level and I've been so looking forward to it."

"You need to rest." Marlee grinned. "The unwinding part, however, will be full of passion and exhilaration."

"Thank God you're driving. If it was me, I'd have to pull over to catch my breath from imagining it." She giggled. "Do you mind if I keep my eyes closed and savor those thoughts for the next little while?"

"Please do." Marlee squeezed Abigail's knee then put her hand back on the wheel and smiled. She loved seeing her lover so carefree and happy.

They drove in silence. Marlee didn't even put on music, as she just wanted to revel in her new life with Abigail.

They stopped for coffee at a roadside café, but were soon back in the car, determined to keep up their pace and get to Merimbula in time for lunch on the beach. Marlee carefully moved them through the hairpin curves on the highway meandering down toward the coast.

"So this is what you had in mind for my driving lesson." Marlee shifted gears at almost every turn, some of which were like J's, and her concentration had to be entirely on the road.

"Wouldn't it be fun to be in a sports car right now?" Abigail rolled her head toward Marlee.

"What's your dream sports car?"

"It doesn't matter as long as it has a gear stick and removable top. And you?"

"I'm in my dream sports car." Marlee grinned, keeping her eyes on the road. "I love this stick shift and can't wait to remove the top on the sexy passenger beside me."

Abigail laughed as she ran her fingers down Marlee's arm. "You're such a flirt."

"Who's the one with their fingers distracting the driver? I might have to pull over, but this isn't really a good place for that." She downshifted while entering another sharp turn and was startled to meet a car going in the opposite direction.

"Oops." Abigail pulled her hand back. "I guess I'd better behave myself."

"Maybe only for now while I'm driving." Marlee gave Abigail's leg a quick tap. "You can be naughty with me all you want in Merimbula."

"I'm planning to be a good student when we get there." Abigail chuckled. "I want to learn all about your orgasmic cake."

Marlee burst out laughing, her libido in full gear. "I can't believe you're sounding hornier than me. Who would've thought Dr. Abigail Taylor, Founder and CEO of AbTay Biosystems, has so much pent-up passion?"

"It's not funny." Abigail stifled a laugh. "One of the things I love the most about science is discovering new and great things. With every breakthrough, I want to learn as much as I can and spend hours studying the revelation. I've just made the greatest discovery of my life with you. Why should this be any different?"

"I'm so glad it's not." Marlee could hardly contain her feelings of love for Abigail. She finally found a place to pull over and brought the car to a stop. "I need to kiss you." She leaned over and inhaled Abigail's mouth as their tongues met in a fury of passion.

Abigail moaned in delight. "Take me to Merimbula. Now."

CHAPTER THIRTY-NINE

Soft sand sifted between Marlee's toes as she peered over the water from the Merimbula Main Beach. A few surfers dotted the rolling waves and she yearned to yell out to beware of riptides and sharks. Of course, she knew they'd never hear.

"I can't believe we're finally here." Abigail strolled into the water up to her ankles and swished it around. "It feels so good. Come in and get your feet wet."

Marlee dipped a toe in. "It's cold and I like the warm sand." She'd removed her sports sandals and dangled them from her fingers as they walked over the beach.

Abigail held out a hand toward Marlee. "Come on. Walk with me in the ocean. I'll protect you."

"I don't want to get our sandwiches wet." Marlee wiggled the small backpack that held their lunches. "Let's find a place to sit down and eat because I'm hungry."

"You did warn me about being a bit of a cranky traveller." Abigail laughed as she skipped out of the water.

"I can't help it when I'm hungry." Marlee spread a large beach towel on the sand and plopped down on her knees to smooth it out. She smiled up at Abigail, taking joy in the simplicity of her lover's happiness. "I only brought one towel, so it'll give us an excuse to sit close together."

"Works for me." Abigail dropped onto the towel and almost rolled onto Marlee. "I feel like a kid again. Where's my spade and pail to play with in the sand?"

"You have me instead and there'll be lots of time to play later, but first we must eat because I'm starving." Marlee dished up vegetarian wraps for each of them as well as two bottles of water. She had been tempted to get a chicken wrap, but opted for the avocado as her vegetarian partner stood behind her when she ordered from the local café on the way to the beach.

Abigail studied her phone. "It looks like we're in luck with the weather for the next few days."

"Good, now you can put it away."

"Let's do a selfie first." Abigail held out the phone to align a photo. "It'll be our first picture together. What a memory."

Marlee leaned into Abigail and smiled. "If we're really going to have an escape from everything, there'll have to be parameters around your phone, like keeping away from your email."

"I wish I could." Abigail sighed. "As much as I want to forget about everything else, I can't let anything slip by me while I'm out of the office right now. I know I left Hannah in charge, but I don't know. I'm concerned." She bit into her sandwich.

"I thought we weren't going to talk about Hannah."

Abigail took her time chewing then leisurely swallowed before answering. "She was on my mind and it slipped out. Sorry. I'll try to be more careful from now on."

"There's no need to apologize," Marlee said. "I don't want you to try to be anything other than yourself when you're around me. If Hannah's on your mind then let her out. The last thing I want is for you to feel trapped between the two of us. Another thing. I know I joked about getting a toaster for recruiting you as a lesbian, but that's just an old saying. If you weren't a lesbian to begin with, you wouldn't get so wet the moment I'm near you. Chemistry or not, lesbian attraction between two women is as fundamental to who we are as water is to life. It just takes some longer to figure it out, that's all." She stuffed the last of her wrap into her mouth.

"Wow." Abigail put her wrap down and leaned back. "That's me told."

"Don't think of it like that." Marlee wiped her mouth with a paper napkin. "I want our relationship to be open and honest all the time. It's so important to communicate our true feelings with each other."

Abigail straightened up and put a hand on Marlee's knee. "This is exactly what I was hoping for with this trip. Things have happened so fast between us that we haven't had time to really get to know each other. I want to learn more about you."

"Go ahead and ask whatever you'd like," Marlee said.

"How did you know you were a lesbian?"

Marlee shifted a little. "So you want to hear my coming out story?"

"Yes and everything else there is to know about you." Abigail brushed an eyelash off Marlee's cheek. "Why don't we walk along the beach and learn more about each other?"

"I wish we could hold hands." Marlee stood and pulled Abigail up.

"Let's do it then." Abigail helped her fold the towel.

"It'll draw attention to us and I don't want that. I'll walk on the edge of the water with you though." Marlee stuffed the towel in her backpack then slung it over her shoulder. "Ready?"

"Let's go." Abigail led them closer to the shoreline. "How long have you known you were attracted to women?"

Marlee considered Abigail's question for a moment, as she still felt awkward about those earlier years. "Forever. I tried to deny it when I was a teenager and wanted to fit in with everyone else. I even dated a guy for a year right after starting university."

"I didn't know you went to uni," Abigail said. "What did you study?"

"Psychology and humanities. I have an undergraduate degree that doesn't qualify me for anything specific, but it helped me grow up a bit. I came out during my second year and became a real slut after that."

Abigail laughed. "You must have broken a lot of hearts."

"I never let myself get too involved with any one person in those days. I loved the sex, but could never bring myself to settle down. I always felt like I hadn't found that special one."

"Until now, I hope."

"Of course." Marlee bumped against Abigail, realizing how empty her life had been back then.

"Did you become a police officer right after uni?"

"I did, and that was a lot of fun too. I especially loved working Pride events, all decked out in my uniform and collecting numbers for future dates."

"I'd love to see you in your uniform."

"I'll show you a picture sometime. And what about you? How are you feeling about your own coming out story?"

"Overwhelmed." Abigail's voice quivered. "I've never felt so happy and alive. It's as though I can't get enough of you."

"Me too." Marlee touched Abigail's arm. "I know I need to be keeping my hands off you for now, but I can't resist these little taps of joy during a conversation like this."

"Maybe we should have asked Tyler to come along to keep an eye on our behavior in public."

"No way. I like Tyler, but there are limits. This is our time and I don't want to share it with anyone."

"I've been wanting to ask you something." Abigail put her hands in her pockets as they strolled along the beach. "How many other women have you fallen in love with like this?"

"None." Marlee stepped in front of Abigail and stopped. She removed her sunglasses. She wanted Abigail to see her sincerity. "It's never been this strong with anyone before. Yes, I've fallen in love with women. Too many times and to the point where I figured I was no good at it. My relationships only lasted a few years at the most and I'd all but given up on finding a happy ever after love. But then I met you. You're my other half. That's the only way to describe how I feel about you."

A tear slid from underneath Abigail's large sunglasses. Marlee brushed it away with her thumb.

"Thank God I was such a wreck and on my own when we met," Marlee said. "If I'd have been with anyone else, or you were…" Her voice started to quiver. She didn't want to think about a life without Abigail.

"I want to kiss you right now." Abigail pulled a tissue out of her pocket. "All my life I've felt something was wrong with me. Now I know why."

"I feel the same," Marlee said. "It's like we've been waiting for each other all along."

"What if we'd never met?"

Marlee put her sunglasses back on. "Why couldn't we have met sooner? Life's like that, don't you think? Things sometimes happen where you just have to go with it because it was meant to be."

"I've always hated just accepting things for what they are," Abigail said as they resumed walking. "It goes against my better judgment and that's why I spend such long hours in the lab. I need to see clear pathways to mapping genomes and understanding how connections are made through the interplay of genetic and environmental factors. I wish I could relate some of that thinking to what's happened between us."

"It sounds pretty obvious to me," Marlee said. "The strong chemistry between us has to be in our matching genetics. As for the environmental factors, I had to come to Australia so we could meet."

Abigail stopped and lowered her sunglasses to look at Marlee. "You're brilliant."

"I told you our genetics match." Marlee smiled. "I have another brilliant idea. Let's head back to our room and share a piece or two of that orgasmic cake I've been promising."

"Lead the way, please."

CHAPTER FORTY

"Are they ever cute." Marlee bent over to pet two grey tabby kittens playing outside the lobby of their luxurious apartment rental near the beach. "I wonder who they belong to."

"They're yours if you want." The woman who'd checked them into their unit appeared from around the building.

"Oh, I couldn't." Marlee straightened up. "I've just moved here from Canada and have enough going on in my life right now."

"How old are they?" Abigail picked one up and smiled as she kissed its head.

"Almost three months and way past time for them to find a new place to live." The woman flicked the toes of her sandals against the cement footpath, as though clearing out sand. "There were four of them altogether, but the orange boys went first. These are two little sisters."

"What are their names?" Marlee reached for the other kitten and cuddled it against her chest.

"Whatever you want," the woman said.

"They're cute." Abigail put hers down and brushed her hands. "I hope they find a good home."

"They love it here," the woman said, "but they won't be kittens forever and the place isn't big enough for them and their mother once they grow up. A loving home is just what they need." She paused, looking between Marlee and Abigail. "I'd better go back to work. Let me know if you'd like them."

"Have you ever had a cat?" Abigail asked as they made their way to their unit.

"I sort of did once when one of my girlfriends moved in with hers for a few months. It was a grey tabby too, and I fell in love with it. The hardest part about ending that relationship was letting go of the cat."

"Why didn't you get one of your own then?"

"I don't know." Marlee unlocked the door and they entered the bright living area of the luxury unit that put her shabby little apartment in Sydney to shame. Even the smell was fresher, with its lemon furniture polish aroma shouting out that it had just been cleaned, and the glass doors to the large private balcony embellished with plants for their own personal jungle.

Marlee kicked off her sandals. "One of my girlfriends was severely allergic to cats, so I didn't want to ever be in the position of having to end a good relationship over a cat." She laughed. "Even though I hung on to a bad relationship longer than I should have because of one. Go figure, eh?"

"My crazy Canadian girlfriend." Abigail pulled her into an embrace and they shared a lingering kiss. "I'd never risk losing you over a cat."

"Do you like cats?"

"I don't mind them," Abigail said. "My work's always been so intensive. I've never thought about getting a pet because I'm too busy to look after it the way it should be cared for."

"I like that you look after people through your work," Marlee said.

"So do you." Abigail rested her head on Marlee's shoulder. "Our work is similar in that respect. Helping people, like you're helping me now."

"I haven't done anything to get you and your company out of this mess. What if I can't save you?"

"You've already helped me so much more than I could have ever hoped for." Abigail gave her another lingering kiss. "You awakened my senses and brought me to discover sexual bliss, a crucial part of me that was missing." She chuckled. "I realize how empty my life was."

Marlee brushed her lips over Abigail's and smiled. "You helped me with my own discovery too. I've never known this kind of ecstasy with another woman."

"Are you still sure about quitting your job to be with me?"

"Positive." Marlee kissed Abigail's nose.

"I imagine it's not easy being a police officer, especially when you see things no person should have to witness."

"Yes." Marlee sighed as her eyes drifted to the far wall and a framed print of a colorful parrot in a rubber tree. "It's not easy sometimes, that's for sure."

"I'd like to know more about who you are as a police officer and what you've experienced on your job." Abigail rubbed Marlee's forehead. "You look so sad right now. What are you thinking about?"

"Something I've been trying to put behind me, but I think it's one of those calls that'll be with me for the rest of my days." The memory was still so painful.

"Tell me about it." Abigail took Marlee's hand and led her to the couch. She put an arm over Marlee's shoulder as they sat. "Go ahead."

Marlee took a few deep breaths, fighting back tears as she realized that if it hadn't been for this call, they'd probably never have met. "About a year ago, I was the first responder at a horrific accident scene. A mother and her five-year-old son were crushed to death in their small car." She paused to swallow, the burnt stench of the deployed airbags and spattered blood still so vivid.

"They were on their way home from the grocery store." Her throat constricted as she fought back a gag. "It was a stupid accident that never should have happened. The driver of the truck was a young university student stoned out of his mind. He swerved into their lane and barely suffered a scratch. How do you make sense of something like that? Why do some people die and others walk away?" A tear trickled down her cheek.

Abigail tightened her grip and caressed Marlee's arm. "I ask myself the same thing all the time. Why does cancer kill so many people, but let others survive? Or even leave many untouched?"

"At least you can offer hope when there's none. I had none to offer the wailing father and husband when he arrived at the scene. It was so heartbreaking to see his loss and pain."

"You were there. It takes a lot of courage to respond to tragedy and that in itself should give hope."

"How can it give hope when your family has just been killed?"

"By caring. Hope for everyone starts with someone else caring." Abigail's voice had a soothing effect. Simple words, but she said them with such conviction.

Marlee looked for a tissue. She still couldn't get that father's face out of her mind. The demand for answers where there were none. "You make it sound so simple."

"That's because it is. Caring has to be one of the simplest things to do in this life."

"But it can be hard too," Marlee said. "I stopped caring about a lot of things after that day. I cry every time I think about it and I'm sure it's why I ended up in Australia. Everything in life began to bother me. My job, my history of unsuccessful relationships, and my personal unhappiness brought me here in search of myself. I put all of my energy into surfing, as though mastering it would help me find my way."

"How ironic. If it wasn't for your misfortune with surfing, we never would have met." Abigail kissed Marlee's cheek.

"Thank God I sucked at it and you came along on that nice boat of yours to save me." Marlee leaned back into Abigail's arms. It felt good to be there. Safe. "Even when you're not working, you help others. I was hopeless until you came to my rescue."

"Now I'm hopeless too," Abigail said. "Hopelessly in love."

"How romantic." Marlee smiled. "I think it's time to change the subject to something more fun because this is supposed to be a vacation." She fondled Abigail's fingers. "I love your painted nails. They're so sexy and feminine in that nice purple."

"Good segue to another topic." Abigail chuckled. "The color's violet, to be exact. Have you ever painted yours?"

"I might have tried once or twice when I was in high school. I like yours, especially with them being nice and short under that polish." Marlee gave little kisses to Abigail's fingers.

"Would you like me to paint your nails?"

"Hell no."

Abigail laughed. "That was quick. I guess it's a no-go for a personal pedicure then too."

Marlee looked at Abigail's matching painted toenails. "I'd be happy to do one on you, if you'd like. I'm sure I could do a good job because I've been known to give awesome foot massages."

"Really?" Abigail swung her feet into Marlee's lap. "I'd love to have my feet rubbed right now. And I'll let you in on a little secret. I'm getting aroused at the thought of you massaging them."

"It must be our genetics working together again because I'm getting aroused too and they're not even my feet." Marlee giggled as she began to caress Abigail's toes.

"I love the way we're exploring each other." Abigail moaned. "Your hands are divine wherever they touch me."

"If you think my hands feel good, just wait until you feel my tongue all over you after this."

"I can hardly wait." Abigail pulled her feet back and jumped on top of Marlee. "I want to devour you right here and now."

Marlee smiled. "I like that my doctor lover is reading my mind."

"Yes, it's all in the genetics. I can feel it in my genes."

"I want to feel it in your jeans too." Marlee reached between Abigail's legs. "Whoops, you're wearing shorts. Guess I'll have to wait."

Abigail giggled. "I love how you make me feel and am so ready for your orgasmic cake."

"So am I. Will you join me for a shower as an appetizer?"

CHAPTER FORTY-ONE

Marlee closed her eyes and savored the moment as she bit into a fresh strawberry. It was sweet, juicy, soft, and best of all being fed to her by Abigail.

"Would you like another bite?" Abigail dangled the fruit just above Marlee's mouth as the two of them lounged naked on the hotel bed.

"Yes." Marlee opened her eyes and smiled. "Then I'd like to taste you." She wrapped her lips around the berry and gently sucked it from Abigail's fingers, squishing it with her tongue and slowly swallowing the sweet pulp.

They'd been feeding each other cheese, crackers, and strawberries, as a prelude to the lovemaking Marlee promised would take their sex to the next level. Marlee watched as Abigail's pupils dilated each time Marlee's mouth covered a strawberry then leisurely tugged it away from its stem. She finally set the bowl of fruit on the side table then wrapped her body around Marlee. "I think I'm finished with the appetizers. Shall we move on to the main course?"

"I like a woman who knows what she wants." Marlee smiled as she swallowed the last of the pinkish pulp.

"What I want is for you to show me what you mean by the next level, including what could be dirty with something that must feel so good."

Marlee's head rolled back in laughter. "There's nothing dirty about what I have in mind. Some might consider it a little X-rated, two women pleasuring each other like we're going to, but it's definitely a good, clean, fun way to heighten sexual intimacy. Let me show you." Her tongue began a trail from Abigail's lips down to her neck and shoulders. "Lay back and enjoy while I continue this journey on downward."

Abigail's uneven breathing increased as she rested her head on the pillow and put a hand on Marlee's head. "I'm afraid you might drown if you go down too far."

Marlee chuckled. "So you're that wet, eh?"

"Don't laugh." Abigail smiled and tapped Marlee's arm. "No one has ever done this to me before."

"Me too." Marlee's soul danced as they shared an intimate gaze. "I'm so drenched in you, Ab, and I still can't seem to get enough." She licked Abigail's lips. "I want you to relax and enjoy. There's no need to worry about me drowning because you've already proven yourself more than capable of rescuing me."

Abigail moaned in pleasure as Marlee's tongue mapped pathways all over her body, meandering from the peaks of her swollen nipples, across her pulsating stomach, down each arm and leg to her fingers and toes and finally toward the depths of her arousal.

Marlee listened to Abigail's uneven breathing and felt her writhing body succumbing to the passion. To know she was giving her lover so much pleasure brought Marlee a sense of fulfillment that went to the depths of her core. She felt euphoric as her tongue reached its target and Abigail's hips thrust upward until her orgasm erupted in a sustained burst that culminated with a soft wailing. Abigail's hips finally dropped back to the sheets.

"Oh my God." Abigail's arm flopped over her brow. "You're amazing."

Marlee sat up and reached for a towel. "You're the one who's amazing." She wiped her face and shoulders. "I'm so hot for you. Look how I'm sweating."

"Come here while I catch my breath." Abigail motioned for Marlee to lie with her. "It'll be your turn soon."

"Relax and savor the moment for now." Marlee rested her head on the pillow, basking in her own joy at knowing Abigail seemed to be so gratified. "There'll be lots of time for me later."

"Are you sure?" Abigail rolled to Marlee and kissed her. "I want you to have pleasure too."

"Oh, I just did. Did I ever." Marlee held Abigail's face to hers. "Maybe I didn't wail or moan like you, with my mouth being occupied and all, but you wouldn't believe how much pleasure it gave me to do that to you, Dr. Abigail Taylor."

"Well now, Sergeant Marlee Nevins." Abigail grinned. "Are you going to deny me my own opportunity for that?"

"Of course not." Marlee kissed Abigail's nose. "But I want this to be about you for now."

"Then I need to at least touch you and give some release." Abigail reached down and began to caress Marlee. "I'd never expect you to make a big sacrifice like forgoing an orgasm for me."

"No sacrifice is too big for you." Marlee moaned. "I would do anything for you."

"I know. And I for you, my love."

* * *

They walked into town for a late dinner at one of the restaurants. Their stroll along the streets and across the bridge into the commercial part of Merimbula was pleasant, but would have been better if they'd felt comfortable holding hands. Especially since Abigail had to grab Marlee a few times before crossing the street.

"I keep forgetting which direction the cars are coming from," Marlee said as they stood at an intersection. "It's like watching a tennis match."

"Always remember to keep an eye to the right before stepping into the road," Abigail said. "We'll have to get you out for more walks so you can get the hang of it."

"I don't know if I'll ever get used to it." Marlee followed Abigail as they finally crossed the street. "It's like you already have driverless cars here. I don't know how many times I've looked at passing vehicles and there's nobody behind the wheel."

Abigail laughed. "I guess it would seem that way to you."

"I keep thinking dogs and kids are driving too when cars whiz by. Isn't it enough everything is upside down here that you don't have to complicate things more with putting your cars on the wrong side of the road?"

"Are you trying to tell me we'd be better off in Canada, with all of its snow and miserable weather?"

"Hey, our snow is nice and the weather isn't that bad." Marlee brushed up against Abigail. "I'm just teasing. I love it here. I could live anywhere as long as it's with you."

"That's good to know. I might have to move my business somewhere else, maybe the States, if things don't get sorted out here soon."

"Really?"

"I don't know." Abigail sighed. "Probably not. I won't leave Josh and I couldn't take him as far away from home as that. I'm getting fed up and frustrated, though."

"Things will work out," Marlee said. "As long as we're together, I can handle anything."

"Me too." Abigail smiled.

They continued along their way, wandering up and down streets in search of a suitable place to eat until Marlee spotted a silver BMW sedan zooming past that resembled Tyler's. By the time she looked at the correct driver's side, only a profile was visible as the car sped away. Short hair, sunglasses resting on the top of the head, and shoulders about the size of Tyler's.

"It can't be him." She stopped, confused as her heart started to pound. She grabbed her phone in case she'd missed a message from him. Nothing.

"What's up?" Abigail put a hand on Marlee's arm. "It can't be who?"

"Tyler. I think he just drove by."

"He's not supposed to be here. Are you sure it was him?"

"No." Marlee shook her head and looked around. "I must have been mistaken."

"It's been a long day," Abigail said as she checked her phone. "Let's just grab a pizza and take a cab back to our unit."

"If it was him, I'm sure he would have told me." Marlee put her hands on her hips and stared into the distance.

Abigail slid the cell back into her handbag. "My legs are still feeling a bit wobbly from all that sex and I think a ride back is in order anyway."

"Pizza and a ride back to our unit sounds good about now." Marlee's jaw tightened.

They picked up a bottle of merlot and a few cold beers to go with their pizza then hired a cab. The two tabby kittens met them at the lobby door again. Marlee put down the bags to pick one up.

"You love them, don't you?" Abigail smiled.

"They're so cute." Marlee brushed her nose through the feathery fur. "I hope they find a good home."

"I'm sure they will. Maybe we can get our own once things settle down. Josh would be thrilled, although I'm sure he'd prefer a dog."

"Dogs are nice too." Marlee put the kitten down and picked up its meowing sister for a cuddle. "I don't know that I'd ever be able to tell them apart, they look so similar."

"I'm sure their personalities would come out once you get to know them." Abigail leaned against the building and scanned her email. "It's all in the genetics, you know."

"My own personal geneticist. How lucky am I?" Marlee released the cat and picked up her bags. "Shall we head in and eat?"

"Yes, please, considering I worked up such an appetite." Abigail smiled as she brushed against Marlee and led the way inside.

They made it an early night to get rested up for a sunrise jog along the beach the next morning. Marlee ensured the windows and doors were securely locked then double-checked around their unit to verify nothing had been disturbed while they were out. Everything seemed fine, even the wind was calm and the surf peaceful as they lay in bed, but Marlee couldn't fall asleep. Something was coming, she could feel it her veins, and her instincts wouldn't let her rest.

She listened to Abigail's even breathing long into a night of inner turmoil over whether or not it could have been Tyler in Merimbula and wondering if Hannah had somehow gotten to him and they were working together.

Marlee replayed their meeting at the elevator earlier that morning. It had been as though Tyler was waiting for them. And then there was the gun. Why had he brought it to Canberra and then not let her have it? Something wasn't right and she was beginning to worry their safety was at risk, especially when Tyler didn't answer any of her messages asking if he'd made it back to Sydney.

CHAPTER FORTY-TWO

A spectacular sunrise highlighted the horizon over the glistening ocean as Marlee and Abigail jogged along the beach toward Merimbula's satellite village of Pambula. The air was fresh and the water retreating. Waves washed the sand to leave a hard-packed surface that captured their footprints along an otherwise pristine shoreline.

"This afternoon it's your turn," Abigail said as they ran side by side.

"Oh yeah? My turn for what?"

Abigail playfully shoved Marlee. "You can't be that much of a saint. Tell me you haven't been thinking of it."

"Oh I've been thinking about it all right, for a long time now." Marlee licked her lips as she corrected her exaggerated stumble. She was still feeling uneasy, but didn't want to dampen the mood with something she hoped was a figment of her imagination. Especially since Tyler finally responded to her messages and she convinced herself he was back in Sydney.

"Sometimes it gets to be too much just thinking about you touching me there like that and I have to block it out," Marlee said between breaths. "I can hardly wait."

"Then why did you hold off until we got here?" Abigail panted. "I can't believe you stopped me yesterday when it was your turn."

"Call me old-fashioned, but I think progressions in our love are worth savoring," Marlee said. "I want us to relish moments like that. It seemed fitting to postpone it until our vacation."

"You're making this sound like a honeymoon of sorts." Abigail chuckled, keeping up her pace.

"Maybe, but I hope we have lots of little intimate trips like this."

"I like that idea. What other holidays do you have in mind?"

Marlee started to fall behind as she reduced her speed. "Can we take a break?"

"Sure." Abigail slowed to a halt and put her hands on her knees to catch her breath.

"When we get over to Canada," Marlee gasped for air, "I want to take you on a little excursion to the States and visit P-town." She flopped onto the dry sand and faced the water.

"And what's P-town?" Abigail sat beside her.

"It's one of my favorite places in the world because it's where we can be ourselves and hold hands or kiss on the streets and I want to be able to do that with you. Like I wish I could now, but people would stare."

"There's hardly anyone on the beach right now. Anyway, who cares if they look?"

"You're going to make a great lesbian." Marlee turned to Abigail and smiled. "Just think of the role model you'll be when you come out to the world. Dr. Abigail Taylor, renowned geneticist and CEO of AbTay Biosystems, is a lesbian and living the best life ever with her Canadian partner."

Abigail laughed. "You're making me sound like your poster girl."

"You are my poster girl. From now on, I'll always have a picture of you in whatever locker I have." Marlee patted Abigail's knee then stood up. "We should keep moving or I'll seize up."

"Are you thinking police locker?" Abigail brushed off the seat of her shorts as she got up. "Is that what you want to do over here?"

"I don't know yet, but I hope to at least have a gym locker because I don't plan on becoming lazy and fat now that I've hooked onto you." Marlee blew a kiss. "Come on. Let's keep going so we can say we jogged from Merimbula to Pambula. It sounds neat."

The rest of the run was leisurely but well paced, and it didn't take them long to reach the main beach near the Pambula campgrounds. A few surfers were putting on wet suits and other beachgoers were setting up chairs or strolling along the sand.

"If you don't mind," Abigail said, "I'd like to visit the public toilet before we head back."

"Good idea. I'll go too."

They used the washroom facilities and were alone at the sink washing their hands. No one else was inside.

"If we go into the town of Pambula," Abigail said, "we can have a rest at one of the cafés then hire a cab back to our unit."

"Sounds like a plan. How long is the—"

Marlee gasped for air as someone grabbed her from behind, thrust her into a headlock, and dragged her to the door. She tried tucking her chin to bite the muscular male arm, but her assailant was ready. A black leather-gloved hand clamped over her mouth while the barrel of a gun jabbed into her rib cage. She was rendered defenseless in a matter of seconds.

They were dragged outside. Marlee watched as Abigail struggled to avoid being stuffed into the back of a white windowless cargo van. Marlee wanted to fight back, get them out of this ambush, and protect Abigail. All she could do was take notes.

There were three attackers in all, each dressed in dark clothes and their faces concealed. Marlee was shoved in behind Abigail, pushed facedown against the unforgiving metal floor of the seatless van. The rear doors clanged shut, two of their attackers closed in with them and the third hurrying into the driver's seat.

"Help! Call the police!" Abigail screamed when the hand over her mouth released its hold. "Let us go." Her arms flailed about in an attempt to break free from her captor. A gloved hand whacked her in the face then tightened the grip around her arms as they bounced around in the speeding vehicle.

"Ouch! You're hurting me," Abigail cried out.

Marlee tried to lunge, but couldn't move as she was pinned facedown, a heavy knee against her spine. A strip of duct tape was plastered over her mouth and her arms were yanked behind her back. She heard the ripping of more tape and felt stickiness binding her hands together. She turned her cheek against the cold metal floor, struggling for her eyes to meet Abigail's and signal she'd find a way to get them out of this. There had to be a way, especially since she'd been trained how to get her hands out of duct tape.

Why hadn't Tyler given her the gun? If only she had a weapon now. Her phone. Yes. At least it was in her pocket, at the ready for an opportunity.

"Who are you and what do you want?" Abigail's cheek reddened from the smack, but she spoke as though in charge. Her assailant cut off a piece of duct tape and plastered it over her mouth. He also wrapped it around her wrists and fastened them to a handle on the side door.

Marlee guessed they were driving away from the nearby town. The ride was smooth and fast, so she surmised they were being transported by highway. Whether to be interrogated or killed, or both, she wasn't sure. She was certain they knew she was a police officer. The way they had been ready for her, two assailants against Abigail's one, and leaving nothing to chance with the hard Glock in her ribs made it obvious. She knew without a doubt that Hannah was somehow involved.

Her eyes scanned the inside of the windowless vehicle, looking for anything that could help get them out of this situation. A sunroof was opened to let in a breeze and revealed a clear blue sky. Their captors remained silent and the driver was hidden behind a curtain blocking out the front view.

Marlee studied the two thugs. Their faces were still hidden and they didn't speak. She deduced they were all Caucasian, two dark haired and one red, judging by the hair on their arms. The redhead was driving.

All were over six feet tall with muscular builds, and wore dark zip-off pants, plain black T-shirts, and black balaclavas. It was though they were a team, or clones, except for the redhead. Musk aftershave permeated the air.

The inside of the van was new and barren, most likely a rental, with the exception of a spade and three digging shovels thrown on the floor near the back. When the vehicle slowed and turned onto a gravel road, Marlee's eyes drifted back to the tools and her heart pounded. They were going to be killed and buried somewhere in the bush outside Merimbula. She was sure of it.

Abigail's frantic eyes urged Marlee to look toward the sunroof. A helicopter hovered against the blue sky, as though keeping in stride with them. It was too high up to know if it was the police, but Marlee hoped for the best. Had Tyler followed them to Merimbula, knowing something was up? Could he have alerted the authorities? Please let it be so because Marlee knew there weren't many other options.

When the helicopter disappeared, Marlee held her breath, yearning for another glimpse as the whirring motor drifted into the silent distance. Marlee finally released her breath and dropped her head in anguish. They were on their own.

Marlee carefully wriggled her hands behind her back, working at the duct tape. She managed to slide it over her wrists and was diligently tugging it away with her fingers. She also loosened the tape over her mouth by discreetly blowing and sucking against the glue. There had to be a way to get them out of this, just like when all seemed lost at sea until Abigail rescued her from the shark. She couldn't give up.

The van came to an abrupt stop. The doors flung open to a wooded area and Marlee was shoved out first. She fell onto the sand and rolled to conceal her loosened hands. Shimmering water off to the right caught her eye and she realized they weren't far from the coast. As soon as she freed her hands, maybe she could grab one of their guns and at least have a chance to protect Abigail.

Abigail's chin hit the dirt when she landed on the ground and her hair had come out of its ponytail. The tape had been cut from her hands and she reached to remove the piece over her mouth.

"Leave it alone." Hannah appeared from behind the van, semiautomatic pistol with silencer in hand and fury in her eyes.

Hannah looked away from Abigail and pointed the gun at Marlee, their eyes meeting in sizzling hatred. "I ought to shoot you right now, but I want you to suffer." She motioned into the bushes near the rear of the van where the three thugs were digging a hole. "Considering the two of you are so stuck to each other, I thought you'd like to be together for eternity."

Hannah snickered, keeping her gun and eyes on Marlee. "I'm disappointed in you, Tay. We were supposed to be best friends and that should mean we tell each other who we're sleeping with, unless, of course, you're ashamed of your Canadian slut. I think I'd be, considering she's a pathetic excuse of a bull dyke that doesn't even have a bite."

Marlee's hands were almost free and she concealed her final tugs on the tape by exaggerating convulsions of anger toward Hannah's hateful words. Her gut feeling had been right all along and she needed to take control. Marlee groaned and whimpered until her hands finally came free. She kept them hidden behind her back as though still tied, and acted like she was reaching frustrated resignation.

"She's a wild one, isn't she?" Hannah sneered. "I didn't realize you liked it so feral, Tay, or I'd have played a little rougher." She turned the gun on Abigail. "Maybe you'd like a little Russian roulette to turn you on?"

Marlee watched as Abigail pointed to the tape over her mouth and pleaded with her eyes to remove it.

"I'll let you speak now, Tay." Hannah waved the gun at her. "Go ahead and pull it off, but if you scream, I'll kill you."

Abigail carefully removed the tape and let out a sigh. "Hannah." She spoke in a soft voice. "What's going on? I don't understand. Why are you doing this?"

"As you like to say when rationalizing a decision I don't agree with, there are a few reasons." Hannah gave a wicked grin. "First of all, there's the money. Why should you get it all?"

Marlee sat quietly, studying their surroundings while waiting for an opportunity to reach her phone and hit speed dial for the police. She studied Hannah's gun and the three thugs in the distance. If only she could get her hands on a gun.

"I've always tried to be fair to you," Abigail said. "You're my highest paid employee and I've been more than generous with your bonuses."

"You don't get it, do you?" Hannah said. "I wasn't just an employee. I helped you build that company. I should have been a co-owner."

"I'm sorry, Hannah. If that's the way you feel, I'll talk to my lawyers and make it happen. Let us go and I'll do whatever you want. You can have it all if you want."

"What I want is for people like you to pay." Hannah swatted a fly with the back of her hand. "People who have everything—money, brilliance, good looks, happiness. I can see how happy you've been over the last few weeks and it makes me sick. Your company's under siege and yet you look the happiest you've ever been. All because of her." Hannah jerked the gun toward Marlee. "Where's your little androgynous friend Tyler?"

Marlee glared at Hannah, her body shaking with anger. The woman was clearly deranged, expecting Marlee to answer even though gagged.

"Where is he?" Hannah screamed and fired a shot in the ground next to Marlee.

"I'm right here." Tyler jumped out of the bushes beside Marlee, hands shaking as he pointed the stolen gun at Hannah.

CHAPTER FORTY-THREE

Marlee lunged at Tyler, grabbed the gun, and aimed it at Hannah with a readiness to kill. She spit the tape off her lips. "I'll shoot if you make the slightest move."

Hannah had raised her gun toward Tyler in the confusion, but it now pointed at empty air as he'd dropped to the ground during the exchange with Marlee.

Marlee motioned and Abigail bolted to her feet. She sprinted to Marlee's side as the three thugs threw down their shovels and reached for their guns.

"Run!" Marlee fired a few shots as they fled into the bushes and raced for their lives.

"This way!" Tyler shouted, leading them through an opening in the brush to a rock face along the shore. "I think we can get down to the beach from here. Follow me."

Their attackers were right behind, thrashing through trees and closing in. Marlee tailed Tyler and Abigail as they slid down the steep rock face to the shore and began to race along the sandy beach. Silenced shots were fired from above as they darted into the concealing trees along the shore. They continued deeper into the undergrowth and finally collapsed behind a mound of dirt.

"Where are they?" Abigail panted.

"They might be driving around." Tyler gasped for air. "There's a road not too far from here."

"Where are we?" Marlee remembered her cell and tossed it to Tyler. "We could use some police support now."

"Good on you." He kissed her phone. "I forgot mine in the car." His hands trembled as he tried to make the call.

"How are you holding up?" Marlee brushed a hand over Abigail's shoulder.

"I'm good." Abigail gave a weak smile. "My two heroes. I'm so glad you're on my team."

"We're not out of this yet." Marlee knew of the danger that still lay ahead.

"I can't get through." Tyler shook the phone. "What a useless piece of shit."

"Fuck," Marlee said. "What's wrong with it?"

"The coverage in this gulley isn't strong enough for your phone and the battery's almost dead. What about yours?" He looked at Abigail.

"I didn't bring it." She groaned. "I wanted to forget about the office for a few hours."

"We should keep moving," Marlee said. "I'm sure we'll find a signal around here somewhere."

They were just about to get up when a branch toward the left snapped. Marlee motioned for Tyler and Abigail to freeze. She held her breath and listened for movement. The next sound came from the right. They were being circled. She spotted Hannah through the branches first, head twisting back and forth like a robot, her gun out in front. They couldn't make a noise, and maybe, just maybe, they wouldn't be discovered.

She spoke with her eyes, staring toward Hannah then at Abigail and Tyler to let them know silence was paramount. A bead of sweat formed on her brow and tickled, but she didn't dare wipe it. Her pounding heart echoed, reminding her of a partridge pumping its wings in the bush, and hoped it wouldn't give them away like the hunted bird often did with its fluttering feathers.

Hannah came into clear view and Marlee's finger hovered over the trigger. A distant branch snapped and Hannah bolted toward the noise, disappearing behind the trees.

"They're over here!" Hannah's voice reverberated to the sound of the others following.

"Now's our chance." Marlee sprang up and looked around then crouched back down. "Which way is the road?"

"That way." Tyler pointed with the phone.

"We need to split up," Marlee said. "As soon as we move, they'll be on our tail. And we need to separate the phone and gun to double our chances of escape."

"I was thinking the same," Tyler said. "Can the two of you make it to the road on your own?"

"We'll have to." Marlee turned to Abigail. "Are you ready to run like hell?"

"Yes, but what about Tyler?"

"I'll scramble up that hill over there." Tyler motioned with his chin. "I should be able to get a signal to call for help."

"We'll go first." Marlee stood up and faced Tyler. "They'll come after us and as soon as they go by, that'll be your chance to sneak away and run for a signal."

"Okay." Tyler handed her the keys to his car. "It's parked just off the road. Use the alarm if you can't find it."

"Oh, Tyler." Abigail grabbed his arm. "What would we do without you? Please be careful. And thank you." She leaned over and kissed his cheek.

"I owe you for this." Marlee squeezed his arm. "Take care of yourself."

"You too." Tyler crouched lower to hide.

"Let's go." Marlee grabbed Abigail's hand and they fled through the trees, racing along the clearest path to the road. It wasn't long before they heard Hannah's voice then aggressive thrashing behind them. The sound of ripping branches was getting louder and Marlee realized they were about to be overtaken.

She pulled Abigail behind the disfigured trunk of a large rubber tree and squished her up against it. "Don't move," she whispered.

Hannah and her thugs ran past then stopped in a distant clearing. "Fuck!" Hannah said. "We lost them."

Marlee watched as Hannah moved in a circle, pointing her gun in all directions and ready to shoot. She shielded Abigail and gripped the stolen pistol, hoping Tyler had made the call and help was on its way.

"Let's spread out." Hannah got closer. "They must be here somewhere."

Marlee was prepared to die, but not until she'd saved Abigail. She put her lips to Abigail's ear and whispered. "I love you. Take the gun and stay here." She slipped the pistol in Abigail's hand, kissed the back of her neck, then slid out from behind the tree and crept away to hide behind another trunk. She waited until Hannah got closer.

"I'm over here." Marlee called out, hoping to distract their captors from Abigail.

Hannah swung around and readied to fire. "Where? I can't see you."

Marlee heard trampling, imagining the thugs rushing to Hannah's side. "I'm by myself and don't have a gun. If you promise not to shoot, I'll step out."

"I'm not promising you anything."

Hannah approached the tree. Marlee's heart raced as she prepared to die. If only she could prolong her life long enough for the police to arrive and save Abigail. That is, if Tyler was successful in reaching help.

"I'm waiting," Hannah yelled. "Come out now or I'll shoot to kill when I find you."

Marlee took a deep breath and stepped forward to face a firing squad of Hannah and the three thugs, her hands raised.

"It's over," Marlee said. "The police are on their way."

Hannah rolled her head back in a laugh. "You're hilarious. Is that how you got to Tay? With stupid jokes like that?"

Marlee stayed silent and kept her eyes on Hannah's, hoping she'd continue talking. She would pretend to listen, give empathy and draw out the conversation. Maybe even build a little rapport with Hannah the way she was taught to do in situations like this. The longer they talked, the better. Marlee had to believe help was on the way.

"Tay thinks she was good to me." Hannah moved closer, gun in hand, still aiming at Marlee, and stomped her foot in the dry sand. "She doesn't know a thing about me. All those studies we did together. All the times I put in extra long hours at the office and went out of my way to postpone my personal life for her. I even slept with her. Did she tell you?" She brushed the point of her pistol over the side of Marlee's cheek, tracing a line from the tip of her eye to the corner of her mouth.

Marlee held her breath and stayed still under the scary sensation of the long suppressor touching her face and threatening sudden death. She resisted the urge to grab Hannah's wrist and pry the Glock away. Heart pounding, Marlee had to keep control and make Hannah believe she empathized.

"She wasn't any good in bed, but I'm sure you know that," Hannah continued, dragging the gun along Marlee's sweat-beaded chin. "You should have come on to me instead. I'm going to have more money than she'll ever have and I could have shown you a good time."

Marlee's breathing became uneven as the tip of Hannah's pistol climbed to her drenched temple and she envisioned a bullet ripping into her brain. Her knees were starting to shake. She had to do something.

"It's not too late." Marlee spoke in a soft voice, hoping to postpone her death a bit longer and keep Hannah distracted, away from Abigail.

"Of course it's too late." Hannah stepped back, her voice loud and strained. "I'm going to kill you. The only regret I have is you won't be able to watch Tay die first."

"You'll be caught," Marlee said. "She knows about you and has gone for the police. They'll be here soon."

"Then I'd better kill you now." She cocked the gun and prepared to fire at Marlee.

"No Hannah, wait!" Abigail stepped from behind the tree, pistol dangling at her side.

"Aha, I knew you were here," Hannah sneered, but kept her aim on Marlee. "The two little lovebirds wouldn't separate. Where's your third wheel? Tyler? Oh Tyler? Where are you? I'm going to kill Marlee if you don't come out."

Abigail gasped. "He's not here. Please don't shoot."

"I'm going to count to ten," Hannah said. "If he doesn't come out, I'll pull the trigger and we'll all watch Marlee die."

"Please Hannah, no." Abigail started to wail "I'll do anything for you, but please, just let Marlee go."

"One."

"You don't have to do this, Hannah." Marlee's throat was constricting.

"Two." Hannah paused between counts.

"Hannah please, he's not here." Abigail raised her gun then screamed and dropped it as a bullet exploded into the ground beside her.

"Three."

"It doesn't have to end like this." Marlee's jaw trembled.

"Four."

"Please Hannah, don't kill her. I'll do anything for you." Abigail fell to her knees.

"Five." She continued as though in a trance.

"Tell me about your sister." Marlee tried to get her talking. "What was her name?"

"Six." Hannah twitched.

"Annabel," Abigail said. "Her sister's name was Annabel."

"What a beautiful name," Marlee said. "You've done so much good work in her memory. She'd be so proud of you."

"Seven."

Marlee readied to lunge for the gun and at least kill Hannah before she died.

"Eight."

Just as Marlee was about to pounce, Tyler bolted out from behind a tree. "Don't shoot!"

CHAPTER FORTY-FOUR

Marlee teetered as Hannah switched her focus to Tyler. She hoped he'd managed to contact the police. If not, they were surely all to die soon.

"Well, well." Hannah kept her gun trained on Marlee. "I love how I can make the three of you appear. My next trick will have the three of you disappear." She turned the weapon toward Abigail, waving it through the air as though a magic wand, and leveling it in position. "I'm going to start with you, my dear Tay. I want your girlfriend to see you die."

Marlee grabbed Tyler's attention and widened her eyes, silently asking if he'd made the call. He gave the slightest nod and tapped his pocket. Yes. Backup was on its way. All Marlee had to do was keep them alive a bit longer.

"Come on, Hannah, don't you at least owe her an explanation?" Marlee edged toward Abigail.

"I don't owe her anything." Hannah's trigger finger twitched.

"She has the right to know where things went wrong," Marlee persisted.

"She doesn't have any rights." Hannah kept Abigail in her sights, but eased her finger off the trigger.

"Please, Hannah." Abigail sobbed. "I'm sorry if I hurt you. I loved you."

"You never loved me." She waved the gun at Marlee, her face twitching. "How could you love that bitch dyke instead of me? All the years I spent working with you. Giving everything, sacrificing my own happiness, and then you betray me with her."

"Hannah, I'm so sorry." Abigail's voice shook. "I never betrayed you."

"Yes, you did!" Hannah resumed her aim on Abigail. "I saw the two of you by the pool."

"Please, Hannah, you're like a sister to me. We're family and have to look after each other." Abigail leaned forward, jaw quivering as she begged for her life. "This isn't you. I want to understand what happened. Is someone making you do this?"

"Of course not." Hannah's face relaxed, the corners of her eyes and mouth twitching upward. "I'm finally in control."

Marlee knew a mentally unstable person could never be in complete control. She studied the armed brutes flanking Hannah. It was scorching, but they still wore their balaclavas. All three used both hands to grip semiautomatic pistols, silencers extending barrels, and stood at the ready to fire at the slightest cue from Hannah.

"I tried to let you do what you wanted in the company," Abigail said.

"No you didn't!" Hannah's face changed to a scowl. "It was your business and you had the final say."

"I always listened and appreciated your brilliant ideas. A lot of people with cancer have hope because of your good work. I don't know what I would have done without you on my team."

"I was dropped from your team the day she showed up." Hannah almost growled at Marlee. "How do you feel about being on Tay's team now?"

"I could never replace you on Abigail's team," Marlee said, visualizing the surroundings for some way to protect Abigail. "I'm not smart enough to understand your work."

"You got that right." Hannah snickered. "Some police officer you are. Is that why you had to leave Canada? So you could smarten up? You weren't even clever enough to protect Tay."

"You're right," Marlee said. "Abigail protected you. She believed in you and was convinced of your innocence."

"But you weren't, were you? And him." Hannah shook her gun at Tyler. "Who the fuck are you?"

"Tyler," he said. "I thought you knew that."

Hannah fired a shot near his feet, the thud of the silenced bullet exploding dirt. He jumped back and threw his hands in the air. "Please don't shoot. I'm the IT hacker guy. I stopped your files from downloading the other night."

"So that was you." Hannah nodded. "I figured Tay's systems team was too stupid for that."

"I can help you with anything on the net," Tyler said. "I'll get you the rest of your files and even more if you want."

Marlee edged closer to Abigail. She was conscious of Tyler's gun on the ground, but knew the likelihood of grabbing it and killing Hannah and her three thugs before getting them all killed was nonexistent. If nothing else, she could push Abigail to safety down the nearby embankment if Hannah moved to shoot.

"I'll work for you," Tyler said. "I'll do whatever you want. I'm the best when it comes to hacking computers."

"Shut up." Hannah waved her gun at Tyler.

"Okay Hannah, I've had enough." Abigail straightened up, putting her hands on her hips as she tried to assert authority. "Let them go right now or I'll fire you."

"Fire me?" Hannah laughed. "Sorry, Tay, but we're not in your company boardroom, in case you haven't noticed. I'm the one who's going to do the firing right now." She shot a bullet into the ground near Abigail.

The exploding dirt stung Marlee's legs. She feared the next bullet would shoot someone. Palpitating heart and hyperventilating lungs, Marlee watched Hannah's hand for any sign it was about to pull the trigger again. She'd managed to get close enough to Abigail to push her down the embankment and take the bullet, if necessary.

Then she heard it. A helicopter was fast approaching. She wanted to raise her arms and flag them down. It had to be the police.

As the whirring got louder, everyone except Marlee watched the sky while the helicopter flew past. She kept her focus on Hannah's gun, which was aimed at Abigail.

Marlee heard the faint snapping of a twig in the bush behind her and hoped beyond hope that a rescue party had arrived. She knew that the next few seconds would be pivotal in defining their fate. Her eyes stayed trained on Hannah as she readied to pounce and push Abigail out of harm's way at the slightest sign of movement.

The ground ambush was sudden and swift with heavily armed police officers emerging from the bushes to surround everyone. Hannah's finger twitched toward the trigger.

"No!" Marlee lunged and thrust Abigail down the embankment into the gully of safety as the gunshots began. The first bullet grazed Marlee's shoulder and the second caught the edge of her abdomen. She fell to the ground, bloody and gasping for air amidst rapid gunfire in the shootout with police.

The pain was unbearable, but she knew it was minor compared to the agony she'd suffer had Abigail been killed. Blood spurted from her side. She was going to bleed to death. Her only consolation was that she'd saved the woman who had rescued her. The woman she loved and couldn't live without. She closed her eyes, unable to do anything else.

CHAPTER FORTY-FIVE

"Marlee!" Was that Abigail? Was she okay?

The gunfire had stopped and Marlee lay on the ground, unable to move. Her eyes were closed and the pain was excruciating. She tried to call out for help, but no sound came.

"No!" Marlee heard Abigail drop on the ground beside her. She wanted to reach out, so relieved that her Ab was safe, but her body had disengaged from her mind.

"You're bleeding. Please Marlee, stay with me." Abigail was crying and Marlee felt warm hands pressing against her abdomen. She must have been shot there and imagined blood spurting out of the wound. Poor Ab.

"Help! I need help over here!" Abigail's voice again. Marlee wondered where Hannah was. Surely she was captured, if not killed in the ambush. She envisioned heavily armed police officers roaming the area to verify that all threats had been eliminated.

"I can help you." Marlee heard a male voice, most likely a first responder. "I have a first aid kit with me. Let's get that bleeding stopped. She felt fingers at her neck, feeling around for a pulse.

"We've been saved Marlee." Abigail's words were spoken in sobs. "Help is here. You just have to hold on for a bit longer. I know you can do it."

Marlee was losing consciousness, her world going black. She fought to hang on to whatever life she had left. She knew she was bleeding to death. The rusty smell of blood was strong and she knew there was a lot of it. The sound of approaching sirens offered Marlee hope that she'd be saved. She had to be.

"I'm here Marlee. I love you." Abigail's soothing voice brought her comfort. She yearned to hug the love of her life.

"I love you, Marlee." Abigail's sobs were getting louder. "Please don't die on me. I love you. Stay with me. Please don't die."

Marlee was in anguish. The pain of her injuries nothing compared to the suffering brought on by Abigail's cries. She wanted to reach out of her body and somehow comfort her Ab. Hold her and tell her everything was going to be okay. It was as though she was already dead.

"Keep fighting for me, Marlee." Marlee pictured Abigail hovering over her lifeless body, wiping away tears. "It's not over. Don't give up. You can't. I won't let you." Marlee felt Abigail's lips brushing up against her ear. "I love you. Please don't leave me. I know you're strong."

Marlee faded in and out, her motionless body in shock. Abigail's soothing words were comforting. Marlee knew she was dying, could feel her blood draining, and was starting to sense peace. She felt as though a cloud of vapor flowed through her inner core, preparing a passageway to release her soul from life. Abigail was by her side, forever the hero as she maintained control and offered words of encouragement. Marlee tried opening her eyes, but her lids refused. She found solace in knowing her quick thinking had at least saved Abigail.

"You're a fighter, Marlee." Abigail sobbed. "I know you can do it. You're my hero, my smart policewoman. I love you so much and need you to stay with me."

There was pain in Abigail's words. Dying was about more than just her. Abigail would be destroyed by her death. She couldn't let it happen. That was it. She was going to live.

"Marlee." She heard Tyler drop to his knees and felt him put a hand on her arm. "The ambulance is arriving now. You have to hang in a bit longer." He choked back tears. "We made it. I just talked with the police and we're safe now."

Tyler. Marlee knew he was a good friend, a real hero the way he risked his life for theirs, and he was safe too. He would help Abigail. Just as she knew her Ab would look after him. They were family now. The bond would be too strong to break.

Marlee tried to open her eyes again and this time her lids cooperated. Abigail and Tyler hovered, their heads almost touching as they smiled through their tears. Marlee struggled to smile back, but started to choke and gasp for air. Her eyes closed.

"We're ready to move her now," said a new voice.

Marlee heard garbled voices in the background and felt many hands carefully lifting her in tandem onto a stretcher and fastening the belts.

"I won't leave you, Marlee." Abigail touched Marlee's good shoulder and walked beside the stretcher.

"It's best if you follow behind," another voice said. "We're bringing her to the airport, where there's an air ambulance waiting to fly her to the Canberra Hospital. Two of us will ride in the back with her so there won't be room until we get to the airport. We need to go now."

"I love you, Marlee," Abigail cried as Marlee's stretcher was loaded into the ambulance. "I'll be right behind and see you soon."

"I'll take you, Dr. Taylor." Marlee pictured a police officer offering a ride. She imagined Tyler and Abigail jumping into the backseat of a cruiser and following her ambulance in a blaring rush of sirens. Then her world went black.

CHAPTER FORTY-SIX

Marlee heard voices. Kerry and Gabe. Eyes closed and body aching, Marlee lay motionless in a cocoon of blankets. How could she be back in Ottawa, her best friend and brother casually chatting at her bedside? Where was Abigail? Had it all been a dream? No. Marlee knew Abigail was for real. She wanted Abigail.

"You should have seen the girls." Gabe's animated voice was quiet and Kerry's soft giggle followed his words. "They didn't know what to do when they saw me dragging my bike up from the ditch, all covered in mud and looking like some kind of wild beast."

Marlee hoped she was still in Australia, wondered if she was even alive. She needed to hear Abigail's soothing voice, feel her caressing touch, and smell the faint coconut aroma of her ponytail. Images of a beautiful smile and memories of tasting luscious lips made Marlee open her eyes in search of Abigail, her all-consuming hero and savior.

"Ab." Voice weak and eyelids struggling to stay open, Marlee's head remained flat on the pillow. She glimpsed a white ceiling and noticed a rack of hospital tubes just above her head.

"I can't believe you didn't get hurt," Kerry said.

Marlee knew they hadn't heard her.

"Ab." She tried again, this time louder. Or so she thought.

"I was lucky," Gabe said. "The puddle of mud helped break my fall."

Pain shot through Marlee's left arm as she tried to move her hand. "Ab."

"Oh my God, she's waking up." Kerry was suddenly at the side of her bed. "Marlee, we're here."

"Ab." Marlee registered Kerry's hovering face and wasn't sure if she'd been heard.

"Hey, sis, it's so good to see you." Gabe kissed her cheek. "I'll be right back. I have to let the others know you're waking up."

"Ab." Why wasn't she there?

"What are you trying to say?" Kerry lowered her ear beside Marlee's mouth. "Are you in pain?"

"Ab. Abigail." Marlee started to panic, her eyes racing.

"Abigail. Of course you want Abigail." Kerry straightened up. "All I can say about Abigail is wow. What a classy woman. You really lucked out with her."

Marlee's eyes relaxed, but an anxious twitch aggravated her jaw. Where was Abigail?

"She arranged for Gabe and I to fly over here as soon we got the news and we're staying at her house." Kerry ruffled Marlee's hair. "What a place and what a catch. No wonder you don't want to return to Ottawa."

Kerry's words started to register and excitement began to build in Marlee. She was in Sydney and Abigail was near.

"Abigail's been at your side nonstop, wanting to be here when you woke up. Of course as soon as we convince her to take a little break, you come to." Kerry kissed Marlee's cheek. "I'm so happy to see you, Marlee. I've really missed you."

Kerry stepped back as the door burst open.

"Marlee!" Abigail dashed to the bedside. "I'm so sorry. I wanted to be here when you woke up."

"Ab." Marlee struggled to smile, relief filling her body and opening up her tear ducts.

Abigail began to cry too. She took Marlee's face in her hands and leaned over so their lips were almost touching. "Oh, Marlee. My hero. I love you so much." She gave a kiss then stepped away to wipe her tears as a doctor entered to examine Marlee.

After the doctor finished probing Marlee and she'd had another rest, she was alert and reclining in her raised bed. Abigail perched on the edge, her fingers entwined with Marlee's. Gabe and Kerry sat in nearby chairs.

"Tyler's anxious to see you too," Abigail said. "He'll be here shortly. I flew him back to Merimbula to pick up my car. He's been such a big help. I don't know what I would have done without him."

"You really had us scared," Gabe said. "I couldn't get here fast enough. I always thought I'd visit Australia someday, but not like this. We even started talking about it more seriously after your decision to move here, but the only Sydney I thought I'd go to this year is in Nova Scotia."

"I hope you'll visit us often," Abigail said. "You too, Kerry. We have lots of room."

"You won't have any problem there," Kerry said and Gabe nodded agreement.

"It means a lot to me that you're here now," Marlee said. "I can't believe I was out of it for so long."

"Your body needed the rest," Abigail said. "You had emergency surgery in Canberra then were flown back to Sydney and have been here for the last four days."

"My own private room." Marlee still felt numb, as though everything was all a dream. "I'm going to have to hurry up and get better. My travel medical insurance is about to run out and I don't think I have coverage for a private room."

"Everything's taken care of," Abigail said. "As soon as you decided to stay in Australia, I added you to my health insurance policy."

"And she's hired me to look after you once you get home." Tyler had slipped into the room, carrying two large helium-filled balloons and a gym bag.

"I've asked Tyler to keep living with us for now and he's graciously accepted," Abigail said.

"What about your job?" Marlee asked him, happy that he'd be staying with them. "Don't you have to go back to work soon?"

"I'm following in your footsteps and I'm going to quit." Tyler placed the balloon weights on the floor and handed the gym bag to Abigail. "I snuck them in so you can show her."

"Perfect." Abigail carefully opened the zipper, peered inside, and smiled. "I have something for you Marlee. It's for us, actually." She reached into the bag and lifted out two tabby kittens.

"Oh, Ab," Marlee gasped, her heart bursting with joy. "The two little sisters from Merimbula. They're so cute."

"They are, aren't they?" Abigail put the little fur balls on Marlee's lap. "What should we name them?"

"You better hang on to the one with the big eyes," Tyler said. "She's rambunctious, like a little Tasmanian devil."

Abigail picked up the kitten and tried to snuggle, but it squirmed out of her arms and jumped back onto the bed. "She is feisty, isn't she?"

"The other one likes to be cuddled," Tyler said. "Go ahead and pick her up, Marlee. She slept on my lap for most of the drive to Sydney. It was as though she was happy to come here."

"So you like Sydney." Marlee lifted the kitten with her good arm and held it in front of her nose. "I like Sydney too and it's a fitting name for a cute little cat like you. Eh, Sydney?" She kissed the top of its head. "What should Ab call your sister?"

"Hmm." Abigail picked up the hyper kitten and tried to steady it. "She definitely doesn't like to be held, but does have a playful look about her. She's kind of mischievous. Ouch." Abigail dropped her to the bed. "You little devil. Her nails are sharp. Sydney and Tasmanian devil. No, that doesn't work."

"Sydney and Tazzie," Marlee said. "How does that sound?"

"Brilliant," Abigail said. "I'm so happy."

"See what I told you a few weeks ago, Marlee?" Tyler laughed. "I knew the two of you would end up like this with a happily ever after kind of life together."

CHAPTER FORTY-SEVEN

Marlee made good progress in her recovery over the next few days, focusing on her health and the excitement of being alive with Abigail, and also visiting with Kerry, Gabe, Tyler, and her two newest family members. Tyler was good at sneaking Sydney and Tazzie in for daily visits and entertainment.

Marlee was finally alone with Abigail in her hospital room, when the others had gone out for dinner. It had been great visiting with Kerry and Gabe, seeing Tyler, and getting to know her new pets, but Marlee longed for private time with Abigail to share their emotions. The moment had finally come for them to talk about the events in Merimbula.

They had each been interviewed by the police, but were avoiding discussions between themselves, mostly at Abigail's insistence on happy conversations to help with Marlee's recovery. Marlee was indeed feeling joyous as her strength improved each day, but she needed to know her Ab was okay behind the constant smiles and loving words.

"How are you doing or going, as you'd say?" Marlee reclined on her raised mattress, wearing pajama bottoms and a T-shirt as she perched on top of the blankets.

"I'm fine." Abigail sat on the edge of the bed and smiled.

"All the focus has been on me over the last while." Marlee spoke in a soft voice as she fondled Abigail's ponytail, tugging it ever so slightly for their eyes to meet. "I know this has been a difficult time for you, and I'm so sorry about how things turned out with Hannah. It must be painful. I want you to know I'm here for you."

Abigail's head dropped as her smile faded to tears. "Hannah was like a sister to me. I can't believe she's gone."

"Come here." Marlee pulled her into an embrace. "You need to let yourself mourn her."

"I'm so angry," Abigail said. "She almost killed you and wanted to murder me too. How could I have been so wrong about her?"

"Don't second guess yourself." Marlee squeezed Abigail's trembling shoulders. "Her mental disorders were far too complicated for that and you did nothing wrong. You were a good friend to her…"

"If I was such a good friend, I should have been able to help her." Abigail stiffened.

"How? You trusted her and she betrayed you." Marlee rubbed Abigail's arm. "Have you been able to make sense of what exactly she did and was planning to do?"

"No." Abigail shook her head as she wiped her nose. "All I know is she was trying to develop some kind of bioweapon to promote deficiencies in fetal development. Kind of like the Zika virus, but one that could target victims based on genetic configurations and produce varying degrees of deformities. Nobody knows who she was working with, other than that the three men killed with her during the police shootout were hired mercenaries from Russia."

"I don't understand. What was she thinking? Why did she do it?"

"We'll probably never know for sure," Abigail said. "I think it was somehow linked to her younger sister's deformity and eventual suicide. When I look back on things, Hannah got so angry and blamed others for her sister's death. It was like she never got over it."

"She obviously had a lot of negative feelings toward you," Marlee said, "and outright hatred toward me."

"She kept her feelings about me well hidden, but not about you, that's for sure."

"What was she planning to do after killing us?"

"I think she was going to return to Sydney, take what she wanted from the company, and disappear under a new identity."

"Was she going to use the name Taylor Williams, as we'd suspected?" Marlee asked.

"Yes. Police found a passport for a Taylor Williams and a large stash of American cash hidden in her unit."

"How did the thugs know where to grab us when we were in the washroom?"

"Hannah hid GPS trackers in the insoles of my shoes." Abigail shook her head.

"She'd been planning this for a while," Marlee said. "It's a good thing I came along and screwed up her plans."

"Yes it is." Abigail smiled.

"Could anyone else at AbTay Biosystems be linked with this?"

"The police are investigating, but believe she was a lone wolf in the company. Thank God. Things are a mess and I have lots of work ahead of me to bring everyone back to a new normal. I'm going to be very busy at the office and am happy Tyler has agreed to stick around while you're recovering." Abigail got up and pulled the curtains around the bed, giving them privacy.

"What are you doing?" Marlee grinned.

"I've been exonerated, by the way." Abigail carefully climbed onto the bed, straddling Marlee just beneath her hips, and leaned forward so their lips almost touched. "Thank you for everything. I wouldn't be here if it wasn't for you."

"And neither would I." Marlee gave her a lingering kiss that turned passionate as they began to sway and grasp at each other. Abigail pulled back.

"Let's be careful. Somebody could come in. I don't want to open up any of your healing wounds."

Marlee smiled at Abigail's nervousness. "I can't wait to go home so we can get naked and hold onto each other in our own bed forever and ever."

"Me too. I've missed you in my bed." Abigail straightened up, sitting back onto her heels. "Let's hope they discharge you tomorrow."

"Forget about hope, it's going to happen." Marlee took one of Abigail's hands and began to smother it with kisses. "How's Josh doing?"

"He's amazing." Abigail smiled. "I told him about us and he thought it was cool."

"That's great. I'm so looking forward to spending more time with him." Marlee paused. "How's he doing with Hannah?"

"He's angry and hurt. Hannah's always been part of his life and they were close. At least, Josh was close to her. How she felt about him, we'll never know."

"Is it safe to come in?" Tyler was at the door.

"Of course." Abigail reached for the curtain and peeked through.

"You can even come into our little tent and have a seat on my bed." Marlee tapped her mattress.

"I sure hope you're decent." Tyler slowly tugged the drape and peeked inside. "Let me know if I wear out my welcome."

"Tyler, you'll always be welcome with us," Abigail said. "Have a seat."

"You're a real hero, you know that?" Marlee said. "If it wasn't for you, Ab and I wouldn't be here right now."

"Please stop." Tyler chuckled as he put his hands over his cheeks and sat on the edge of the bed. "You're embarrassing me."

"I'm serious," Marlee said. "You saved our lives. How did you know to follow us to Merimbula and why didn't you say anything?"

"Because I wasn't sure," Tyler said. "It was just a hunch, nothing else so I didn't want to ruin your trip."

"I saw you drive by," Marlee said. "You had me scared that maybe you were somehow involved."

"I figured you might have seen me and I panicked. I stopped for a few minutes, and by the time I returned, you were gone. I convinced myself that you hadn't noticed my car and were carrying on with your evening so I just left it at that."

"How did you know where to find us in the bush?" Abigail asked.

"I saw someone who looked like Hannah that morning. I didn't recognize the car she was driving, but thought I'd follow her while the two of you jogged along the beach."

"You knew we were out for a jog?" Marlee asked. "Were you spying on us?"

"I was keeping an eye on you," Tyler said. "Anyway, I wasn't sure it was Hannah driving the car I was tailing so I just kept following to see where it was going."

"Didn't you get nervous when she started driving into the bush?" Marlee asked.

"Not really. I had a full tank of petrol and the gun under my seat. Besides, it was a nice day and I had nothing else to do."

"Why didn't you let me know?" Marlee asked. "You should always have backup."

"Who was your backup?"

"I didn't think I needed any." Marlee was almost afraid to ask her next question. "What happened to the gun?"

"The police have it," Tyler said. "All's good. It was registered in my name all along. Can you believe it? My ex had a criminal record and couldn't get a gun license so he falsified the documents. In the end, I just went back and took what was mine. He probably doesn't even know it's gone."

"Tyler told me all about the gun." Abigail sighed. "From now on there'll be no more secrets between the three of us. Okay?"

"Sounds good to me." Tyler twitched his eyebrows toward Marlee as he rubbed his hands together and giggled.

"Wait a minute," Marlee said. "There'll definitely be secrets kept from Tyler. He knows I don't kiss and tell and I don't expect you to start either, Ab."

Abigail rolled her head back and laughed. "Of course not. He'll need to find his own secrets in that area."

"I think visiting hours are over," Tyler said. "Are you ready to go?"

"Yep." Marlee nodded.

"I wish." Abigail gave her a kiss then climbed off the bed. "We'll see you tomorrow."

"Gabe and Kerry said goodnight," Tyler said. "I left them by the pool, playing with Sydney and Tazzie. They'll visit tomorrow if you aren't discharged."

"Tell them I'll see them at home tomorrow," Marlee said.

* * *

"Tyler's waiting outside." Abigail put the last of Marlee's things into a small shoulder bag. "He's our chauffeur and says he loves driving my Prado."

"That doesn't surprise me." Marlee stood beside the bed and put her good arm around Abigail. "I'm so happy to be going home with you today."

"Are you ready for this?" Abigail kissed her. "The media has been eager to meet you, to see the Canadian police officer who saved my life."

"Yes, I think so." Marlee took a deep breath. "What are you going to tell them about me?"

"The truth."

When they got to the front doors, a line of reporters, cameras, and onlookers were waiting for them. Abigail squeezed her hand then led them on through, smiling and focused on Marlee as they stepped outside.

"Before answering any of your questions, I would like to introduce Marlee Nevins, the woman responsible for saving my life." Abigail kissed Marlee on the lips, lingering the act to demonstrate her point to the world. "She's my forever hero. I love her with all my heart."

At first there was silence as mouths hung open, then someone started to clap and the rest joined in, adding cheers and congratulations. Marlee was overwhelmed, excited beyond belief about her future, and so in love with Abigail. She stepped into the spotlight, smiled at the cameras, and caught the ultimate wave as it crested into her new life.

Bella Books, Inc.

Women. Books. Even Better Together.

P.O. Box 10543
Tallahassee, FL 32302

Phone: 800-729-4992
www.bellabooks.com